THE ATLANTIS CRYSTAL

by M.L.Rigdon

ISBN-13: 978-1481106996

ISBN 10: 1481106996

Cover design by: Stephen D Case Casegrfx.com

Visit the author at M.L.Rigdon.com

An excerpt from *Seductive Mines*, the next book in the series is included.

Dedicated to Judith Post

For Jo:
Thanks for the
Paintings, the friendship, the
music. Love Mary Lo

Chapter 1

Chicago Suburbs
June 1997

Phil dug through forgotten candy bar wrappers and loose papers to search the bottom of her briefcase. She growled under her breath, "Fine way to start a vacation. Keys that hide. A missing uncle. Industrial espionage. What's next?"

When she arrived at work at the University of Chicago, a special messenger waited by her office door. The package from her Uncle Cal's lawyer contained two keys. A recent burglary attempt to pry open the front door of her uncle's apartment required a lock change. Due to her push to get everything done at work before taking time off, she had not had time to pick up the new key.

She was still shaken from the lawyer's call and confusing information. Her Uncle Cal's attorney informed her that the questions surrounding her uncle's longtime disappearance had been resolved with the delivery of his ashes. He requested she pick them up and resolve the deluge of requests for the release of her uncle's personal papers about his famous crystals.

More than a few considered Uncle Cal a nut case for insisting that his synthetic crystals came from Atlantis. When the furor of that pronouncement died down, the rush for the lucrative aspects began.

She finally found the metal ring with its dangling tags and used the larger key to open the door. The replacement lock felt stiff and resisted until she did some strong-arm convincing.

The other key labeled with a bank's name and address was for a safe-deposit box she'd known nothing about. Long ago, Uncle Cal had given her, his only heir, power of attorney and full access to his private papers and estate. She'd go to the bank later to check out the mystery box. For now, she needed to be near the things that belonged to him—to think things through and sort out what to do next.

She closed the door, locked it, and glanced around the living room. Everything looked the same as when she was there two years ago, only dustier. Her uncle used only one apartment in the fourplex he owned. The other three were left vacant for the storage of his artifacts and boxes overflowing with forty years of field notes.

Dr. Persis Calvin Hafeldt rarely came home from the field—a greasy film of neglect verified his extended absence. The furnishings were utilitarian, the décor uninviting, and all with a studied lack of personality and the smell of musty neglect

The first place to check was his office. Before she could get there, the doorbell rang. Collecting her wits, Phil ordered her heart to stop pounding from the unexpected interruption.

She hesitated in front of the door and stared at the wood, stilled by a vague sense of unease. When she started to reach for the doorknob, an internal shout of instinct flung her sideways.

Four loud thuds splintered the closed door and slammed into a moldering high-back, tapestry chair that stood directly in line with the door. Puffs of dust hovered around four bullet punctures in the fraying material.

Phil frowned at the smoking holes. It appeared she wasn't the only one who thought that her uncle was still alive.

She flattened her back against the wall and waited for the doorknob to turn. Two more rounds blasted off the deadbolt. The door burst inward, ripping free of its hinges from the kick of a booted foot, and landed on the tapestry chair.

Phil waited for the intruder to make the first move. A scuffed black boot rested cautiously on the threshold.

An Army-issue pistol held in a two-handed grip appeared. She focused her energy and readied to move. The man's tanned and tattooed forearms had not yet cleared the doorway.

Years of training fast-forwarded a mental picture of what came next. She'd wait until Tattoo Guy got in up to the elbows, then knock free the gun, and go for the kneecaps. A blow from behind to the base of his skull, high on the back of his neck, would knock him out.

She unconsciously raised her fists protectively close to her chin, balanced her weight, and stood poised for the perfect moment to strike.

A nanosecond before she moved, the intruder was shoved from behind and sent flying forward. Her strike fanned empty air. Instead of connecting with Tattoo Guy, Phil was intercepted mid-movement and pushed out of the way by a second man. The brief contact told her that he was strong, enjoyed his strength, and his perfect control of it.

Tattoo Guy landed face first, sprawled across the kicked-in door. The second uninvited guest used the heel of his pricey loafer to slam Tattoo Guy's elbow into the door, causing the pistol to fall from numbed fingers.

Phil staggered upright and searched for the closest object to use as a weapon. She yanked a hammered-metal mask from the wall.

She was ready to Frisbee the mask across the room when Tattoo Guy pushed up from the door, knocked aside the second intruder and escaped, leaving his pistol on the grimy carpet.

Footsteps pounded on the landing and down the steps. The first-floor entry door rattled open and banged shut.

"What an amateur," her unexpected rescuer muttered as he straightened up from a near fall and adjusted his suit coat.

Phil's heart and breath chugged to a halt. There on the threshold stood every woman's fantasy—a confident, rugged, mouth-watering male. What was this Hunka-hunka Burnin' Luv doing on Uncle Cal's doorstep?

She took a moment to chastise herself for not being at least a little wary of this menacing stranger, but something about him looked familiar. She felt a bit distracted by the weird impression that she'd seen or met him before.

Worry about her uncle must have scrambled her brains. She'd read about immediate physical attraction but never believed it. Until now, with Mr. Centerfold-of-the-Century staring down at her as if she were an unimportant species of bug. Her skin felt on fire and she didn't for a second believe that this was a menopausal hot-flash moment twenty years too soon.

Phil forced her mouth closed and lifted her chin. How embarrassing! To be caught gaping, like a teen groupie.

A thrill skittered up her arms. She was rarely intimidated by anyone. She assured herself that her nervousness was merely a crude physical response that she could and would control. After all, elemental reactions were all rather basic and explainable. She used the diversion of propping the mask against the wall to collect herself.

Mr. Hunka got right down to business. "Who are you, and what are you doing in Hafeldt's apartment?"

Phil was still preoccupied with the realization that there actually was such a thing as "chemistry" to reply.

Magnetic dark eyes swept over her rumpled clothes. "I asked you what you're doing in Dr. Hafeldt's apartment."

Phil took the offensive and slid into snooty mode. "More appropriately, I think it's time you told me who you are."

He didn't answer right away. He folded and slipped a switchblade she hadn't noticed earlier into his breast pocket.

He glanced at the pistol on the floor and said, "I'm here to see P.C. Hafeldt."

"I don't think you should touch that gun."

His smirk was annoyingly masculine, all confidence and condescension. "I do."

He leaned over, swept up the Beretta from the floor, switched on the safety, and ejected the magazine. Still grinning, he dropped the ammo clip into the side pocket of his suit jacket and tucked the pistol into the spinal groove between the waistband of his fashionably faded jeans.

The brief exposure of his backside sidetracked Phil. When he tugged the jacket back into place, she said, striving for a lofty manner she couldn't quite achieve, "You have yet to identify yourself."

"You haven't said who you are, either."

Phil gave her spectacles a thoughtless push up the bridge of her nose. "I'm P.C. Hafeldt."

He didn't bother to hide his surprise. "You?" He took a long step closer and stuck a once-broken nose and an incredulous expression into her face.

"*You're* Dr. Hafeldt?"

Phil took an involuntary step backward, something she often did when an aggressor advanced. She liked room to maneuver, but her reaction this time was sparked by the intensity of the man's presence.

She covered her momentary lack of balance with haughty nonchalance. "Which one do you want?"

"There's more than one of you?"

"Not at the moment. My uncle's gone missing."

"Gone missing? Sheesh! Haven't heard that one since the last time I watched Masterpiece Theater."

"I didn't ask you for a critique. I asked you for your name."

"Don't go all prickly on me, and call me Rod, honey."

"Rod? Well, Rod *Honey*, I could also call the police but would feel decidedly at a loss as to how to explain what happened in the last five minutes."

"Go ahead and call. Tell'em Rod Chaucer's here and saved your butt."

She shoved the glasses up her nose again, wondering if the frames got bent from the manhandling. "You expect me to believe that melodramatic nonsense? Oh, I can hear it now. '*Rod Chaucer, here, on the case.*'"

Rod smiled. "It does sound kinda cool, and you didn't thank me for coming to the rescue."

She stared up at him, profoundly unimpressed.

He sighed and suggested, "Let's go someplace neutral and have a chat. You need some time to cool off."

Suspecting that he was the one who needed to calm down, since she felt fine, she headed for the kitchen. "This is neutral enough for me."

He strolled after her and didn't let the swinging door—that she tried to smack him in the face with—hit him. She ignored him for a moment to consider the problem of Mr. Centerfold nurturing the impression that he had to save her. Phil could take care of herself in any situation, but she'd eat a bug before volunteering that information. That was one of the many lessons she learned while compiling ideas for her how-to book titled *A Thousand Easy Ways To Turn Off A Guy.*

Rod glanced around the kitchen. "How come this is so different from the rest of the place?"

She rinsed out the coffee carafe and set water on to boil. "I don't recall granting any interviews for *Architectural Digest*, Mr. Chaucer."

"Like I said, call me Rod."

"I'm still thinking about calling the police."

"Now, doc, we won't accomplish much talking in one-liners and non sequiturs."

Phil scowled. She dropped a filter into the drip coffeemaker and measured coffee. "Let's start with you telling me why you're here."

She watched him pause, no doubt to dredge up a devious answer. "Try not to strain yourself, Mr. Chaucer. Should I repeat the question slowly?"

"Rod, remember?" He pursed his lips, still working on his answer. "I had an appointment with your uncle. Are you sure you don't have any idea where he is?"

She swallowed and used the task of putting away the coffee bin to hide her response to his puckered lips. Her hands were shaking.

What's going on here? Get a grip, Hafeldt!

Phil gently cleared her throat. "Uncle Cal's attorney says that he's dead, but I think he's alive."

Rod arched a dark eyebrow, pulled out a chair, and swung it around to straddle it. "Now, you're talking! What makes you think Dr. Hafeldt's still alive?"

"What makes you think I'll tell you?"

He winced and shook his head. "Back to that again, are we? Water's boiling. And you're pretty calm for having gone through a life-threatening situation."

She'd been in scarier corners, but she wasn't about to tell him that. The way he refused to answer a question was annoying. He wasn't exactly making it a secret that he knew something she didn't.

His elusiveness brought to mind the old adage about keeping your friends close and your enemies closer. The difficulty was that she couldn't rationalize why her brain was telling her one thing and her body another. She wouldn't mind having him much closer than across the room, planted on a chair.

What makes him so intriguing? And what's with this curious tingle? She mentally shook herself. *Stay on task, Hafeldt!*

She shoved away from the counter she was leaning against and poured steaming water over the grounds. The brew's dark fragrance spiraled around the room. Her mouth began to water. Smooth and rich—that's how she liked her coffee and chocolate. She'd already checked out the food on hand. The kitchen cupboards contained an assortment of uninteresting cans. The chocolates in the candy jar were white and grainy from serious aging.

Phil inventoried the pantry shelves for unopened cookie packages while the coffee dripped. Glossy packaging winked at her from the back of the cupboard. She stood on tiptoe to reach the cookies and felt Rod's gaze on her back, checking out her legs, she was sure

At least my legs are nice, even if the rest is rather nondescript.

After she poured coffee, she hoarded the cookies on her side of the table. It was fortunate that he seemed to like his coffee black, since she had no intention of offering anything else. There was no milk and only enough sugar for her coffee.

He eyed the cookies. *Silly man.*

"They look fresh," he ventured suggestively.

She curled her arm around the crinkly package. "The only sustenance I give to the enemy is something to drink. You can't have my cookies."

His gaze dropped to her chest under the oversize gray silk blouse and maroon suit jacket. The intensity of his meaningful look made her cheeks burn.

"Well, darlin', if I can't have your cookies, I guess I'll have to settle for coffee. Which is good, by the way."

"Mr. Chaucer, whenever I commit time to any given project, I do it as perfectly as may be allowed, which is why the kitchen looks like this. I did all the cooking for Uncle Cal whenever I stayed with him."

He glanced at the expensive copperware hanging above the butcher block. "You mean *gore-may* stuff?"

Her reply oozed scorn. "Southern French."

He sipped appreciatively. "So, now that the big, bad guy has taken off, what's next?"

Phil tried to see what was going on behind his amused stare. "You still haven't told me what you're doing here, Mr. Chaucer."

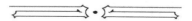

Rod grinned at the adorable dweeb sitting on the other side of the table. She had a protective arm wrapped around the macaroons, which weren't his favorite, but he liked teasing her. She had the cutest little nose, which she wrinkled whenever she heard something she didn't like. The nose thing made her glasses slip and slide and gave him a chance to enjoy those eyes—so big, blue, and direct.

The lady didn't realize that slouching over the cookie package presented some of her best assets on the table like an entree. Rod felt one corner of his mouth twitch and covered it by lifting the coffee cup

Keeping up the obnoxious macho-macho man act was tedious but necessary. He had to talk to the uncle, whose expertise and experience would provide the answers Rod needed to finish his work in progress. The trouble with being a successful writer was coming up with bigger and better ideas on the heels of the last one. The premise of his next book, and nine months of hair-rending toil, hinged on Hafeldt's learned response. He absolutely had to find the elusive anthropologist and to do that he had to figure a way around his current predicament—the suspicious and delectably prickly niece.

Everything about Hafeldt's niece screamed defensive control. The emotional signage she kept carefully suppressed, while her steady gaze shrieked that she didn't trust and wouldn't share what she knew.

He wondered how much of the truth he could tell her. Not all, of course, but enough of a story to keep her interested in the bait. A sudden epiphany made him inwardly smile; staying in her company was fast overriding his need to question the uncle. And she was so deliciously easy to provoke.

He pretended to reach for the cookies just to watch her crush them closer. "Does your uncle usually have guys come visiting with guns?"

She scowled. Her glasses slipped. "I'm the one asking the questions."

"So ask."

"What was your business with Uncle Cal?"

He paused then said in fun, "Hired me as bodyguard."

She thought about that. Her eyes darted around the room, and she started whispering under her breath. Rod covered his smile by taking a sip of coffee. She was too involved in her thoughts to notice his amusement.

"Earth to doc! Anybody ever tell you that talking to yourself could lead to problems?"

She hushed him with an impatient flip of her hand. "Be quiet. I'm thinking."

Allowing her time to ponder, he let his gaze cruise over her honey-colored hair. She had it done up in one of those complicated single braids women use to snug their hair to their scalps like a helmet. Dr. Persis Calvin Hafeldt's highbrow niece also had drowsy, bedroom eyes and killer gams. Definitely a big-brain type.

Her next question was a stunner. "Since Uncle Cal isn't here, would you consider working for me?"

He scrambled to collect and redirect his naughty thoughts. "Doing what?"

She made an impatient noise. "If Uncle Cal thought he needed a bodyguard, it goes without saying that I will need one. What do you bench-press?"

"Around four hundred."

"Done any rappelling?"

He frowned before answering. "A little."

She selected another cookie. "Are you interested in the position?"

"Depends." He watched her examine the macaroon for flaws and used the interval to carefully consider his reply.

She removed an offensive speck from the macaroon. "On what?"

"Can you take orders as well as you give them?"

Her deprecating stare told him no. "Perhaps you didn't understand, Mr. Chaucer. I would be the employer, and you would be the employee. In those instances, the employer commands the employee."

Oh, yeah, this was going to be fun. He warped a budding grin into a grimace of resignation. "Whatever you say, boss. But I got to know that you'll do what I say, when I say it, if things get sticky."

She popped the cookie into her mouth and munched. After a pause for chewing and thought, she said, "Define sticky."

"Like what happened at the door a few minutes ago."

"Oh. In those cases, should they arise, I shall defer to you, Mr. Chaucer. I must assume that Uncle Cal reviewed your credentials, such as a background check and training."

"I didn't bring anything with me, since that was already taken care of. But I'm Coronado trained and I have no felony convictions, if that's what you mean."

"Coronado?" She rolled her eyes. "Oh, wonderful. A SEAL type."

"Best training in the world. Where'd you get yours?"

"I'm the interviewer, Mr. Chaucer. This is all about retrieving information from you."

"Then let's cut to the chase. I'm housebroken, not inclined to sniff strangers in embarrassing places, and have all my shots. What more do you need to know about a guard dog? I'd still like to know where you went to school and what kind of doctor you are. After all, I told you mine. Don't I get to know yours?"

She tapped a thoughtful cadence on the crackly cellophane. Her fingernails were trimmed and unpolished.

"A number of schools, including Amherst, Stanford, Oxford," she said.

"*The* Oxford? As in England?"

"Yes. I later switched to Cambridge."

"Sheesh! I guess I won't be one-upping you in the education department. What's your field?"

"I studied romance lit, history, and library science."

"OK, since you're the one with all the brains, why not tell me about the guy with the tattoos. What was he after?"

She was going to hedge. Some people were gifted liars. Philadelphia Hafeldt was not one of them.

"My uncle was in possession of an item that either challenged or piqued the interest of some fairly ingrained institutions. Starting with the least likely, there are a few radical and far right religious groups that have been sending him threats for years."

"You're thinking the guy with the tattoos was hired by Moral Majority types?"

"I said *least* likely, Mr. Chaucer. I haven't seen many born-again evangelicals introducing themselves with the aide of an Army-issue weapon. It's true that some factions, including talk-radio charlatans, have spurred the outrage of their gullible listeners. Uncle Cal has been added to their list of lying spawns of the devil."

He forcibly suppressed the urge to laugh at the way she talked. He loved the way she sounded like a prissy throwback from the previous century.

"Why are they out to get your uncle?"

"For uncovering and insisting upon the existence of cultures previous to the Garden of Eden. Never mind that such cultures are mentioned in Genesis and carved into numerous examples of Maya stele."

"So you don't think your intruder is a site-challenged abortion clinic bomber."

"Very doubtful, Mr. Chaucer."

"Who are the other likely suspects?"

"Utility companies or certain government agencies could be possibilities."

"Not good, doc. Attracting the interest of the government is never a smart move. And the utilities are always hardball players. Your uncle doesn't pick fights with sissy boys, I'll give him that much."

"Uncle Cal never initiates conflict."

"I'm relieved. Enough chitchat. Let's get this show on the road. I expect you want to find your Uncle Cal before the boys with the guns do."

Phil stood when he swept up their cups and took them to the sink. His ploy of initiating a domestic task to confuse her first impression of him worked. He covertly watched her struggle not to mutter under her breath as she revised her opinion of him. He waited for her next remark, which would be an attempt to retake control, and reminded his lips not to smile.

She clutched the package of cookies in a territorial grip. Impatience sharpened her tone. "While you're there, you should rinse those, Mr. Chaucer. I may not be back for a while."

He sprayed them with water, shut off the tap, and shook the water from his hand. "What's next?"

She shoved the cookies into a drawer. "There's something I have to get before we go. Wait here."

Oh, yeah, like that's going to happen, he thought and watched her leave. He waited for a few minutes after the kitchen door closed to follow her.

Chapter 2

Phil went to her uncle's office, which was in every way different from the rest of the apartment. That was where he actually lived and where she would have started her search if Tattoo Guy hadn't rudely interrupted.

The scent of pipe smoke lingered in the air, a sweet tang of cherry-blend tobacco, evoking memories of the summers of her youth spent with Uncle Cal. They walked endless dusty roads and hacked trails through sultry jungles that writhed with enormous snakes and voracious insects. Even that was fun. Until the Yucatan labyrinth. The fun ended there. That was the last summer field trip.

Phil smiled as she glanced around the office—not a single boa or pesky mosquito in sight and none of the concealed dangers of Site Fifty-four and its twisting corridors. She hadn't had a nightmare about the incident in the labyrinth for months.

Shelves of books and photographs of her uncle with famous people covered all available wall space. She favored the pictures of small groups from the remote sites. Rangy and lean, her Uncle Cal towered over the scantily dressed dark-skinned men of South America.

She stopped to glide her fingertips across the frame of her favorite photo. Amazonian males, sporting colorful regalia on semi-nude bodies, glowered at the photographer, herself. A grinning Uncle Cal stood amid them in worn jeans, floppy hat, hiking boots, and a glowing tan. He held a shiny object in his open palm—the smallest of the hexagonal crystals she had helped him find. That was the best summer of all.

Phil rubbed the sting from her nose with the back of her wrist. She wouldn't cry and refused to believe the attorney. Her uncle couldn't be dead, but he was in trouble. There had to be evidence, a clue of some kind somewhere in the office, if she could only find it.

She touched the photo of him in his desk chair with her on his lap holding a crystal. She remembered that day well. They had ice cream after his best friend and colleague in the Anthro department, Mike Richardson, snapped the picture. Then they went to the Field Museum, and later had a picnic lunch by Lake Michigan. That was the day she told her uncle that crystals sang to her. It was the only way she could describe the humming vibrations in her head and the heat tickling her palm when she held them.

Uncle Cal relieved her fears when he told her that she was one of the "chosen" and special. Phil would rather be normal; she only used her so-called gift to humor or help her uncle.

Summer trips with Uncle Cal were thrilling and often dangerous. While guiding and protecting her, Uncle Cal taught her to be self-reliant and resourceful. He enrolled her in martial arts and outdoor sports to counteract her sedentary reading habits. His confidence in her made her confident in herself and eager for challenges. She bloomed in the radiance of his pride in whatever she did.

When had her life become so boring? She loved being a librarian and the everyday comfort of being surrounded by thousands of books, but she felt she'd become as dry and brittle as the paper pages.

Boring and bored. She needed Uncle Cal to get her back on track. And, it seemed that he also needed her.

Phil blinked away tears and was about to turn away when something about the picture made her pause. She looked at it again and then around the room. Something was missing. There was no hum. The black crystal, one that usually sat on his desk as a paperweight, was gone.

The oblong chunk of sparkling stone was her uncle's favorite. He discovered the stunning piece while compiling information for a paper on the Peruvian Nasca.

An identical crystal, although much smaller, was found twelve years ago in the Amazon. Phil had directed her uncle to the crystal he held in the picture with the Amazonian men, who called it a "set free" stone. That crystal, an opaque, six-sided quartz, remained continuously on loan to the geology departments of various universities. Its composition suggested that it had been man-made, a discovery that ignited a tumult of interest in the field synthetic crystal production.

The academic world continued to remain perplexed as to what an Amazonian tribe living in the heart of the jungle was doing with a synthetic stone. Industrial conglomerates were more than interested. The desktop was littered with unopened letters stamped with famous logos—a number of them from businesses involved in military laser applications.

Phil understood the business world's interest in synthetic crystals but didn't trust corporate intent. Her uncle was an anthropologist, not an engineer or a scientist. That his theories were believed boggled her, but not the industry's attraction to the potential commercial applications, which were immeasurable.

And where was the paperweight crystal?

The thought was swept from her mind by the feeling of being watched and she turned around. Rod Honey stood in the doorway like a smirking dark angel.

"Mr. Chaucer, I believe I said that you were to wait in the kitchen."

"Yep. You did. This is what I call showing employee initiative."

He stood in the doorway, his grin and virile confidence as lethal as a double order of curly fries.

No, more like the sinfulness of crème brulée.

She had to stop with the food association thing and keep her mind on track. Chaucer could be an enemy too dangerous to keep close, but if she cut him loose now, she would miss out on so many opportunities to use him. She suspected she was going to need all the help she could get. The absence of the black crystal, removed by her uncle or someone else, screamed a warning.

Phil grabbed a well-used satchel style briefcase from a chair and left the office.

Rod followed her back to the kitchen. "Where to first?"

She began to transfer items from her smaller briefcase into Uncle Cal's larger one. "To the funeral home to pick up the ashes."

"I thought you said he was alive."

"They aren't his. I know it."

Chapter 3

A blast of heat, like the opening of an oven door, rushed out of her uncle's ancient Plymouth. Phil rolled down the window and slid in behind the wheel. The bench seat crunched and seared the backs of her legs. She waited for Rod to get seated before handing him a pewter urn full of ashes. He grimaced and set it on the car mat, using his feet to hold it in place.

She pulled the rusting sedan out into the traffic on Roosevelt. "That's not Uncle Cal."

He kept a wary eye on the container. "How can you be so sure?"

"I know, that's all. Uncle Cal is alive, and I'll find him."

"Where to now?"

"To the bank. The estate lawyer gave me a safe-deposit box key." She decided not to mention the fact that it was a stash she knew nothing about.

He said, "I expect you know that it'll take more than a key."

She flicked on the left turn signal. "It's in both our names. I'm his heir and cosigner on everything. When he works in the field, he often goes to places where there is a dearth of ATMs."

"A dearth, huh?"

She ignored that. "Long ago, we decided that I should handle his affairs while he's gone. I also arrange for shipments of whatever he needs."

He acknowledged this with a lift of his chin. They stopped at an intersection and a refreshing breeze off the lake pushed through the window on his side. His hair had a tendency to curl and ruffled in the wind.

From covertly watching Rod, Phil was reassured that she hadn't abandoned all logic by hiring him. Her newly hired bodyguard kept his attention focused on the outside mirror, scanning the streets. He did this casually, as if sightseeing and not searching for lurking thugs with tattoos and automatic weapons.

The closest parking space to the bank was almost a block from the entrance. Phil made Chaucer wait in the car with a stranger's remains while she entered the sterile, air-conditioned chill of the bank lobby. Her skin cringed from the attack of cool air through her sweat-damp clothes.

After Phil was left alone in the vault, she opened the safe deposit box. The hum from the crystals inside increased. She quickly sorted through the documents, setting aside familiar papers, and exposed the row of glittering crystals that lined the bottom of the metal box. Discordant melodies rose up from the assortment of stones. She selected the black, hexagonal one that her uncle usually kept on his desk and dropped it into the oversize, leather briefcase.

A manila envelope with her name scrawled on the front contained a rubber-banded roll of bills in large denominations. A note and photos of jungle sites filled a business-size envelope. The inscription inside the unfolded note was brief: You know where I am.

Phil dropped her uncle's note back into the box, took half the cash and the envelope of pictures. She returned the familiar documents and closed the lid.

A few minutes later, she stepped out of the bank and into the sun's glare. Something hit her from behind—a brutal shove between the shoulder blades that sent her stumbling to the sun-baked pavement.

A youth made a grab for her briefcase. Phil resisted the urge to retaliate and held onto the straps, forcing her attacker to drag her on her right hip across the hot cement. The thin cotton of her skirt began to shred. She held fast to the leather straps and crushed the briefcase to her chest.

A pair of men's brown leather loafers glided past her face. In the next second, she was released and her shoulder hit the concrete. She sprawled on the sidewalk, blinking to get her bearings.

She sat up and saw that her bodyguard had her teenage assailant restrained, holding him still with one hand. On closer examination, she saw that Rod's thumbnail was pinched into the back of the youth's hand. The pressure on the nerve between the sensitive bones held the boy immobilized.

Phil looped the long straps over her head and tucked the briefcase securely under her arm. She awkwardly stood up, hugging the leather satchel to her body. Angry at herself for being caught off guard, she worked to calm her pounding heart that threatened to burst from her chest.

Instinct brushed a warning across her senses. She pivoted. Using the heel of her hand, she blocked a second assailant's attack, a tire iron aimed at Rod's head. Utilizing the assailant's momentum, she flipped the youth onto his back on the pavement. The boy's head cracked against the cement. His eyes wobbled in the sockets before he passed out.

Phil picked up the tire iron and gestured at the squirming youth that Rod held immobile. "What do we do with Bevis and Butthead?"

The youth held prisoner began to curse. Rod increased the pressure and the teen buckled with a shriek. He landed on his knees on the sidewalk. When Rod released him, the teen leaped up and ran off, abandoning his knocked out friend.

Rod glanced down at the unconscious teen on the pavement. "Let them go. They're just kids, and it's best to leave before the police get here and delay us with a ton of questions."

"Just leave him here on the sidewalk?"

Rod strode back to the rusting Plymouth, lobbed her the keys she'd left in the ignition, and got in the passenger side.

"Come on, Phil. The police will be here any minute. They'll hold us up with hours of questioning and forms. Bring that tire iron. It's got your prints."

She exhaled a sigh and tossed the tire iron onto the back seat. As she slid the car into the downtown traffic, Rod asked, "That was a neat move back there. Where'd you learn it?"

"An elderly Aikido sensei. The technique isn't seen much these days."

"It looked so quick and smooth. It knocked the kid out. I've never seen anything like it."

She glanced in the rearview mirror, memorizing cars, checking for a tail. "It's the utilization of one's own concentrated chi and the attacker's momentum. Your style is military, like the usage of the pressure point on the back of the boy's hand. All quite aggressive."

He shrugged. "It's a guy thing. Where are we headed?"

"To your hotel to pick up your clothes. After that, O'Hare. Where are you staying?"

"O'Hare? Where are we flying to?"

"Colorado. That's where I think my uncle is."

"Not smart, doc."

"A word of advice, Mr. Chaucer. It is never wise to insult one's employer."

"It's part of your brilliant plan to lead the creeps right to him?"

Phil tried to sort through his question and weave through downtown Chicago's kamikaze traffic at the same time. "What do you suggest?"

"Can you afford to take a roundabout route to your uncle?"

She smirked. "I've got enough cash with me to hire a private jet."

"That'll work. Besides Colorado, where else in the U.S. did your uncle spend time working?"

"How about Florida?"

A half grin lifted one side of his mouth. "Hot at this time of year but great roads for driving. We'll fly into West Palm. From there we'll drive around and fly to Denver from another airport."

"We have to stop and collect your rental car and luggage first."

"Never mind that. Go straight to O'Hare. I took a cab to your uncle's and the hotel can send my luggage home. We need to get out of Chicago. Too dangerous here."

"What's the matter, Mr. Chaucer? A tussle with a few boys out to prove themselves to their gang buddies put a fright into you?"

"It's not the boys, doc. It's the goons who hired them. And there're two cars tailing us."

Phil jerked her attention to the car mirrors. "Which ones?"

"The beat-up blue Buick and the newer Chevy sedan three cars back. The Buick is the decoy. Your uncle has some serious enemies. I think the Chevy might be federal."

"How do we elude them?"

"We don't, and slow down."

Phil made an impatient noise. "Perhaps I failed to explain your position, Mr. Chaucer. You are the bodyguard. I am the employer. Do I need to be more specific?"

"No, doc. In fact, it's my turn to be specific. We *want* them to follow us. It's *good* to know where the bad guys are. We want them to tail us away from here. We'll lose them later, when and where it's good for us. Get it?"

Phil thought about that for a moment. "Like the Everglades?"

"Now you're getting it, doc."

Phil headed for the closest I-90 on-ramp that would take them directly to O'Hare.

Chapter 4

The argument they got into at the ticket counter attracted a crowd. The disagreement started when Rod insisted on seats at the rear of the plane. The glaring resentment of the passengers waiting in line intensified Phil's embarrassment. She tried to point out the benefits of the seats closest to first class but he refused to listen.

A tug on Phil's sleeve interrupted the furiously whispered dispute. She turned and looked down.

A pair of sly, age-faded eyes glared up at Phil. The lady's startling outfit upstaged her scowl. She wore trendy purple biker tights that looked two sizes too small. A fuchsia warm-up jacket covered a magenta silk shell. Her tiny waist was encircled with a garish pink fanny pack. Short, silver hair was expensively cut in a spiky, youthful style that contrasted with her age. Her complexion was tanned to black-walnut stage—the tone and texture of worn leather—a testament of too many years of sun worship. The embodiment of a Florida retirement community refugee, she lacked only one appendage—the golf cart.

Her escort was a giant young man who appeared to possess no personality and enough muscle mass to qualify for a building permit. His bland, smooth complexion remained impassive until his elderly companion spoke, at which time a crease of concern appeared between his almost nonexistent eyebrows.

Like a yappy lap dog, the retiree barked, "Hey, you two! Make up your minds already. I got a plane to catch."

Phil gave Rod a warning scowl before answering. "I'm sorry, ma'am, but we're almost done."

The wink and smirk Phil received in reply was not grandmotherly. "If I had something like that, I wouldn't waste my time arguing with it."

When Phil was unable to curb a stunned glance at the huge escort to check for his reaction, the older woman cracked a laugh. "Naw, that's my grandson, the nose tackle. Don't much care for the bulky types, myself. I tend to go for the baseball players. They've all got those great buns."

Phil felt her cheeks brighten. Grandmothers weren't supposed to talk like that! She jerked around, resolved to hide her embarrassment and ignore Rod's amusement.

"Hey, doc, aren't you going to introduce us?"

Always ready to create a complication, Rod broke off their argument to bestow on the feisty senior a naughty smirk and questioning expression. She immediately stuck out her hand.

"I'm Estelle, sweetcakes. What's your handle?"

"Rod."

Estelle grinned hugely and looked up at her grandson. "Get lost, Teddy. I got me a new guy. A guy with a *real* name."

The brief spasm of pained helplessness that came and went on Teddy's face was replaced with grim determination. "Dad said I had to stay with you, Granny. Remember what happened last time?"

Estelle narrowed her eyes. All eighty pounds of her wiry frame vibrated indignation. "I changed your diapers,

Theodore. How'd you like it if I stopped by after practice for a locker-room chat?"

"Grandma!"

"Go home, sonny. I found me a new beau." She turned back to Rod and suggestively waggled her eyebrows. "How about it, Rod? You and me."

"Estelle," Rod said, "I gotta admit I'm tempted, but last week I saw your grandson take down a three-hundred pound offensive lineman. I think I'll stick with the ball and chain I already got."

Phil rolled her eyes and muttered, "I can't take any more of this. Sit wherever you want. I'm going to make a reservation for a rental car. Meet me there."

Eager to escape, Phil headed for the baggage claim area. She started at the first counter in the row of rental agencies, not stopping until she confirmed a reservation in West Palm Beach.

Rod waited for her on the other side of the area roped off for customers. As she turned away from the desk, the man behind the reservation counter said, "Are you traveling with Bud?"

Phil stared. "Are you speaking to me?"

"Yeah. Isn't that Bud Gameson over there?"

Phil forced her face to stay absolutely expressionless. "You know him?" She darted a glance at the agent's badge, "Larry?"

"Everybody in Chicago knows him and his family. Bud went to college with my sister. He was on her tennis team."

Phil's mind raced. She forced a smile. "You must have him confused with someone else."

Larry smiled back, shrugged, and turned to the next customer. Phil took off at a fast walk, her thoughts in a jumble.

"Hey, doc, slow down."

She allowed Rod, alias Bud, to take her arm and wasn't happy about the way she liked the feel of his holding her. The guy was definitely a liar. But she'd known that from the first, so why was she so angry to have her suspicions confirmed? The point was to keep him around until she figured him out. She put aside her worries as they approached the check-in area.

She was grateful that there were no long lines. She made sure that the clasp on her briefcase was securely fastened and set it on the conveyor belt. She slipped off her watch and emptied her pockets into the plastic tub before going through the archway.

Her necklace set off the alarm and she waited to be checked over, oblivious, as the wand swept along her body. Her mind was working on what to do about Rod. Or Bud.

Cleared, she slipped on her shoes and met Rod, who had passed through without a hitch.

He handed her the briefcase. "What's in that thing?"

She glared. "Funny you should ask, *Bud!*"

He didn't react, just stared until someone coming out of the checkpoint area made an impatient noise. Rod gently drew her out of the way. Still holding her arm, they moved toward the departure gates.

"Haven't heard that in a long time," he said.

Phil made a skeptical noise. "Quite the coincidence that the guy at the car rental should recognize you."

Rod frowned. "You're right. What did he look like? I wasn't paying attention to the people behind the counters."

Phil jerked her arm free. "I've got to stop in here before we board the plane and get rid of these torn pantyhose."

She felt Rod's gaze on her back as she went into the restroom. Still angry with herself, she glared at her image in the mirror. A toilet flushed. The glass reflected the stall door behind her opening

Estelle came out and grinned when she discovered Phil. She now wore a sleek pair of sunglasses on top of her head. Silver spikes of hair sprouted around the expensive shades.

"Hi, doc! Looks like we're going in the same direction." Estelle washed her hands and talked as she looked at Phil in the mirror. "I always have to take a tinkle before getting on the plane. Can't stand the smell of those boxy, little toilets. And the seats are always ice cold. Makes my bladder tight as a tick. Can't squeeze out a drop when that happens. Do you think it's true that they flush right out into the air as the plane is flying along?"

By this time, Estelle had her hands dried and was waiting for an answer. Stunned by the images, Estelle's candor, and the subject, Phil mumbled an apology and ducked into an empty stall. The wily and vivacious Estelle was gone when she came out.

Exhaling a relieved sigh, Phil washed her hands, checked the contents of her briefcase, patted her clothes into place, and exited around the doorless corner. She stifled a moan when she saw Estelle talking to Rod.

A hand shot out and grabbed the straps of her bag the second she cleared the doorway. Phil leaned back and jerked the man off his feet. He landed on the floor, still gripping the strap.

Phil broke his hold with a kick to his right elbow. He sprang up, ready to make another grab for the straps with his good arm. His right arm hung limp and useless but he was still game.

A streak of purple flashed in front of Phil. Estelle poked the man with something in her hand. The assailant's eyes rolled and he staggered.

Rod grabbed Estelle around the waist from behind and pulled her away. Phil's assailant scurried backward in a frenzied retreat. He fled through the crowd, heading for the departure gates.

Rod pried the Taser from Estelle's hand. "Where'd you get this?"

Enjoying herself, Estelle piped, "My fanny pack."

"Your..? How'd you get it through the check-in?"

Coy and satisfied, Estelle chortled. "I just acted senile and sent it through in the coin tray. It doesn't look like a regular one. Must be running out of juice. Didn't knock the guy out."

Rod shook his head, disgusted. "You're not taking this on the plane." He looked at Phil. "I'll meet you at the gate. This has to be turned in to the airport authorities."

Phil nodded and looped the straps of the briefcase over her head and across her shoulders. Estelle toddled after Phil as she moved to the departure gates, spry as a gymnast and talking all the way. Her chatter distracted Phil from worrying about what Rod was doing while he was out of her sight.

"Are you two married?" Estelle asked. "If you aren't, do you think he'd date me?"

"Do you have to talk so loud?"

"So are you married or anything?"

Phil stopped walking. "You should be ashamed of yourself. He's half your age!"

"Listen, honey, sex doesn't end when you turn forty. It just gets better. You know what? You act like you haven't had any since high school, and you've got no excuse with that guy hanging around. So, if you aren't going to make use of that gorgeous thing, can I have him?"

"You lost your sunglasses in the shuffle."

"Some kid'll pick them up. Let's talk about the hunk. Is he taken or not?"

Desperate, Phil muttered a lie. "I hear my flight being called. You'll have to excuse me now."

Phil stared meaningfully at Estelle until the older woman grinned and took off at a trot in the direction Rod went.

The waiting area for their flight to Florida was empty. No one was at the counter. After making some phone calls, Phil sank into a chair and closed her eyes. She had finally been able to contact her uncle's maintenance service. Someone would have the apartment door taken care of before the flight departed O'Hare. It was a relief to know that the door they'd propped into place would be repaired immediately. How nice it would be to have everything else in life fixed so easily

Maybe Estelle would hog-tie Rod. She'd make the flight in peace, blessedly alone.

Twenty minutes later, when passenger seat assignments were being announced, Rod was still nowhere in sight. Phil was furious with herself for caring and wondering. He showed up as the last of the passengers were boarding.

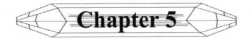

Chapter 5

The late afternoon flight in midsummer to Florida had plenty of seats available. Phil clutched her briefcase to her chest and walked up the narrow aisle. Rod had gotten his way and reserved seats at the back of the plane, the very last row.

Phil sidled across seats to the window. Exhausted, she leaned back and closed her eyes. The plane wouldn't be taking off for a while. She could rest her eyes for a minute.

A deep voice murmured against her ear, his breath warm and moist against her cheek. "Buckle up."

She opened her eyes, startled that she had actually dozed off. Disoriented, she blinked at the man sitting next to her. Rod reached over and slid his hand down the side of her hip to search for the belt buckle.

Phil sat still and watched him insert the clasp and adjust the fit. Her hip burned where he searched for the elusive belt. When he leaned back into his seat, she thought his cheekbones looked slightly flushed.

A grown man blushing?

The plane jerked and the tarmac began to move outside the window. A woman with strong, tanned legs, wearing a bright orange vest, waved signals to the pilot. In moments the plane was rumbling down the runway, then thrusting up into the air. The wheels clunked into place.

Outside the window, the sunset on the horizon disappeared when the plane banked and headed south.

This had been an event-filled day. Not at all boring. When had she become such a stick? She tried to think back and discovered that she had eased into mediocrity. Sort of oozed into a bland monochrome life.

She could tell that Rod thought of her as a geek. She used to be fun and do fun things. When had she given up on life? When had she given up on men?

Phil looked at Rod. He was focused inward, dissecting a private thought. She studied the backs of his broad hands resting on his thighs. She liked his hands, and the way he held himself, so self-contained, confident, and relaxed. He was a little like Uncle Cal but more like her father.

That odd comparison struck her as significant. Her father was the stereotypical egghead, forever lost in the workings of his mind, the quintessential intellectual.

Rod, who looked yummier than a bowl of double-dipped chocolate covered peanuts, acted like her father, content to think, happy inside his head. The combination of academic and stud didn't fit into the neat equations that ordered her life. Perhaps that was why she found him so intriguing and made so many excuses to keep him with her.

She frowned. If Rod acted true to intellectual type, he should be bursting with interesting things to talk about. It was a cruel disappointment that most of what came out of his mouth sounded dismally testosterone-driven.

Phil sighed. Oh, *well. When a guy looks like Rod, who needs conversation?*

Oh, dear, she hadn't realized that she harbored that little seed of sexism. She shook her head, chastising herself for allowing fantasies of the horizontal mambo with Rod to distract her from her uncle.

Rod unexpectedly reached out and took her hand. "What's the matter? Nervous?"

His warm fingers completely encased hers. Her mouth went dry. "Uh, no. Why do you ask?"

"You look…concerned."

"Just thinking." *Damn. Why is he taking his hand away?*

"A penny for them."

She thought a smile was in order. It came off sort of crooked. "They're rather convoluted, I'm afraid. Mostly about Uncle Cal."

He settled back in the seat. "Tell me something about him."

"What would you like to know?"

Rod's killer lips twitched with a smile. "Like why an anthropologist insisted on taking his niece to work with him wherever he went."

"Oh. That."

Like, she was going to tell him the truth? She learned that lesson a long time ago. She wasn't about to confess the weird fact of her being a human crystal magnet and send him screaming from the plane. Whenever that topic came up, her male companion invariably zoned-out and redirected his attention to her chest or the other women in the room.

She glanced out the window. Night darkened the sky above the fading sunset. Small towns twinkled to life below. It wouldn't hurt to tell him a little; it might be comforting to talk about her uncle.

"Uncle Cal allowed me to come along mainly because I asked. I love being with him. Always have.

38

Some kids dream of having their very own fairy godmother. I have a fey uncle. He ended up being more of a parent than my own ever were."

"You lived with him full-time?"

"No. I went to private schools and spent the summers with him. The holidays were with my parents. Mom was usually gone on sabbatical or teaching out of the country. Dad always held down the home fort."

"What does he do?"

"Research. Mother was an educator."

"Was?"

"She died the day before my high school graduation. A car accident."

They were interrupted when the flight attendant asked their choice of beverage. They were handed annoyingly small packets of peanuts and useless paper napkins the size of postage stamps.

When the attendant moved the cart down the aisle, Rod dipped a hand into his suit-coat pocket and came out with three candy bars and a bag of cashews.

Phil gaped at the goodies. Saliva gushed in her mouth. "Oh! You have risen to the heights of divinity, my god in jock's clothing."

"Shame on you! And here I was sure you looked more like a Presbyterian than a pagan. But I can do pagan."

"I'm Methodist and will do you serious physical harm if you don't give me that chocolate. Now!"

His treacherous grin and next comment sidetracked her from the candy bar. "Oh, baby, I do like it when you talk tough rough. Do you play that way, too?"

He laughed silently at the expression she hadn't been able to quell and peeled back the candy wrapper.

"Close your mouth, honey. I may like my love life rowdy but not with an audience."

Dazed by imagery, Phil accepted the chocolate. When she held it motionless in a limp hand, he broke off a piece and slipped it between her parted lips.

"Now, chew."

She did and pried her stare away from the enticing mischief in his dark gaze. Her mind refused to part with the vision of Rod's rowdy love life. *Yikes!*

After swallowing, she choked out, "Do you really like it that way?"

Rod averted his face. She could tell by the way his shoulders shook that he was laughing at her spontaneous question. Her uncle always bragged about how much he liked her ingenuous curiosity. She often ended up embarrassed by the questions that flew out of her mouth.

She poked his arm. "Don't laugh at me, Chaucer. The question may be impolite but it was honest."

Merriment glinted in his eyes when he turned back to seriously respond, "Oh, honey, I'm just a guy. You should know by now that we men like it any way we can get it."

She scowled at him and munched the chocolate in silence. After the snacking mess had been cleared away, the interior lights were lowered. Passengers snuggled into comfortable positions to sleep.

"Hey, doc."

She pulled her attention from the black world beyond the window. "What?"

"You were telling me about your uncle. Why is he considered—"

"A crackpot?" she finished for him and gave him a few points for being kind about her uncle.

"I wouldn't have put it that way."

Phil smiled. "His Atlantis theories have made him famous and infamous at the same time. The controversy helped him to make a great deal of money on the book about his finds. He even turned down a movie option."

"Why'd he do that?"

"Oh, I guess he thought his ideas were laughed at enough. A movie would make the world take his ideas less seriously."

"Exactly what are his ideas?"

"Since childhood, he's been fascinated with Plato's writings on Atlantis. When he was ten, he went to an Egyptian artifacts exhibit and saw a circular shaped calendar. It reminded him of pre-Columbian calendars. Then he got to thinking about Native American wheels. All of this began to tie together in his mind. That's how he came to believe that Atlantis really existed."

"Because of the frequent occurrence of circular patterns?"

"No, that's more of a mathematician's point of view. Uncle Cal is strictly right brain. What he really noticed is that almost all ancient cultures are similar in physical appearance."

"Black hair and dark skin?"

"Exactly. This led him to believe that the similarities stem from a mass migration from Atlantis after the continent's catastrophic end."

He thought about that and shrugged. "Not a crazy deduction. So, how did he find evidence to support it?"

"Some DNA studies have been done in the last years that support his migration theories and a number of obvious historical occurrences in different parts of the globe happened at the same time." She paused then asked, "What's wrong?"

"Nothing, actually. It's more of what's right. You just answered a question I had. Tell me more about the migration thing."

"As I said, it's based on historical occurrences and the sudden high level of scientific, agricultural, and cultural understanding. There were also a zillion pyramids popping up from the Middle East to Central America and Asia around the same time. Then there're the crystals."

"Crystals have been found in all those places?"

"He didn't find any in Asia, but I wasn't with him for those trips. He's searched Brazil many times. He believes there's an outpost or buried colony still intact somewhere in the Amazon. He wrote the book because he lacked financial backing for a final venture. He was setting up the trip when I last talked to him."

"When was that?"

Phil wedged a thin pillow behind her back and twisted sideways in the seat to face him. She watched him drape a blanket over her lap.

"You're very nurturing for a guy."

"You think so? I thought it was a gentleman thing."

She grinned. "You must have a nice mommy."

He thought about that. "She's kind of hard-nosed about manners. Other than that, pretty easy to live with."

Phil didn't bother to hide her shock. "You still live with your parents?"

Rod grimaced. "Do I look like somebody who still lives with Mommy and Daddy? Back to your uncle."

"Where was I?"

He narrowed his eyes and began to tick off the details on his fingers. "He's figured out that the world's scattered dark-skinned cultures were descendants of Atlantis, which isn't altogether outfield. It might explain the Nasca drawings and mound builders, and the Cro Magnon having a larger brain capacity than our own. There's also the circular building patterns of ancient civilizations in North America and elsewhere." He paused when he noticed her astonishment. "Uh, I have a friend who is really into this stuff."

She searched his face. "Why act like a musclehead when you're smart?"

"What's the matter? You got something against jocks?"

She squinted at him, fed up with his games. "Something tells me you're not a jock or a womanizer."

Her heart lurched when his hand slid under the blanket. "I could be both."

She muffled a squeak and grabbed his hand when his fingers got too personal. He chuckled and withdrew.

His stare pinned her to stillness, a visual challenge that conveyed a purely masculine dare. She felt the heavy thumping of her heart inside her chest and instinctively withdrew. The ridge of the window bit into her spine. Her breathing sounded loud. The world contracted into the place where they sat, looking at each other. The space felt too confined.

A snore came from one of the forward seats, breaking the spell.

Phil whispered, "You always do things to distract me from finding out what you don't want me to know. It makes me curious."

"Nothing wrong with curious. In fact, I'm curious about exactly where your uncle found the crystals."

Suspicion made her pause. "Which one?"

"Let's start with the small one."

"In a box of rocks from Florida."

"What made him pull it out of the box? Does it look different from other crystal formations?"

"No, but the one I have and the one on loan have the same markings."

"Markings? You mean tags?"

"No, I mean markings. They're both etched on their bases with what Uncle Cal thinks are glyphs."

"He thinks Atlanteans used glyphs instead of script?"

Oh, but she loved a guy with brains! Excited, she shifted sideways in the seat to face him. "Actually, he thinks that they used both. When I found the big one—"

"Whoa! Did you just say that you found it?"

Chapter 6

Phil growled under her breath for revealing that bit of information. *Stupid, stupid, stupid!*

She huffed a sigh, disgusted with herself, especially when she noticed the glint in Rod's gaze and the private-dick-on-the-trail-hits-pay-dirt smirk. She hated that grin. It made her spine tingle.

Noting her anger, he expanded his smile and leaned closer. "Oh, baby, you are *so* busted."

His voice was low and honey-smooth. His breath on her mouth carried Essence of Hershey. The fiery promise in the liquid dark of his eyes made her heart speed up.

She came to her senses and pushed him away and back into his seat. "Yeah, yeah. Save it for somebody who'll fall for that act. I know my priorities. Give me some more chocolate."

"You mean the sex substitute?"

Phil grabbed the half bar he was waving under her nose and snarled, "You've been reading too much *Cosmo*. By the way, what did you do with that item you picked up off the carpet at Uncle Cal's apartment?"

"Locked it in the trunk while you were in the bank. Let's get back to that bit where you said that you found the crystal."

There was no way she was going to tell him about that. She'd scared off too many guys when she told them about her "knack" of tuning into the music of the spheres.

Annoyed with her compulsive bent for fairness, she accepted her attraction to him and the rare event of having a man interested in her. A girl didn't bump into men with confidence and GQ looks every day. Instinct told her that this guy was bonafide. Sort of. So she wasn't going to screw it up with trying to explain the occasional hum in her head whenever a crystal was in the vicinity.

She ran the tip of her tongue across the square of chocolate stuck to the roof of her mouth. She savored the rich flavor, making it last, even though it gave her a temporary speech impediment to have it lodged there.

"Leth's thalk inthead about yo' bwilliant idea uff 'ow da geth da Colah-rado."

"What did you say?"

She repeated it after swallowing, and added, "Via Florida, of course."

His expression told her that this was no problem. "Use some of your wad of cash to get us on the first flight out to Denver. I'll take it from there."

"Whatever." Phil turned her head and used the back of her wrist to hide a yawn. "You're welcome to do the vampire thing, but this girl's got to sleep. Wake me when we get to West Palm."

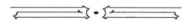

Rod reached up to switch off the overhead lights. He watched Phil snuggle into a comfy position. She surprised him when she fell asleep, suddenly and soundly.

He stared, shook his head slightly, and looked away. Sleep that fast and deep meant that she had to have an honest heart. On the other hand, he was looking at some serious sleep-deprived psychosis. And he'd told more fibs today than he had in his entire life. He'd stretched the truth to the screaming point so often that he might never sleep again.

Unable to control the urge, he turned his attention back to Phil. He smiled. Philadelphia Casca Hafeldt. He remembered being surprised when the administrative office at the University of Chicago connected him to the Regenstein Library where he asked for "good old Hafeldt" to come to the phone. The chuckling response of the person on the other end of the line was not unexpected, but there was a subtext underneath the affectionate humor that sent up a warning flag.

After many minutes on hold, the library informed him that Dr. Hafeldt was not available. They refused to give any information over the phone. His plan was to stop at the university if the elusive anthropologist wasn't at home. The discovery that the unavailable Hafeldt was not a middle-aged academic was another surprise. Meeting the niece turned out to be the best part of trying to hunt down the uncle. And what a surprise to get some of the answers he needed from the uncle in a casual conversation with the niece.

His gaze cruised over the sleeping woman and he hoped that she might find a way to make herself re-available. He liked her sass and quirky temper. The obstacle was that she acted like she'd been more than merely bruised in her relationships with men. He was going to have to tread carefully. He knew a keeper when he saw one.

Wisps of caramel-colored curls fringed her brow. She would not be pleased that the single braid had lost its tight perfection. She was so deliciously uptight. Women like that sometimes used a prim façade to mask the tumult underneath.

What an interesting thought. Dr. Hafeldt, demure librarian, concealing a bit of wantonness under a prudish shell.

One of the buttons on her blouse had popped off, revealing a glimpse of seductive underwear. He liked lace and baby blue. *Oh, yeah. The librarian's definitely a hottie in disguise.*

"Can't fool a fooler, " he whispered and lightly ran the tip of his forefinger over her lower lip.

Her only response was a sweet little snorty snore. Rod grinned and stood up.

He maneuvered with care along the narrow aisle, heading for the gentle glow and faint click of computer keys.

The laptop belonged to a chilly blond, who made it known with a glare that she was not happy about being disturbed. He gave her his best smile. She thawed.

He leaned down. "I'm sorry, but I am in desperate need. No, I'm not here to hit on you. Just want to send an e-mail. Can you go online with that?"

Astonished, she blinked. "Yes. Are you sending to a private address or a business?"

"A company."

"Then I suppose it'll be fine. I won't be sending until I reach the hotel later this evening. Do you still want me to do it?"

"Yeah, thanks. By the way, my name's Rod."

"I'm Stephanie."

He shook her hand when she offered it. She was in business; he could tell by her firm, brief grip.

Rod gave her the online address. After she tapped it in, he said, "Make it to Binky."

When Stephanie sent him a you've-got-to-be-kidding look, he clarified, "My assistant."

"Right. So what do I tell Binky?"

"Cell phone temporarily out of order. Stay by yours. I'll be calling. Run a preflight check on the plane yourself. Rod."

Stephanie grinned. "I guess Binky isn't a bimbo, then."

"Uh, not even close. Thanks. Is there anything I can do for you? If you'd give me your business card, I'd like to show my appreciation."

They were interrupted by a sardonic cackle. "I just bet you would."

Rod looked up from the screen's soft blue glow. Estelle stood in the aisle. "Hi. What brings you from first class?"

"I thought I smelled a cupcake. Care to introduce me to your friend?"

"Estelle, this is Stephanie. Another new acquaintance."

Estelle wasted no time. "You'd better look out for this one, Stephie. He's got another cutie tucked away in the last row. Besides, I saw him before you did, so hands off."

Appalled, Stephanie stammered, "I'm married!"

Estelle snorted. "What's *that* got to do with it? So's he! At least, he says he is. I have my doubts. You could say I'm something of an expert about marriage, and I'm betting they're not hitched. They don't act like it. And you don't want him anyway. His nose is too small. I don't care what anybody says. Big noses, not big feet, are the way to tell. Sometimes big hands, but the nose is the best way. My second husband had a *huge* nose."

Rod held up a hand to silence her. "Uh, Estelle, if you would be quiet for a moment?" He smiled apologetically at Stephanie; an innocent helper and bystander didn't deserve this. Stephanie's bright cheeks and horrified expression sparked the temptation to strangle Estelle and fling her off the plane.

"Stephanie, would you excuse us? It was a pleasure meeting you, and thanks again for helping me with that message."

"Give my regards to Binky when you see her," Stephanie muttered, eyeing Estelle in fascinated dread, as if she were a bomb about to explode.

Rod herded Estelle down the aisle toward first class before she could spout another tasteless innuendo. He plunked her into an empty seat and took the one across the aisle, well out of her reach. Best to be safe. He feared she was a groper. Estelle proved his suspicions by leaning across the aisle to tuck something into his suit coat pocket and feel around while her hand was inside.

Rod jerked her hand out and tugged the business card from her fingers. She smirked and elevated her eyebrows. "Just making sure you had my number, lover."

Rod glanced at the card and tucked it away. "All right, Estelle, what's it going to take to turn you up sweet?"

Her smile was coy. She played with the uneven ends of her pricey haircut. "What have you got?"

"Nothing for you, if you don't promise to behave."

Disgusted, she waved a hand. "Well, I suppose I can. You don't have a big nose, so why should I waste my time getting my hopes up for a letdown."

"Believe me, Estelle, nose size is no indicator."

She laughed. "Yeah, I know. My first husband had a pug nose and he had the second one beat by an inch."

Rod *had* to get her off this subject. "You said you lived on Sanabel, right?"

"Almost forty-seven years."

"Impossible! You can't be a day over forty-five."

Estelle's faded-green eyes twinkled. "Whatever you want, stud muffin, you just tell me and it's yours."

"I need an alibi. Sort of."

She sat up in her seat, intrigued. "This sounds like fun. You and the girl in trouble?"

"Not really, but you may be questioned. You took down that guy at O'Hare in a public area and were seen talking with us."

"I knew you weren't married."

"Not yet, but I'll get her in the end."

Rod hesitated. *Where did that come from?*

Estelle dove into the breach. "You mean it. I can tell. In that case, tell me what you want me to say."

"If anybody asks, and they will, tell them you overheard us saying that we hired a boat and plan to do some fishing in the Keys."

"No problem. I'll make it sound convincing. My fourth husband had sailboats. Uh-oh."

Rod glanced up, following Estelle's stare. Phil had left her seat. She stood in the aisle, and from the look on her face, had been listening. He mentally scrambled to remember what he'd said.

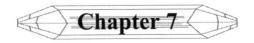

Chapter 7

Phil thought Rod looked guilty and wished she knew why. Anyone in Estelle's company was bound to suffer some form of humiliation, but she suspected it was more than merely getting ensnared in another predicament—episodes she was beginning to think of as Estelle-capades.

Her lips felt stiff when she tried to cover her feelings with a smile. "You two having a nice chat?"

Estelle leaned into the aisle and whispered, "She doesn't look happy, Rod. Maybe I better take my toys and go home."

Phil watched Estelle spring from the seat and hurry away. She slipped through and jerked shut the curtains between first class and coach.

Rod followed Phil back to their seats. She glared at him when he sat down beside her. "I don't think it's wise to encourage that woman."

"I have to agree. She's a little frightening. How much did you hear?"

"Enough to know not to use nose size as an indicator for something. We won't go there. I'd rather live my life blissfully free of yet another Estelle-ism. I lost my watch during the bank confrontation. How long did I sleep?"

"Not more than twenty minutes. Have you thought about what you want to do after we land?"

Phil refastened her seat belt. "Actually, I have. But I thought you wanted to organize the travel plans."

"Not especially. Just a few pointers now and again. You know where your uncle is and I don't. What are your thoughts?"

"Pick up the rental car, get on the turnpike, and go north. Take the first exit and go west. At some point, I have to buy clothes. My jacket barely covers the rips in my skirt, and what I'm wearing isn't appropriate for where we're going."

"You've said you know your uncle is alive and in Colorado but not exactly where."

"He's not in Colorado but that's where we're stopping first. We'll drive or hire a small plane from there."

"I've got to admit that you know how to show a guy a good time. Life's not boring when you're around. Why the look?"

Phil shook her head. "The recent activity is unusual for me."

"You call what we've been through today just activity? Anyone else would say that you live in the fast lane, lady."

"Today was an exception. I consider myself rather dull, plodding along, doing my job, day in and day out. And my life is pretty boring, compared to the years I spent with Uncle Cal."

"That must have been a trip, exploring with an archeologist."

"He's a cultural anthropologist. He uses archeology to substantiate his work."

"After spending so much time with him, I'm amazed you didn't follow his lead. Why didn't you major in that?"

She made a face. "I like the exploring part but not the study of it. What little I know, I picked up from being around Uncle Cal."

"Have you ever heard about the legend of the crystal skulls?"

"Do you mean the Skull of Doom?"

"Yeah. My friend goes on and on about it."

They were interrupted when the captain announced that they would be landing in forty-five minutes.

Phil said, "I've changed my mind about driving anywhere tonight. I've got to get some sleep."

"So we'll find a place to crash after we pick up the car. There's got to be lots of places near the airport. Tell me what you do know about the skull legend."

She raised her hand to cover a yawn. "A thrill seeker named Mitchell-Hedges alleged that his daughter found a polished crystal skull with a moveable jaw under a Maya altar."

"When did that happen?"

"The late 1920s. Later on, it was revealed that Mitchell-Hedges had bought it at a private auction and planted the item."

"So it's a made-up story?"

She shifted in her seat. "Not entirely. Further studies suggested that the Skull of Doom is over twelve thousand years old, much older than the Maya site where it was supposedly found."

"Twelve thousand, did you say? Bet that ticked off a few fundamentalists."

Phil sleepily smiled. "Religious and academic."

"You look beat. Are you too tired to talk?"

"Not me. My life is spent in the stacks or in front of a computer screen. It feels good to actually talk to a living body."

"I guess I've been called worse. Give me the micro-lecture, doc."

"Going back to the scientific aspects of the skull's age, the question about its age and authenticity stems from the argument that ancient peoples of the area didn't have the skill to grind and polish the crystal. It was later confirmed that the native peoples of Mexico made use of grinding wheels."

"So the skull is authentic?"

"Its history is considered something of a conundrum. Why are you grinning like that?"

"I love the words you use. Conundrum. Haven't heard that in ages. What's made the Skull of Doom into a conundrum?"

"Under laser-beam testing by a reputable lab, the skull was proved to have been polished from a single crystal, which took over three hundred years to grind and polish. The puzzle stems from the skull's interior optical qualities, as if lenses had been placed in it."

"Interior optical qualities. Like reflective or laser applications?"

"I know very little about lasers."

Rod nodded. "So it sounds like the guy's a fake and the skull is real?"

"Only as far as the testing standards of today can ascertain."

Rod thought for a moment. "Has anything been said about where the stone originated?"

"The only thing I've heard was that it came from Calaveras County in California. There was one mention of Mexico."

"Curiouser and curiouser. Why is it called the Skull of Doom?"

"Other skulls with moveable jaws have been found. There is an ancient legend about a world-scale catastrophe occurring when all the skulls are located."

"How many skulls in all?"

"I can't remember for sure. Most likely thirteen, which is a sacred number for the Maya. They may not all be crystal. One is supposed to be gold and another one, emerald, I think."

"How many have been found?"

"Five, the last I heard, but it could be more by now."

"Skull of Doom. What a great book title! I bet your uncle loves the skulls. Did he ever look for them?"

"No. But he does think that the interior optical peculiarities of the Mitchell-Hedges skull proves his hypothesis. At least the part about Atlanteans being highly evolved and technologically advanced."

"You're using those big words again, doc."

"It's how my mind works. I tend to see the words written on the page when I recall."

"Must come in handy, being a librarian. Just how advanced does your uncle think Atlanteans were?"

"Air transport worldwide, nuclear capability, widespread cloning, dependence on sun-generated, laser-enhanced power."

"Sounds like they were a lot farther along than we are. How come they just disappeared without a trace?"

"Uncle Cal says they didn't. Only the land mass did. Proof of their existence is scattered all over the world."

"Like the huge stones found under the water in the Caribbean?"

"There's a lot more than that. Some of it is archived in museums and they don't know what they're looking at. Uncle Cal has found a great deal of corroborative history in the tablets of the North American mound builders."

"You mean, the stuff is just sitting in boxes and crates? Doesn't everything get inventoried as soon as it arrives?"

"Have you ever seen the archival storage areas of the big museums? They're immense. Piles and rows of containers crammed full of artifacts and papers, much of it yet to be inventoried."

"Not my kind of job. So the skulls are apocalyptic?"

"That's one of the legends. Uncle Cal is more interested in verifying that Atlantis existed. He's fascinated with their advanced technology, especially the use of lasers and synthetic crystals."

"I guess that's why he's being hunted. You only have to look online to see how the field of synthetic hexagonal crystals has advanced. How will your uncle prove that the crystals he has weren't recently made?"

"Age has already been established, as far as I know. He's had one crystal on loan for years to various universities. Studies have shown that the composition is definitely synthetic and far in advance of our present day capabilities."

"No wonder the bad boys are after him. Just think of the applications."

The red fasten-seat-belts sign came on and the attendant reported that it was ten minutes to landing. Rod became silent and contemplative. Phil wondered what he was thinking. His basic understanding of anthropology and archeology seemed to lean more to the gloom and doom aspect rather than sorting through historical mystery. His rapid deductive capability shot to pieces his dumb jock routine.

"Hey, doc. Does your uncle have one of those crystals with him?"

"The synthetic kind? I said that the only one he had was on loan."

"Has he ever seen one of those skulls?"

"I believe he has."

"Have you?"

"I've never had an interest in seeing one." *The power of the vibrations would knock me out for a week.* "I'd rather return to the Amazon and look for the famed lost city that is supposedly buried in the Brazilian jungle."

"Sounds dangerous."

"It is. One of the most famous South American explorers that ever lived disappeared trying to find it. If there was a way to get rid of the snakes and bugs that live there, I'd go exploring tomorrow."

"I'm not fond of slimy things myself, but it would make a great story."

Phil tightened her seat belt and pulled the briefcase from under the seat in front of her. She clasped it close to her chest. The crystal inside droned a gentle hum. "You know, you've mentioned that twice."

"What?"

"That an idea would make a good story for a book. Why don't you write one?"

"A story?"

"Or a book. You seem to latch onto the kind of scenarios that intrigue the general public."

"They say everybody has a book in them. How about you?"

"I used to teach, so I had to publish. Every academic I know is published. I wasn't talking about nonfiction. You sound like you have an imaginative mind. You should think about it."

He turned his head to look out the window across the aisle. The flickering lights of the city and airport twinkled below in the distance. The plane banked and leveled off, reducing speed and altitude.

Rod looked back at her. "I just might do that. What was the name of the explorer who disappeared in the Amazon?"

"Lieutenant Colonel Percy Fawcett."

"When did this happen?"

"The mid-twenties, if I remember correctly. Why the thoughtful look?"

Rod said, "Right about the time the skull was found."

"Before it, actually, but I never thought of that. You also have a knack for connecting the dots. I really think you should try writing a book. Perhaps a mystery."

He didn't reply as the plane dipped and abruptly sank lower to land. The touchdown was rough, rocking the plane, drawing Rod's attention across the aisle to the view out the window. Flashing lights sped by and slowed as the plane taxied. The captain announced that it was a hot and muggy night in West Palm Beach and apologized for the bumpy landing.

Rod kept staring out the window. Phil knew he was avoiding her and wondered why.

Chapter 8

Phil only cared about two things regarding the rental car they were to collect at Palm Beach International. It had to have air-conditioning that worked, and there had to be a rental agent who didn't know Rod. Her luck held and the desk clerk at the closest hotel didn't know Rod either.

Located so close to the airport, most of the rooms were booked. The only accommodation that would work for them was something called a petite suite. Phil was so tired she didn't care if they had to share a room and registered a vague relief to hear that there were double beds in the suite. She handed over the cash and let Rod fill out the forms.

The elevator ride seemed to take forever. She leaned against the mirrored wall and closed her eyes. After Rod opened the hotel room door, she walked straight to the closest bed, set down the briefcase, stretched out on the bedspread, and immediately fell asleep.

A familiar tune woke her in the morning; Rod's phone was programmed to ring the Star Wars theme.

Phil growled, staggered out of bed, and went to the dresser to shut the thing off. Since the phone's owner was singing off-key in the shower and she was feeling ornery, she flipped it open and briskly rubbed her face before speaking.

"Hello."

A basement basso asked, "Roddie?"

"Can he call you back?"

"Sure. Hey, is this Dr. Hafeldt?"

"This is his niece."

"His niece? *Shut up!* You're *the* Dr. Philadelphia Casca Hafeldt? Author of *Souls of Romance* Hafeldt?"

Perplexed to full wakefulness by the question, Phil took the phone away from her ear and stared at it. A distant, tinny voice, squawking with excitement, drifted up from the device cupped in her palm.

She returned the phone to her ear. "This is Philadelphia Hafeldt."

"Dr. Hafeldt, what an honor it is to talk to you! I really loved your book. I especially liked the chapter about the Bronte sisters and your supposition that some of the themes of their books could have stemmed from scandals and local legends."

The raspy voice kept chatting on and on until she felt a touch on her shoulder. She turned and her mouth fell open.

Oh, my stars!

Rod, in nothing but a bath towel, stood in dripping glory by her shoulder. He slipped the phone from her hand, leaving behind a tingling wetness on her fingers.

"Hey, Binky. I guess you got my message."

Phil tried to keep her eyes on the moisture beads twinkling on his collarbones. She blamed a long-denied libido—quite naturally driven by gravity—for drawing her gaze lower.

The dark indentation of his navel was surrounded by swirling hair. The idea of nuzzling her nose in that tempting fuzz and tickling him in the same spot distracted her from Rod's odd conversation.

"Is…Kitty in any shape to fly?" He glanced at Phil, noticed that her attention was otherwise engaged, and lifted his stare to a blank wall to finish the phone call.

"Good. Get her ready to fly as far as Denver. I'll contact you later about where to set down. Hire a twin engine. I'll need outdoor wear. Oh, and tell Mom I won't be coming home for a few weeks." He listened. "No, Binky."

Rod paused. "I said, no!"

Phil raised her fascinated gaze to Rod's frown. She lifted an eyebrow, a silent question. Rod shook his head at her and turned slightly away.

"No, Binky. Just get to Denver. Absolutely not. No, I don't have time to stop at a bookstore."

Rod snapped the phone shut. His expression was sullen, mildly disgusted.

Phil asked, "What's wrong?"

"Binky says you've written a book. What is it? Some piece of romantic fluff?"

"Fluff? I'll thank you to take that sneer out of your tone, Mr. Chaucer. It's a comparative study of romance in twentieth century literature."

"I guess that's better than that mushy stuff."

The fine hairs on her arms lifted, like hackles. "Mushy stuff? Oh, be still my heart, I am being graced with yet another glowing review from an informed reader. Is this a jock's incisive, well-thought-out opinion of romance?"

Rod set the phone on the glass-topped dresser. He leaned into the bathroom doorframe and folded his arms across his impressive chest. Whorls of damp, black curls momentarily distracted her from the point she wanted to make. She always assumed that the covers of romance novels were greatly enhanced. Rod was the real thing, standing close enough to touch, living proof that enhancement was not always the rule.

He brought her back to task. "Do you really want to know my opinion of romance?"

His tone hardened her heart. "I'm all atwitter waiting to hear."

"If it doesn't fold out of the center of a magazine, it's not gonna move me, babe."

That crack threw fuel on the waning flames of her argument. "Oh, fine! That's *so* like a man. And I suppose half the people who ever wrote over the last three centuries aren't worth your time either! After all, nothing ever folded out of the center of *their* books."

He gave that a moment of serious consideration. "You're right about that."

"I don't know why I'm amazed that your taste in reading material hasn't advanced beyond pop-up level."

That snared his interest. He lifted his eyebrows. "Porn makes pop-up figures now?"

"Very funny and I know all about your type. So you think that romance is only *mushy* stuff? Did you know that romance novels sell over a billion dollars a year?"

"I guess I should think about investing." He straightened up from the wall and took a step closer. "You know what I heard, doc? They say women read books like that to get hot, get themselves all worked up. So, tell me, doc, what's the difference in that and when a guy looks at the swimsuit edition?"

He had a point, but she couldn't relent. "Why am I not surprised to have your choice of reading material affirmed? Heaven forbid you'd show an interest in a book without pictures."

His smug grin told her how much fun he was having tweaking her temper. Phil couldn't stop herself from responding. She didn't know what she wanted to do first, smack him or kiss him, and was horrified that she might do both. She was also scared that the towel knotted on his hip would slip loose and fall.

And it did.

In no hurry to pick it up, Rod grinned. "Oops."

Phil slapped her hands over her eyes. "Cover that up!"

Peering through her fingers, she watched him pick up the towel and tie the knot in place at his waist.

Phil lowered her hands. "Get dressed. We've got clothes to buy and another plane to catch. And I'm hungry."

"I can help you there, babe. I'm feeling a bit peckish myself." Rod reached for the towel knot. "Must be from all that talk about sex."

Phil squeaked and turned. She peeked over her shoulder in time to take a direct hit from his stare. There was no mistaking his intent.

"Not for that, Chaucer! I meant food."

"You're no fun, Hafeldt." He waited for another moment before breaking eye contact. "There's a pancake house not far from here."

"That'll do. Will you please put on some clothes?"

The glint in his eye turned into a twinkle, and a corner of his mouth twitched. "I won't be much longer. I can get us checked out, while you get dressed."

Phil looked down. She dimly recalled getting up during the night to use the bathroom, taking off some clothes, and tossing them to the foot of the bed. Always slow to wake, she hadn't realized that she'd jumped out of

64

bed to answer the phone in nothing but blue lace underwear.

Phil watched him saunter back into the bathroom and beat down her disappointment. The men she'd known had never looked or acted like Rod Chaucer. He was the type that went after what he wanted until he got it. What was it about her that made him hesitate?

She hid under the covers and waited until he left the hotel room. Flipping back the bedspread, she leaped up and dashed for the bathroom the instant the door closed.

Rod had not been idle while she slept. A clear plastic pouch sat on the clean vanity counter, a high-end travel kit. She studied the contents—all the items a gal on the run would consider indispensable. She gratefully brushed her teeth while arranging deodorant, mouthwash, and powder in a row to be used after a shower.

When she left the hotel room, she noticed a breakfast cart waiting in front of the door across the hallway. Her stomach grumbled, and she hurried to the elevator. The door swished open and a man stepped out. His red and black uniform had a smiley face and "May I park your car?" embroidered beneath the hotel's logo. His employee nametag was missing.

Warning bells clanged in her head. What was a parking attendant doing on the ninth floor?

Phil retreated a few steps and prepared for another attempt to snatch her briefcase, but the attendant raised his hand, palm out.

"Please, Dr. Hafeldt. I only want to talk."

Phil took the man's measure in a glance—slimy weasel, an errand boy, not an enforcer type. His unfortunately close-set eyes were colorless, his olive skin, greasy. A protuberant nose did nothing to help a face plagued by narrowness. The thought flitted across her mind that Estelle would have found the attendant's nose a redeeming feature.

In need of caffeine and sustenance, she was in no mood to exchange social niceties. "What do you want?"

Lowering his hand, The Weasel said in a placating tone, "A moment of your time. That's all. We simply want to warn you about your traveling companion."

"Does the warning include trying to steal my briefcase?"

"We apologize for that unfortunate incident. You do know that the man you're traveling with is not who he says he is."

"Go on."

"His real name is Rob Gameson. He was hired by a West Coast utility consortium."

"And who do you work for?"

"The FBI. I have identification."

This lump an agent for the FBI? I'm so sure!

Phil waited until he reached for identification. She rammed a fist into his solar plexus. The Weasel hunched over for air. She grabbed the back of his neck and shoved his head down into the upward thrust of her knee. His nose gave way with a distinctive snap and squish.

She glanced up and down the hallway, and seeing no one, she towed The Weasel by his shirt collar to the stairwell. A hasty search of his pockets showed that he had no ID and had been reaching for an EpiPen syringe. She doubted he carried it for medical reasons. It looked like an item covert types would use to sedate a captive. She tucked the tranquilizer dart into her briefcase and took the stairs to the lobby.

Rod folded the newspaper and set it aside. He stood up and casually followed her outside into a torrid Florida morning. He acted impatient when Phil stopped to touch the tender pink petals of the azaleas tumbling over the borders of the brick planter in front of the hotel.

"Rod, let's walk to the restaurant."

"It's sultry. It'll be like walking through water."

"So what if we get a little sticky. I'd love some fresh air and exercise. We can take the side streets. They won't look for us on foot."

His smirk told her what was coming next. "There're other ways to work up an appetite, babe."

"Give it a rest, Chaucer."

"I figured you'd think that way. Look what I picked up this morning."

She accepted the white paper bag, peeked inside, and found a steamy novel and a massive, two-pound chocolate bar. "Your carnal imagination exceeds the extent of my appetite, Chaucer."

He strolled away, saying over his shoulder, "Oh, I don't think so, doc."

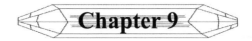

Chapter 9

They left the rental car at the hotel and called a cab to meet them at the restaurant and take them to the other side of town. The plan was to use a smaller car-rental agency and utilize Rod's license this time.

Still feeling cranky, Phil asked for cereal when they sat down at the IHOP. When they didn't have her favorite brand, she ordered pancakes the way she liked them—with chocolate chips.

She was halfway through her pancakes when she recalled Rod's opinion that she used chocolate as a sex substitute. She ignored his smirk when he asked the waitress for the bill and a refill of her hot cocoa.

Phil slid out of the booth. "Excuse me. Lady's room."

Rod frowned. "Don't take too long. The cab should be here any minute."

The rest room was cleaner and larger than most. She washed her hands and face, tidied her hair, and made a check of the contents of the briefcase. When she came out of the stall, she saw a heap of rags in the corner that was not there when she came in the rest room.

The rags moved and lifted, exposing a face almost completely shielded by ratty, mouse-colored dreadlocks.

"Lady, you got any change you can spare?"

Phil didn't like the idea of street beggars but was unable not to give. She took three singles from her wallet.

The bag lady stood up from the tile floor and shuffled closer. Phil started to hand over the bills but stopped when she noticed the beggar's odd way of talking. Her lips didn't move, like a ventriloquist's, and she had manicured nails.

The beggar grabbed Phil's wrist instead of the money. "Be careful, Dr. Hafeldt. You're being followed."

Phil prepared to break the hold, and the bag lady tightened her grip. "No, I'm not here to hurt you. I'm here to warn you. I'm going to take the money, and then I want you to listen to what I have to say before you go. Keep your face to me so they can't read your lips."

Phil froze in place. *A bugged bathroom? That's sick! How could they bug a bathroom? We just got here.*

She watched the beggar dig around amid the welter of ragged clothes and pull out a tiny pocketbook. She enacted an elaborate ritual of putting the money inside while she kept her head bowed and talked.

"How much has Bobbio told you?"

Phil bowed her head and whispered, "Who's Bobbio?"

"Wakefield. Bob Wakefield, the guy you're traveling with. Look at yourself in the mirror. Fuss with your hair or something."

Phil turned on the tap and tried to keep her facial expression neutral. "Who are you?"

"We'll get to that later. Have you got the crystal with you?"

"No."

"Damn. Then we'll have to wing it. There's a tan Buick sedan in the parking lot. The windows are smoked so you can't see inside. Get in the back. The driver will take you someplace safe."

"Why should I trust you?"

"What an unexpected question from somebody who travels with a man whose name she doesn't know."

"Maybe I'm letting him hang around to keep an eye on him."

"Knowing Bobbio, you'll have more than an eye on him before the day's over. I'm going into the stall at the far end to change. It's right underneath the camera."

"What camera?"

"The window. The camera's on a wire stuck through the louvers. Be careful when you look."

Two minutes later, a slim female in a tight purple leather skirt, four-inch red heels, and an abbreviated tube top exited the stall. Her cropped hair was fashionably tousled. An obscene ornament dangled from a bellybutton ring. In sixty years, she would look like Estelle.

She crammed her bag lady costume inside a huge shopping bag and stuffed it into the trash receptacle. The prostitute tottered to the sink, smeared lipstick on her lips, and pulled a travel-size container of hair spray from the shopping bag.

Phil didn't know why she did it, but she stepped back at the same time the hair-spray nozzle was brought up to her face. She turned her head and threw up an arm. Wetness soaked into her blouse sleeve.

Pivoting on her right foot, Phil kicked with her left and connected dead center on the chest of the beggar-turned-slut, who got knocked into the wall.

The crack of her head connecting with the tiles was loud enough to let Phil know the woman was stunned. The pretend hooker shook her head, kicked off the stilettos, and stood up.

Phil huffed a weary sigh. OK, so she was tough.

Hands and bare feet positioned for quick movement, the prostitute said in soothing voice, "It wasn't lethal, Dr. Hafeldt. Just something to make you sleepy."

When Phil didn't reply, the pseudo-slut advanced with caution. "I really am sorry about the spritzing business, Dr. Hafeldt. It's not as accurate as the propellant kind, but I hate those containers. They're so ecologically unsafe. And I never use anything with fluorocarbons."

Phil raised her fists and slowly circled. "I've been recycling as far back as I can remember. Who are you working for?"

"That would be telling. Does this state recycle?"

"Don't know." Phil feigned a straight-armed jab. The responsive block revealed pseudo-slut's training. A second sweep at the floozy's chest confirmed a background in karate. Phil inwardly grinned. *Piece o' cake.*

Phil took two quick steps back and was rewarded with her opponent's immediate advance. Brushing aside the expected strike, Phil targeted her opponent's nose and dropped her left-hand guard to grab the prostitute's purse and tossed it into the sink while the nose jab was being blocked.

Phil hissed a warning before swinging into a whirling kick that she didn't expect to connect. She never used spinning kicks, but the prostitute didn't know that.

The trick worked and her opponent backed up, giving Phil a moment to dump the contents of the purse into the sink and snatch up the spray bottle. She lifted and pointed the nozzle in time to stop pseudo-slut's next move.

Phil advanced as the pretend prostitute backed away. Keeping the hair spray container at arm's length, Phil tucked her nose and mouth into her bent elbow and spritzed. Pseudo-slut blinked, yawned, and collapsed.

Phil tucked the spray bottle into the bodice of her opponent's cheap tube top and murmured, "Send a girl."

Snatching her briefcase from the edge of the sink, Phil darted out of the bathroom and collided into Rod.

He craned to look around the closing door. "Phil, what was going on in there?"

"I'll tell you later." She grabbed his hand and tugged him away from the door. "Is our ride here?"

"It's waiting at the curb."

He pushed open the exit door and they hurried out into the humid heat. Phil didn't wait and yanked open the cab door. In the backseat, she looked out the rear window and saw a tan Buick glide out of a parking space and stop behind the cab. A man jumped out of the Buick and entered the restaurant.

The cab driver asked over his shoulder in a thick Australian accent, "You're wantin' to go to airport?"

Phil shoved a handful of bills through the window. "No. Just drive until I tell you to stop."

Rod used the passenger side mirror to watch the Buick. "Do you know who they are?"

Phil checked her clothes to see if anything had come undone during the scuffle in the rest room. "How should I know? But they know you."

He glanced at her, his expression blank. "Oh?"

"Is that all you have to say for yourself, *Bobbio, also known as Bob Wakefield?*"

He looked uncomfortable. Knowing she had him cornered, she pressed the issue. "So, what is your real name?"

"Wakefield is my middle name, but I'm not Bob."

"Very well, *Not Bob*, why did you tell me a fake name?"

"Back at your uncle's apartment, I couldn't be sure who you were at first. Then I saw your I.D. and—"

"When did you see my identification?" She clutched her violated briefcase to her chest.

"That's not important now. I know who you are, and you should know by now that you can trust me."

Unable to calm her escalating voice, she yelled, "At this point, all I trust is that you're *Not Bob!"*

"Phil, let's talk about this later. We've got to get rid of whoever is tailing us." He leaned forward and tapped the cabdriver's shoulder. "Go a little slower. Is there a big parking garage around here?"

"Two blocks and around the corner."

"Does it have more than one level?"

"Five levels. It's next to the shopping center and courthouse."

"How much did she give you?"

The driver grinned in the rearview mirror. "Enough to take you to Miami and back."

"Not quite that far. Just to the parking lot. Her ex-husband is tailing us. He likes to use a baseball bat and ask questions later."

"I hear ya, mate."

"When we get to the ramp, we'll jump out on the second level. You keep going and stop at a doorway on the top floor."

"You want it to look like you took the elevator?"

"That's the idea."

The driver nodded. "You want any of the fare back?"

Rod looked at Phil. She shook her head. Rod said, "Keep it."

"In that case, I'll lose'em. No worries."

The driver pulled into the parking lot, snatched a ticket, and scooted the taxi up the ramp and around a corner. When the cab screeched to a sudden stop, Phil and Rod leaped out and ducked behind the wall.

The cabdriver gunned the car and shot away from the door. Phil and Rod dashed into the stairwell.

Standing to one side, Phil peeked through the door's small window. The Buick cruised by a moment later and followed the cab's taillights.

Phil started down the stairs ahead of Rod. They exited on ground level and ran along the back of the strip mall, staying close to the buildings. Rod jerked her through an open door.

Phil glanced around. They were in a clothes boutique. Rod pulled a few items from the rack and pushed her toward a changing room. Phil grabbed items more to her liking and in her size.

When Rod slipped into the changing room with her, Phil protested, "What are you doing? Get out of here!"

He rolled his eyes and sat down on the padded bench. "If they ask, say we're married. Take off your shoes. Make it look like you're trying on clothes."

She hooked the hangers on the door peg. "How did you know women take off their shoes to try on clothes?"

He leaned back on the bench, lifted his feet, and planted his size twelves on the wall to keep his feet from being seen under the half door. "Duh. Men take off their shoes to try on clothes, too. And do you take me for some kind of pervert who looks at women's feet while they're in changing rooms?"

"Close your eyes."

He heaved a sigh, shut his eyes, and dropped his head back against the wall. Theatrically discouraged, he muttered, "You really do think I'm a pervert."

"If you promise to keep your eyes closed, I might change my mind. Why are you smiling?"

He quickly straightened his lips. "No reason."

Suspicious, she demanded, "What?"

He shrugged. "Oh, it's just that I think you're protesting too much."

She snatched up a blouse that matched the khaki slacks, grateful to be rid of the stained and wrinkled clothes. "I'm only expressing what I think. It's not healthy to keep angry feelings contained. And I'm willing to bet that you can't tell me where that saying comes from."

"You mean the "doth protest too much" line? I'm supposed to tell *you?* Excuse me, who's the lit major in the room?"

His reflection in the glass proved that his eyes were closed. She didn't answer and quickly turned around in front of the mirrors to check how her fanny looked. She glided her hand over the curve of her butt. She snatched away her hand when he spoke.

"What's up, doc? No snappy retort?"

Miffed at being caught checking out her backside, she said, "One might not be surprised that a question involving Shakespeare would boggle a PE major."

A rumbling purr preceded his reply. "Ouch! Keep it up, honey. I love it when you talk tough. And you look nice in that, doc. Course, any gal with a sassy tush and gams like yours would look good in slacks. But what I'd really like to see you wearing is a pair of boots and tight jeans. Oh, baby!"

His eyes were definitely open now. Phil didn't know whether to be angry or flattered. He liked her butt? She wished she could sneak another peek at what was so likeable about it but there were standards to be maintained. After all, one should never sink to the enemy's level.

She turned up the collar of the blouse and assessed the effect. "You're disgusting, Chaucer."

"You love it."

She arranged a scarf. "Cretin."

He grinned. "Snob."

"Right-winger."

He tsked, unfazed. "Closet bimbo."

She whirled around. "Lech!"

"Existentialist."

She gasped, horrified. "I am not! I'm a pragmatist."

"And a Methodist, too. But I still like your bra."

She snatched up her purse and clothes. "We're leaving. I'm buying this outfit."

He grandly swept open the changing-room door, smug with victory. "Can we stop at a guy place now, so I can undress in front of you?"

"You've already done that," she snapped, hating that he could get under her skin so easily.

She paid cash for the clothes and the two pairs of panties that she surreptitiously whisked from a bin on the way to the counter.

Her tormentor was busy looking out the display windows for possible lurkers. She hoped he found one. At the moment, nothing sounded better than vigorous activity, such as a fight. She wouldn't mind seeing Not Bob get that infernal grin smacked right off his face.

Chapter 10

They took the Florida Turnpike north. When they got off and turned west, the empty stretch of highway in front and behind verified that they weren't being followed.

She'd forgotten how much she liked traveling by car across Florida. Undulating cane fields bordered the highway where egrets waded in ditches. Their beaks and legs looked blacker than black against the pearly iridescence of their pristine feathers.

The three hours it took to get to Orlando seemed to fly, passing without incident or much conversation between them. Rod only mentioned how much he liked driving in Florida and appeared to enjoy the view as much as she did. She was grateful for the peace to make plans and to discover that her traveling partner could be a restful companion.

The traffic congestion increased the closer they got to Orlando. Phil pointed to a roadside sign that promised fast food at the upcoming exit. They stopped to use the facilities and buy munchies to quiet Phil's tummy noises.

The car wasn't out of the exit before she unwrapped a double-decked burger topped with everything. She took a huge bite and moaned. A loving stroke of her tongue swept the sauce from her bottom lip.

Rod munched on fries and split his attention between her sensual enjoyment of the food and the increasing traffic congestion.

"Hey, doc, care to tell me how you can eat junk like that and still keep your girlish figure?"

She sipped a drip of sauce from her finger. "You don't like fast food?"

"To be honest, I don't remember when I last stopped at a place like that. My diet is mostly protein and greens. Binky likes to cook, and I consider myself something of a master at grilling."

A terrifying epiphany forced Phil to stop chewing for a moment. "I don't know if life would be worth living without carbs."

Disturbed by that thought, she took another huge bite. She banished the foolish notion and asked, "Are you going to eat that other burger?"

"Help yourself. So how do you do it?"

"Stay fit? I have a workout room at home and spend one to two hours every day burning off the calories I take in."

"That's quite a workout."

"Depends." She unfolded the foil wrapper on the second burger, pressed it out flat on her lap, and lifted the hamburger's lid to align the pickles. "I use the time to catch up on the news and listen to books on tape. May I have some of your shake? I saved my straw."

Smirking, he handed it to her. "Finish it."

Because Rod thought her comment about the straw was funny, she defiantly used his and sucked the few inches that remained in the container down to a loud, rattling end. After finishing Rod's scorned burger, she gathered up the wrappers, cups, and paper napkins and crammed everything into a bag.

"You like things tidy," he commented.

"Yes. Don't you?"

"As a matter of fact, the word anal was once mentioned in describing my room when I was a kid. My mom got worried when I liked things organized and hired a shrink for some family *sharing* sessions. She was terrified that she'd done something to jeopardize my future manliness."

Phil laughed. "Just because you were neat in your habits?"

"For a while there, I was a bit more than neat. I got a little freaky about anybody touching my card catalogs and disc files. Mom wasn't much for spoiling me, but Dad was. He bought me a new PC every Christmas. All the games and upgrades. I wouldn't have come out of my room at all if they hadn't made me."

Phil frowned at the blurred view of oleander bushes flying by the window. The images of what Rod was telling her didn't gel. She tried to see him as a boy but it didn't work. She couldn't get the memory of him standing in dripping masculine glory after his shower to morph into a boyish face and figure. All she could come up with was a miniature Rod Chaucer that oozed testosterone and smug confidence.

The grown up Rod was blessed, a person who appeared to be totally comfortable with the man he'd become. He talked about the boy he'd been as if his childhood were lived by another person. But then, when a person is lucky enough to end up looking like something that stepped off the front page of a magazine, there's no need to feel regrets about what went before.

She was unable to get the dripping image of him out of her head and couldn't help comparing Rod to the men she'd dated. Dismal as the recollections were, she tended to review them over and over at bedtime. The nightly reruns refused to reveal a clue as to why things never worked out for her with men.

She glanced at Rod. He smiled companionably and returned his attention to the road.

Rod would be fabulous in bed.

That part had always been a trial. None of her experiences had lived up to her expectations. There was the old feminist adage of a real woman being responsible for her own orgasm, but Phil had always hoped that she'd find a man who could at least help out with the process.

She had a question she knew a man like Rod could answer. The hitch was that it was a touchy subject that she hoped to approach it in a clinical manner.

"May I ask you something?"

He recklessly said, "Sure."

"Do all the women you sleep with have orgasms?"

The car swerved, chewed up the gravel on the verge, and popped back up onto the road.

Rod cleared his throat. "That was unexpected. I guess I should know by now that most of your questions come fully loaded."

Stung, Phil snapped, "I apologize for the personal nature of the question. I certainly didn't mean to startle you, but I felt sure you could supply an empirical answer."

"Don't get all tweaked out of shape, doc. It's just that you surprised me, asking something like that out of the blue."

"I'm sorry."

"It's OK. No need to poker up and get all embarrassed about it. You just asked a question." A moment passed. "Yes."

"What?"

"Yes. They do."

When she didn't say anything, he glanced at her. "Why do you have that look on your face? Don't you believe me?"

"Of course I do. Why are you so defensive?"

"Good question." He paused to consider. "I guess it's because it sounds like I'm bragging. Now it's my turn to ask."

She squinted at him. "This isn't going to be a truth or dare type game, is it?"

He pinched his lips to hold back a laugh before saying, "Relax. It's not what you think. I was wondering what you have in that briefcase that everybody wants."

She looked down at the leather satchel by her foot. "I'm guessing that they think I've taken something from the bank."

"You did."

"The only thing I've got in there that would be of interest is cash. There are some aerial photographs of a Maya ruin, a change of underwear, and a rock. That's about it."

"It can't be the cash. What's the rock?"

"A crystal. It's monetary worth isn't much."

He took the off-ramp for the Orlando airport. "What about the photographs?"

"The site is documented. Out of the way but known."

"Where?"

"Southern Yucatan Peninsula."

He stopped at the end of the ramp. "Which way to the airport? The way you say Yucatan sounds like you speak Spanish."

She pointed the way. "And some other languages nobody bothers to use."

"Such as?"

"Cheyenne and Aztec. Some of the up river Portuguese dialects."

"Not much call for those around here. I'll drop you off in front by the check-in. You can get the tickets while I get rid of this car."

Their luck held. They flew out of Orlando on the first flight to Denver, arrived after midnight, and walked to the nearest motel.

Feeling the drag of flight hopping and the stress of being chased, she was relieved when Rod said he needed a full night's sleep.

When Phil woke up the next morning, Rod was standing at the foot of her bed. He tossed a folder full of paperwork onto the bedspread, showing that he'd rented a car. She pulled the covers up and secured the sheet ends under her armpits. He extended a large paper cup of steaming coffee as she struggled to wake. Blinking didn't clear her vision. The aroma of hot coffee did.

"Come on, doc. Let's get a move on it. Daylight's burnin'."

She tenderly clutched the disposable cup he was holding under her nose and took a fortifying sip. Kona Blend. Oh, yeah, the day could now commence. "Get me something to eat while I shower."

He opened a white cardboard box and waved it under her chin. The yeasty perfume of freshly baked doughnuts bathed her face with morning's most sublime fragrance. Saliva gushed in her mouth.

Low and seductive, the evil man whispered, "Chocolate frosted."

That got her up and moving. She made Rod do an about face, wrapped the bed sheet around her, secured a doughnut in her mouth, and headed for the bathroom. She wasn't pleased that he ate most of the doughnuts while she showered. He made up for it by offering to buy more once they were on the road.

Rod gave her directions and had her drive the nondescript rental car to an airport outside of town. He pointed to the hangar at the end of the row. Rod got out, held the door open with one hand, and ducked down to look at her.

"Park the car and wait inside the hangar. I'll be done in a minute. Do you have any information on where we're going?"

Phil pulled out a slip of paper she'd prepared earlier with the coordinates. She watched him walk to a private jet, the size and kind businessmen use as a measure of their clout. It was black, sleek, and expensive-looking, not in the least utilitarian. Somebody's power-trip toy.

A man appeared in the jet's open exit door and came down the boarding steps. He shook Rod's hand when he reached the tarmac.

Phil drummed her fingertips on the car wheel and watched the men talk. They knew each other well. There were no signs of male territorial posturing. They chatted amicably as they went up the boarding stairs and into the jet. They turned in the doorway and entered the cockpit.

It was too late to worry about flying with strangers. She had already agreed to Rod's idea of taking a private plane to Wyoming to lose their trackers. Might as well stick with the plan. She'd had her fill of international airports. The thought of spending more time breathing manufactured airplane air infused with everybody else's germs roiled the doughnuts in her tummy.

Phil parked the car and went into the hangar, which was empty except for a single-engine plane with its motor torn down. Parts and tools littered canvas sheeting on the cement floor. The interior of the huge Quonset smelled brackish and dusty. The acrid smell of oil and grease hung in the air even though the doors were fully open.

She stood in the shade between the hangar doors and waited for Rod. The men had exited the plane and stopped to talk at the foot of the stairs. Even from where she stood Phil could see that the guys were exchanging male bonding type humor. Her attention was drawn away when she heard footsteps.

The man coming from the hangar's office had on the typical jumpsuit she imagined most mechanics wore. His looks were standard American mutt—unexceptional, pleasant, and wholesome. The problem was that he was wiping his hands on an oil-stained cloth and his hands were clean.

Phil straightened up. She hugged the briefcase to her side and waited for the pretend mechanic to make the first move.

The mechanic smiled. "May I help you?"

Phil glanced at the immaculate fingernails, just to let him know that she knew, and shook her head.

The man's gaze never left hers. "I see you're not fooled. You're Dr. Hafedlt."

"Keep talking."

He tossed the cloth into a trash barrel. "Before I forget, Estelle says hello. These days, a Taser at the airport calls for extensive follow-up. In doing so, we discovered you."

"What do you want with me?"

"We've been trying to locate your uncle for some time. You haven't contacted him in over a year and your movements in the last twenty-four hours suggest that you're about to join him. Please, don't be alarmed. I'm going to reach into my pocket for a business card."

He used two fingers to withdraw the card and kept his other hand away from his body but not in a way that she might suspect he was trying to redirect her attention.

Phil accepted the card. "There's only a phone number on this."

"When you call, ask for Bill. That's all you have to do."

"You're a Fed?"

His smile was benign, meant to be enigmatic. "In a way. If you or your uncle need help, please feel free to contact us. And we would appreciate it if your uncle would use that number. The synthetic crystal he's been lending to different universities has some of our best minds twisted in knots. With his permission, we'd like to convene a think tank to discover how it was constructed. We want him to act as an advisor."

Phil paused to let him think that she was considering what he had said. She wasn't, but he didn't need to know that.

"Well, *Bill*, it's like this. We aren't too sure who we can trust at the moment."

"It's never easy to know who your friends are when you're popular."

"Something like that. This think tank you've got in mind wouldn't have cement walls and bars on the exits, would it?"

"Not at all, Dr. Hafeldt. It's an open-ended position."

"In that case, I'll mention it to him the next time I happen to see him."

"Fair enough. When you ring that number, you'll get your confirmation that we can be trusted. And here's a cell phone. We cancelled Mr. Chaucer's account a few minutes ago. This way we can locate you anywhere. Please keep it with you at all times. It has a homing device. You don't even have to activate it. It won't need recharging."

"Will I glow in the dark if I keep it on my person?"

He smiled. "It's not nuclear."

Phil dropped the phone into her bag. "I'll consider your offer, Bill."

"Thank you, ma'am."

"Do you belong to that jet?"

"That sort of entry on my expense report would get me fired. It landed about ten minutes ago. I'll be getting intel on it in a few minutes."

"So, do you know Rod Chaucer?"

Bill's smile was genuine this time. "Everybody in the office knows who R.W. Chaucer is!"

"R.W. Chaucer?"

It hit her then. She must have passed by confirmation of Rod's identity a dozen times traipsing through airports. All she had to do was look on the back cover of his latest bestseller. And she'd been playing with the silly notion that her feeling of knowing him before was some sort of romantic predestination.

She pretended to refasten the buckles on her briefcase to hide the heat flushing into her cheeks. Thinking fast, she started to ask questions about her famous bodyguard, recalling for the first time that he never asked about wages. The worst of it was the mocking fact that traveling with a celebrity was not the best way to keep a low profile.

Chapter 11

Rod stood on the baking tarmac and tried not to look at Phil talking to a man at the hangar. "What's she doing now?"

Binky leaned a hip on the stair rail. "Just talking. How'd you meet her?"

"Do you know who that guy is?"

"How would I know. I just got back from getting the other plane set up. If you're so attracted to him, go introduce yourself. I thought you were interested in Dr. Hafeldt. If you're not, can I have a crack at her?"

"In your dreams." Rod decided to switch topics. "Did you have any trouble getting the jet?"

"It wasn't scheduled. The last few months it's been doing nothing but gathering dust."

"Any questions asked when you requested to use it?"

Binky's grin was not a pretty sight. "No, she didn't ask. *Yet.* But you know damn well she will, and then, look out."

Rod couldn't stop himself. He had to know. "What's she doing now?"

Binky knew which "she" he meant and scoped out the hangar without moving his head. "Still talking. Looks like they're wrapping it up. I still say she's too good for you. Are you sure you want a woman who can whup your ass?"

"How do you know that?"

Binky shrugged. "I know everything about her." He paused to smirk. "Look at you. You're dying to ask. Come on, beg me."

"You should be fired."

"Won't work. You'll never talk her into it. And just because I hurt your feelers, I'll tell all about the fascinating librarian. Stop trying to look over your shoulder. They're still talking and it'll take her a while to walk over here. So, do you want the intel?"

Trying hard to hide his annoyance, Rod nodded.

Binky unwrapped a stick of gum and folded it into his mouth. Rod grit his teeth until Binky got the gum softened up. At least it wasn't bubble gum. He hated it when Binky started with the endless, thoughtless popping of bubbles.

When Binky stopped chewing, and covertly focused his attention on the hangar, Rod asked, "What is it?"

"The guy just gave her something. Small. Handheld. I told you something was fishy about that guy."

"Consider me warned. What about her background check?"

"She's got more degrees than God and possibly the same IQ. Not much in the way of family. Her father's still alive. He's some kind of research geek. Mother died over a decade ago, which resulted in the kid taking care of the father kind of situation. When she wasn't in school. Graduated early everywhere. Got the black belt before she hit her teens and stopped formal training in martial arts before she was out of high school. Still studies it privately. Prefers the Tae Kwon Do discipline. Studied everything from ninjitsu to that stuff they do in Thailand. I think it's called Muay Thai. The one where they can kill you with a knee or elbow."

Rod interrupted, "Do you know if she's dating anyone?"

Oddly, Binky didn't use the opportunity to tease. "She's sworn off men. Last one was a doozie. A former TA from when her uncle taught at the U of Illinois in Urbana. Don't exactly know what the jerk did to her, but must have done a good job. She sticks to a pretty boring routine of work and not much else."

"Did you learn anything about her uncle?"

"He's her only living relative beyond her father. He's considered a nut case by some and a visionary by others. Been missing for a while. She's very close to him. Spent her summers with him when Mommy and Daddy were busy with their careers. The uncle took her with him everywhere he went from China to the Amazon backwaters. She got around for a little kid. That stopped for some reason right around the time she hit her teens. From then on, her parents sent her away to one of those prestigious summer camps. The kind where they keep big-brain kiddies occupied so they won't build thermonuclear devices or clone themselves. That's where she met her best friend."

"She's never mentioned a friend and this is stuff you can't get off the net. Who's the source?"

Binky hesitated. "She's leaving the hangar."

"We got a few minutes yet. How'd you get this info, Bink?"

"I called in a marker. Got somebody to arm-twist her boss at the library and then weaseled the rest out of her assistant. Some of it's common knowledge around campus."

"What about the ex-boyfriend? Is he still hanging around?"

"Not likely. I heard he bad-mouthed her a lot behind her back. Called her frigid."

"She isn't. Makes me wonder what he has against her."

"He can't have much in the line of smarts. Ticked off, that lady could take him apart and put him back together wrong. It's also rumored that she has a temper. Doesn't show it, but there's talk. Most of it is self-directed. Her assistant said that Dr. Hafeldt's mind works so fast she gets impatient."

"How close is she?"

Binky lowered his head to remove the gum. He stuck it on the underbelly of the plane and murmured. "She'll be here in half a minute. Bet I can make her like me best."

"Do and you die, frogman."

Chapter 12

Phil strode to the jet after picking Bill's brain. The information she pried from him wasn't much but gave her some interesting details. It helped her fit together the puzzle pieces of her traveling-companion-cum-bodyguard.

She tried not to think about how lowering it was to be a librarian and have it pointed out that she was traveling with R.W. Chaucer, the famous writer. But then he wrote those smarmy thrillers about industrial espionage. She worked in front of a computer screen at a university library and never bothered to look at newly published fiction.

Rod and the other guy were still talking when she approached. It wasn't until she was a few feet from them that she fully looked at the man conversing with Rod.

Tall and topped by a blond crew cut, the mass of bristling sinew and muscle smiled. And it wasn't just any old smile—he beamed. The welcoming expression softened his terrifying appearance and lent a definite charm to his craggy features. She wasn't fooled; his Cheshire cat smile masked a tiger ready to leap.

Phil had a thing about not allowing anything or anyone to intimidate her or encroach into her space. She put on her best predatory smile and aimed it directly at Mr. Testosterone USA.

Out of the corner of her eye, Phil noticed Rod's boyish bonhomie fade and sensed jealousy. A zing of feminine victory sang along her veins followed by a lowering splash of reality. He'd lied to her about his identity and everybody seemed to know more about him that she did.

Rod was taking up too much space inside her head. Her original idea was to keep him around, maybe for a fling with the steamy side of life. He'd worn out his usefulness by becoming too distracting. No fault of his own, of course, but no one should be driven to the mistake of overlooking an object as intimidating as a blond bulldozer.

Negative thoughts flew out of her head when Rod surprised her and his companion with the territorial move of taking her arm. The tips of his fingers caressed the inside of her elbow and slid higher. The backs of his fingers sizzled against her side near her breast and squeezed just enough to convey his intention. Her heart fluttered at the novel experience of being the object of a man staking his claim.

Don't be so quick to get rid of this guy, Hafeldt! When was the last time a fellow went he-man for you? Use your smarts and keep this radical chick magnet around.

Since she had temporarily lost the ability to speak, Rod filled in the gap. "Phil, I'd like you to meet a friend of mine. He's a fan of your work. Binky, this is Dr. Hafeldt."

Phil gathered her wits, pulled her arm free, and stuck out her hand. "A pleasure to meet you, Mr. Binky."

"Just Binky."

Up close, Binky looked middle-aged. The weathering of his features made it difficult to pinpoint the exact number of years. His ropy musculature was the result of long-term weight training. This was a guy who was serious about body image. His palm was hard and rough, but the careful pressure of his handshake told her everything she needed to know. She relaxed.

"Hullo, Binky. I believe we've met through a phone conversation. You called Rod at the hotel."

"Yes, ma'am. And I brought a copy of your book with me. It's on board. Would you mind signing it?"

It was Phil's turn to beam. "I'd love to!"

She followed Binky up the boarding steps, gratified by the unexpected pleasure of having her boring tome acknowledged. Rod's sulky glower of thwarted possessiveness was an unexpected bonus.

Gee, this jealousy thing might work for me after all.

The jet's interior was air-conditioned and plush. Binky escorted her to a rosewood table. A copy of her book was the only thing on the glossy surface.

Binky handed her a pen. "What made you write this, Dr. Hafeldt?"

"Call me Phil."

"I don't think I can do that, ma'am."

"Actually, this was my doctoral thesis, and since you're one of the ten people who bought it, you can call me anything you like. Do you prefer to read the old romantics?"

"Literature was my major, too."

She ignored Rod when he strolled into the cabin and plopped down on a taupe leather couch attached to the wall.

Phil asked, "Are you flying us to Wyoming, Binky?"

"No. I'll wait here until you get back. There's another plane reserved to take you to Wyoming. It can land anywhere. This baby needs a bit more tarmac to stop."

"Ah. I'm curious, what nationality is the name Binky?"

Rod's derisive laugh was smoothly covered by Binky's reply. "It's not my real name, ma'am."

Phil stood up and handed him the book and pen. "Let me guess. You also trained at Coronado?"

Binky's wide brow creased with a thoughtful frown. "Why, yes, I did. Do you know someone else who made it through?"

"That lump over there."

Binky glanced over his shoulder. "Him? Nah! They'd never have him, and he'd never make it through hell week."

Phil glared at Rod. "You told me you were a SEAL."

"No, I didn't, smarty pants. You assumed it. I said that I was Coronado trained. That meant trained by a SEAL."

Binky grinned and winked at Rod. "His mommy hired me to baby-sit her little boy and toughen him up. She didn't like her baby getting sand kicked in his face."

Delighted with this tidbit, and angling for more, Phil laughed. "You're kidding!"

Binky was on a roll. "Yeah. She's got friends, you know what I mean? And she called up a few and said that she wanted the meanest UDT grad around to put some grit in her precious baby's craw. Said her Roddie always needed a tough binky to chew on to keep him occupied when he was teething."

Rod stood and shot them with a scowl. "You know where you can stick it, Bink. Where's the plane?"

Binky gestured for Phil to leave first. A framed picture attached to the cabin wall stopped her. A hard body thumped into her back. She could tell by the enticing tingle that it was Rod. His fingers momentarily gripped her waist for balance and were slow to withdraw.

She pointed at the photograph of a distinguished couple—a silver-haired man with laughter in his eyes and an ultra-chic matron. A scrawny, geek-boy stood between them—the sort that always got picked on at school. But this kid was no victim. There was a mulish glint in his eyes that couldn't be hidden by the frames of oversize, horn-rimmed glasses.

Rod's gentle shove urged her forward.

Phil swatted his hand away. "No, I want a closer look at this. Is that really you, Chaucer?"

Binky's rumbling laugh came from the rear. "That's our little Roddie. I used to call him "squirt." Pissed him off somethin' awful."

Intrigued, Phil looked over her shoulder. Rod's glare at Binky should have scored off a layer of skin, but Binky only smirked affectionately and gave Rod a playful cuff.

Rod rubbed his arm. "You can be replaced."

"No, I can't, squirt. And make nice or I'll tell Mommy that I've let you off my apron strings."

Phil asked, "What happened to your glasses?"

Rod said, "The wonders of laser surgery. What did you do with yours?"

"I only need them for reading."

Phil sorted through the interesting details of Rod's youth as she descended the steps. She could sense his lingering dissatisfaction with Binky in his disgruntled silence. But how does one go about reprimanding a person so impervious to intimidation as Binky? He looked fit for anything and was every boot camp trainee's nightmare of a drill instructor. It was no wonder that Rod was so confident and physically at ease with himself.

Binky only went as far as the bottom step. "It was a real pleasure meeting you, ma'am. And don't worry about getting the rental car back. I'll take care of it."

"Thank you, Binky." She tossed him the keys. "Will I see you again?"

"Sure. Take care of this piss-ant for me. If he gives you any lip, let me know."

Not entirely opposed to any sort of lip action Rod might opt to provide, Phil was hesitant to reply. She started to walk away and turned back.

"I wish you were flying us there. I've had more than my share of encounters with unhelpful strangers in the last forty-eight hours. Are you available to fly us to Wyoming?"

"Excuse me," Rod interrupted, "but if we're ever going to get the show on the road, it's time to break up this little love-in. Where's the plane, Binky?"

"Back of the hangar. It's good to go. There's a change of clothes in the aft overhead compartment and equipment in the hold. Maps and paperwork are on the seat. I'll be standing by on radio if you need anything."

Phil grabbed Rod's arm. "Chaucer, tell me that you're not flying us there."

Binky laughed and started back up the steps. "Not to worry, Dr. Hafeldt. He had the best instructor there is."

Phil blinked and asked hopefully, "You?"

Not stopping his climb, Binky replied over his shoulder, "No. His mommy."

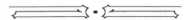

Phil had to be fair. Rod did know his way around a plane and flew them to the border of Wyoming before dark. She gave him directions to an airfield that was so small and out of the way that the runway was packed dirt. Dust billowed and blew across the sun-bleached grass as they rolled to a stop.

Rod handed her his cell phone. "Call for our ride."

She flipped it open. There was no dial tone. She didn't say anything about his phone account being cancelled and went through the motions of trying to make the call. She handed back the phone. "The batteries must be dead."

Rod checked the small screen. "It says it's fine. Must be something else. Now what?"

When she pulled the phone from her purse that the Fed had given her, he asked, "You said there was something wrong with your cell phone. When did you get that one?"

Two can play the game of omission, she thought. "Back at the airport."

She cut off his follow-up question. "You might want to see if Binky packed something suitable for riding. We'll be on horseback the rest of the way. I forgot to ask, can you ride?"

"Sure." He looked at her wrinkled linen slacks. "What about clothes for you?"

"I'll borrow from my friend."

Rod slipped off his headset, unbuckled his seat belt, and moved to the back of the plane. He withdrew a duffel bag from an overhead compartment.

Phil looked away as he started to change and stared blindly at the rolling prairie while the phone rang in her ear. She let it ring until someone answered.

"This is Jimmy."

His voice made her smile. "Hey, Sky-eyes, Phil here."

"You must have taken the long way from O'Hare. Have you landed?"

"A few minutes ago. We're parked about a half mile from the tree line."

"I'm just leaving work. See you soon."

Phil closed the cell phone and tucked it under the seat. That's all the Feds were going to get from her. For now. She was fairly sure that Bill was the real thing. He had the anal retentive air of a governmental, quasi-military drone. She didn't want them listening to what Uncle Cal had to say and yet wanted to keep them in the proverbial loop. It was too soon to cut all of her options. It was also dangerous to play with the Big Boys, but government types had their uses. And it felt good being the user instead of the used.

"Who were you talking to?"

Phil looked over her shoulder. "Our ride."

"Sounded like a man."

Phil faced forward in her seat and tried not to smile. "Mighty big ears you've got, Granny."

Chapter 13

Jimmy's truck appeared as they stepped down from the plane. Rod kicked chocks into place under the wheels and made a slow, circling check of the plane. He had changed into jeans, hiking boots, and Cubs baseball cap. Phil saw him come around the back of the plane just in time to see her give Jimmy Sky-eyes a bear hug.

Phil didn't mind that Jimmy never hugged her back. She knew he loved the affection even if he pretended otherwise. She smiled up into his smooth, dark face. Pale blue eyes gleamed with humor under the brim of his Stetson.

She pressed her hand flat on his chest. "I've missed you. How is my favorite forest ranger?"

"He's wondering why it has taken you so long to return to the land of the standing people and never call unless you want something."

"I'm here to harass Uncle Cal." She turned to confront Rod's hard stare and said, "Jimmy, this is Rod."

Phil watched how quickly Rod recovered when Jimmy didn't offer his hand and gave Rod a cold visual assessment instead. She broke the strained moment by heading for the dust-coated truck.

The drive to Jimmy's place was made in silence. The ruts in the road and the truck's ancient wheel shocks made for a jolting ride. She tried and failed to ignore the rub of Rod's hip and thigh against her own. Since the seat was long enough, he'd stretched his arm across the back, careful not to touch their grim-faced driver. Rod didn't seem to mind her shoulder cupped under his armpit or that the back of her head brushed his bicep every bump. It was a relief and a disappointment when the truck turned onto the dusty turnoff that led up to Jimmy's cabin.

As they climbed the porch steps, Phil asked, "Jimmy, you're sure Uncle Cal is still up there?"

"He must be. He would stop here before going away. Little sister, what are you doing with this Taker?"

"Don't be impolite. When did you see him last?"

Jimmy opened the front door. "It's been a few months. The Moon of Making Fat."

Rod followed them inside and closed the door with unnecessary force. "Do you two mind speaking in English?"

Phil winced. "You don't have to shout. Sorry, Chaucer. We'll stick to English from now on."

Jimmy grinned. He liked spunk and had little patience with people lacking a backbone. "Make yourselves at home. I've got chores waiting. Phil, I put some gear for you in my room and Josie sent up a change of clothes. Chaucer, you get the couch. I'll sleep in the barn."

Phil ducked into Jimmy's bedroom to change and to avoid Rod's questions.

She didn't see Rod when she came out. The shower and change of clothes invigorated her spirit and body. Full of energy and thoughts of her uncle, she pulled blankets, pillows, and a sleeping bag from the closet and made a place to sleep on the couch.

With no sign of Rod or Jimmy, she grabbed an apple and went out onto the back porch to listen to the night sounds. She stared at the truck tire swing, hanging still and suspended from a tree limb. A coyote's yipping howl filtered through the pines. A moment later, a canine chorus began. She tuned it out and gazed blindly at the alpine forest beyond the fence line.

"Looking for chocolate bunnies?"

Startled, Phil turned to Rod, who stood beside her. "You sure know how to sneak up on people."

"I wasn't that quiet. You were deep in thought. Worried about your uncle?"

She went down the steps and lobbed the apple core into the brush. "A little. I'm more concerned about why all this is happening."

Rod's hand slipped into hers. He tugged her toward the tire swing. Phil grabbed the scratchy rope and crawled through the frayed inner circle. Rod pushed her in silence. The rope creaked, disturbing the creatures lurking in darkness beyond the fence. Nocturnal sounds slowly returned to normal levels, merging with the creaking protest of the rope and tree limb.

Phil used her booted feet to aid the swing's momentum. "Where have you been?"

"I went out to the barn."

"Jimmy let you help?"

"Nope. He hates me. I'm going to tell Mommy."

"Jimmy doesn't hate anybody. Well, maybe a few politicians. What have you been doing?"

"I walked around and checked out the place. The only vehicle is that rusted-out truck we came here in. It might be quicker to go to the nearest town and rent an SUV."

"It's a two-hour drive to a town big enough to have a rental agency. There's a graded road that goes up to the cabin, but it's a winding drive and often washed out. The fastest way to get up the mountain is on horseback."

Phil found herself eager for the shove of his palms on her shoulder blades. Each pushing release brought a sense of abandonment, followed by the anticipation of renewed contact. There was something exciting and yet immeasurably comforting about his touch and presence. She had never felt this way before, not even with Jimmy. It was odd and emotionally unbalancing to feel so safe with a man she couldn't trust.

The muffled thumping sound was not enough warning. The swing rope came apart. Rod caught her before she tumbled onto the ground. He helped her to stand and step out of the tire.

Rod leaned over to pick up the frazzled end of rope still attached to the tire. "It's rotted through. How long has it been since this was used?"

Phil wrapped her fingers around the piece of rope left dangling from the oak's sinewy arm. "Probably since we were kids."

"Jimmy taught you to speak his language?"

"His mother did. Thanks for catching me."

"My pleasure."

Rod hesitated and then stepped closer. She looked up. Porch light glowed on one side of his face. The night sounds seem to fade and recede.

Phil's heart slowed and then began a frantic beat. "You know, Chaucer, up close, you're a lot bigger than you look."

His fingertips skimmed along her jaw. "Up close, you're a lot prettier. Beautiful."

Phil swallowed. Nobody had ever called her beautiful before. She needed to burn this moment into her memory. It was like a fantasy coming to life—an exciting, deliciously male man was irresistibly attracted to her. The notion of keeping him at arm's length seemed so pointless. Even wasteful.

She heard her name whispered and waited in breathless wonder. He leaned down to her upturned face. His fingers touched her neck and slid around her nape, drawing her forward. His lowering head blocked out the light and the night. His breath was warm on her mouth. She moved, answering the gentle pressure of his caressing fingers that drew her nearer and lifted her closer.

The back porch door squeaked. "You two want something to eat?"

Phil blinked. Rod's hand slipped away. She looked at Jimmy, not really seeing him. He was leaning out the screen door, waiting for an answer.

Phil searched for her voice, surprised when she sounded normal. "Uh, got any pizza?"

"Only pepperoni."

"Sounds good to me. How about you, Rod?"

She couldn't look into his eyes and settled for his chest. Her train of thought got sidetracked when she noticed the rise and fall of his deep breaths. She couldn't remember moving into his embrace, but her fingers were definitely in contact, resting on the ridge of muscle by his shirt collar. His shoulder felt like iron under the plaid material.

She recalled the sense of his excitement and the thump of his heart against her chest moments before. He might not be telling her the truth about some things, but he wasn't lying about being attracted to her. She dared to look up. A mistake.

His lips curved into a smile. "Whatever you want, doc."

A jolt of electricity zinged along her arms. She felt her eyes widen and her body lean into his.

So this is what babe magnate means.

Feeling dangerous and powerful, she savored every tingle. Out of her depth and yet assured that she could control the encounter, she licked her lips and brushed her fingertips along his arm. Rod shivered. The muscles bunched in his jaw. His gaze moved from thoughtful and distant to hard and calculating. She felt the subtle power shift. She was undermining his control. She let him see her savor the power by curving her lips into a confident grin. His fingers tightened on her arms.

Jimmy cleared his throat, bringing them back to earth.

Phil stepped back, her face burning. Rod was hazardous to her mental health. He made her feel things she'd never experienced before and enticed her in ways she'd only read about.

She had lost her head for a moment—a heady plunge into the intriguing play of the old-as-time man-woman game. That wasn't safe with Rod. His type liked to play the field. He was the kind of guy who took what he wanted and moved on. The question was—could she be the sort of woman who could take what she wanted and move on before he could leave her?

Chapter 14

Night settled around Jimmy's cabin. She'd forgot how quiet it can be in the backwoods. Moonglow flooded the narrow bedroom with bright blue light. She could see the beadwork design of Jimmy's fringed jacket on its hanger across the room. A dream catcher hanging in the window outlined a pattern on the hardwood floor.

Unanswered questions gnawed the corners of her mind. Realizing that she wouldn't sleep until she talked it out, Phil sat up. She dug into her briefcase beside the bed and found her cell. There was enough juice left to make a call. Jimmy's cabin was situated on the edge of tower reception. To use his cell, he had to walk to the start of the long, winding drive to his house to get a clear connection. It was a beautiful night, she couldn't sleep, and perhaps a walk would help.

In the cabin's main room, Rod hung half on and half off the couch, lost in the deep sleep of the unconcerned. She wouldn't go so far as to say guiltless. She eased the screen door open and shut and stepped out on the porch. Boards creaked as she tiptoed around the worst of the known squeakers and down the steps.

The parched grass felt crispy under her bare feet. The driveway's powdery dirt soothed her soles. Moonlight lit the way for the mile plus walk to the end of the drive where she stopped. She pressed the auto dial for her best friend's home number.

A groggy voice answered, "Huh?"

"Maddie, wake up. It's me, Phil."

"Just a minute." A few moments later, Maddie grumbled, "Since you never call me in the middle of the night, I know this has got to be good."

Maddie was one of those annoying people who can come fully alert soon after waking. Her brain went from zero to sixty the instant she hit an upright position, her ability reflected in rapid-fire questions and a perky tone. "Where are you? Cancun? Getting any nooky? Please tell me you are, because I'm not."

"Actually, I'm calling from Colorado, not far from the Wyoming border."

Maddie's jaw-cracking yawn snapped through the connection. "Sorry. Glad I got that out of my system. Go ahead. Start at the beginning. I'm going to get a snack while you talk."

Phil outlined everything that had happened from the time she got the keys delivered, the Tattoo Guy invasion, people trying to find her uncle, Rod and his many names, zooming through Florida, and ending with flying to Jimmy's place.

When Maddie didn't comment, Phil paused to listen to the background sounds coming across the line. "I hear slurping noises. You're eating something. What is it?"

"If you're at Jimmy's, you don't want to know."

"I can hear you moaning and licking a spoon. Tell me."

"Ice cream. Made it this afternoon. My own recipe. I call it Choco-coffee Double Latte Orgasm."

Phil groaned. "I take it back. You are *not* my best friend."

"Yeah, I am. I made a pint for you and stuck it in your freezer when I picked up your mail."

"Since I can't get my hands on it, let's talk about something else. I need a background check on Rod, alias Bud, Bob, Rob, Bobbio."

Maddie smacked her lips and mumbled around another spoonful of bliss, "What's his last name?"

"Chaucer."

Silence on the other end of the line and then Maddie murmured, "Rod Chaucer. Why does that sound familiar?"

"Get me everything you can find."

"An hour from now I'll have everything from his latest video rental to his condom preference."

"I don't want to know about that last bit."

Maddie chortled, "Ah-ha. You sound nervous. Is he that good looking?"

"Why do you assume that?"

"Cause you're scared. I know you, Hafeldt. Describe him in detail. I want to know the good stuff, even though I'll have his driver's license photo in no time flat." When Phil refused to comment Maddie whispered, awed, "That good? Better than I'm-God's-Gift-Jeffrey Ferrall?"

"Well, not quite as handsome. He's more like Banderas and Connery in steroid overdrive."

Maddie choked and groaned with great affect. "And you are not in the sack with him at this very moment? Shame, Hafeldt! You tolerated the abominable Jeffery and pass on this guy? And I'm down to my last two bites of Orgasm. Hey, do you mind if I go over to your place and use your computer?"

"You don't fool me, Maddie. You just want my ice cream."

"Hey, be reasonable. You got the real thing. I've got to settle for a substitute, which means, now that I think about it, I won't get Rod's background check to you for two hours."

"Actually, I don't need it for a few days. Maddie, this cell is just about out of juice and there's absolutely no chance of reception at Uncle Cal's place. Jimmy's cabin is right on the edge. I don't have a charger with me, so I have an alternate number for you. It's a cell the feds gave me. They said it works anywhere."

"Then why not take that with you?"

"Duh, Maddie. And your IQ is what?"

"Higher than yours and everybody else living or dead. I guess you don't want the feds knowing where you are. You're thinking that the fed phone has a tracker?"

"I know it has. They're after Uncle Cal, too, and would love it if I lead them right to him, but I'm not going to need that info on Rod until we get back to his plane."

"Oh? He flies and looks yummy? Have you ever thought about the Mile High Club thing?"

"Maddie, you need therapy."

"No, I need a man. Maybe two or three, and guess what. I'm going to get them. As many as I want."

Concerned, Phil asked, "What exactly do you mean by that?"

"Phil, I'm tired of guys ignoring us or ditching us because we're smarter than they are. I've decided to get back a little of my own."

Phil shot directly beyond concern to worry. When her friend got mentally bored, Maddie liked to flirt with trouble. "And you're about to tell me how you're going to do that."

Maddie chortled. A spoon clanged into a metal sink. "For starters, remember that program I've been shopping around?"

"You sold it?"

"Oh, yeah, to the tune of six figures, and they commissioned another one. I'm going to use a sizable chunk of that money to make myself over. A new me. I'm thinking Miss America meets Ms. Porn USA in haute couture. What'd you think?"

Phil smothered a groan. She loved her friend's typical New York City look. Born and reared in Manhattan, Maddie always wore black, a stark contrast against her pale, freckled complexion and flyaway red-gold hair. She didn't have to be sitting next to her best friend to see the sly glint in Maddie's hazel eyes, a sure sign that her friend was cooking up a scheme, which she did with frequency. A brain as agile and brilliant as Madelyn Blomberg's bored easily and required challenge on a minute-by-minute basis, hence the nickname she acquired at MIT, Bomber Berger.

Phil phrased her reply with care. "Am I going to recognize you when it's done?"

"Sure. At first I thought I'd just get an enlargement, you know the kind. Huge ones that draw the drooling attention of men but make women of intelligence long to kick them in the gonads."

"Maddie, what are you putting in the ice cream recipes? You're starting to sound physically aggressive and that's so not you."

"Give it a rest, Hafeldt. I was just kidding. I'm only going as far as clothes, make-up, and haircut."

"That's a relief. You don't need plastic work, Maddie. You've got a perfect figure. A simple change to bright colors from black will make more than enough difference, I'm sure."

"Yuck. You make me sound so boring. No wonder no one ever asks me out. Hey, are you going to start something ribald with Rod, Bud, Bob, Rob, Bobbio?"

"I couldn't possibly consider it until I see your report."

"Phil, if you didn't sound like an elementary teacher with an elocution pole up her butt, you might get a date with somebody unlike Jeffrey Dahmler."

"Don't call him that!"

"Hoo, honey, Jeffrey's not worth your loyalty. He screwed you over every way from Sunday."

"Then it's my fault for falling for it, Maddie, not his."

"When you get back, we're going to work on that passive aggressive thing you've developed about men. You weren't that way until Jeffrey Penile Compensator took over your life."

"Well, he's gone now, and I've got someone more difficult to deal with. And my cell is fading. Call me the day after tomorrow. I should be back to Jimmy's by then."

"Please, Philadelphia Casca, my dearest and best-est ever friend, don't be an embarrassment to all womankind. Promise me you'll jump his bones."

"Oh, go eat your ice cream!"

Phil flipped the phone shut. To relieve the tension of merely thinking about doing something exceptionable with Chaucer, she muttered some bad words under her breath.

"What's up, doc?"

Phil whirled, ready to strike. Knowing her, Rod stayed well out of range. Sans shoes, he stood in the middle of the road, hands on hips, still bleary-eyed.

Phil tucked the cell phone in her pocket. "How long have you been standing there?"

"Just got here."

"You're lying."

"Yeah. Where'd you get that cell phone? It's not the one you had on the plane."

"I had it. Just didn't want any overages."

"Pull the other one. Why are you running a background check on me?"

Caught in a fib, Phil stuck her nose in the air and started back to the cabin. "An employer has that right. No one gets hired theses days without one."

Rod yawned, scratched his head, and fell into step beside her. "Isn't it a bit after the fact?"

"Better late than never."

"Whatever. That couch is a torture rack. The hay in the barn might be comfier."

Phil snorted. "He has an inflatable bed for company out there. Even his nephews and nieces refuse to sleep on his couch."

"And I thought the Indians were getting their fill of revenge with the casinos."

"No casinos around here, so Jimmy's people don't get fat checks in the mail. You're closest, so you're it. Watch your back, White-eye."

"Now she tells me."

Chapter 15

The next morning, Rod was given proof of his suspicions about Jimmy's not liking him when their host led two horses from the barn.

Jimmy extended the reins for a scrub-tailed Appaloosa to Rod. The stallion eyed him and laid his ears flat. The Appy's pink-freckled muzzle wrinkled, exposing yellowed teeth. Before this, Rod had never known that horses could snarl.

Rod wasn't going to let the horse push him around. He grabbed the headstall near the bit and wrapped the right rein around the saddle's horn, making it impossible for the horse to bite during mounting or to lower his head and buck. He was on the stud's back before the horse could retaliate and held the reins short to keep the ornery horse's head up.

Jimmy smirked. "So, Chaucer. You know how to ride."

Rod looked down and quelled the urge to do something with the heel of his boot to rearrange Jimmy's annoying grin. Sometimes words worked better.

"White man getting heap big pissed off at Injun pain in the ass."

Surprisingly, Jimmy laughed. He lifted and resettled his Stetson. "You act smarter than the average white man. A bit of advice about riding Jake. Look out for trees. He'll run into one just to get rid of you."

"Terrific choice of mount for me. Thanks."

"He'll never tire, doesn't spook, and will run over a grizzly if you ask him." Jimmy's eyes hardened. "I don't hold with guns and glad you don't carry one. If you're followed, ride Jake at them. He hates strangers and eats other trail horses for breakfast. The fuss he'll make will give Phil time to get off the trail."

Rod and Jimmy exchanged a silent visual conversation. After reaching an unspoken truce, Rod nodded.

Phil directed her horse into the pines, following a narrow path. Behind her, Rod said, "This looks more like a deer path than a trail."

"That's because it is a deer path. The trail we want is farther up the mountain. We have to take an old logging road to get to it."

They rode in silence until they broke through the pines and onto a dirt road. The country lane had been widened to accommodate the rigs hauling logs. Rod directed Jake forward to match his pace with Phil's placid bay.

He checked out her horse, noting the prominent speed bump on its rump. "No fair, doc. Jimmy loves you best. You got the fast one."

Phil leaned forward to glide her palm along the mare's sleek neck. She looked at Rod, squinting as she considered his words. "You know horses. Where did you learn?"

"Played polo and spent a large part of my youth riding the fire trails."

"Polo? Really?"

"Had my own string for three years. I spent a lot of time daydreaming and riding in the hills when I was a kid. Southern California is all fire trails."

"That must have been nice. Jimmy told me all about fire trails when Uncle Cal and I went to his graduation from Marine boot camp. I asked him about all the dirt roads cutting up the foothills, and Jimmy said—with that completely straight face of his—that he and his buddies made them from running drill every morning. I believed him at the time."

"That joke's been around a while. How old were you?"

Phil lifted her feet from the stirrups and stretched her legs. She dangled her feet, enjoying the sway and rock of the mare's movement and lazy bob of the horse's black-maned head and neck.

Feeling the penetration of Rod's gaze, she finally answered. "I was eleven and the victim of a major crush. Jimmy looked great in uniform."

"I'll bet."

She glanced at him. "Were you in the service?"

"No. I learned all I ever wanted to know about agonizing physical discipline and submitting to authority from Bink." He gestured at the saddlebags resting on the bay's glossy hips. "Those look interestingly lumpy. Bring your candy bar along?"

"I keep that snug and safe in my briefcase. Those are some bacon sandwiches Jimmy packed for breakfast. Want one?"

They munched as the horses plodded in unison. The morning air was fresh and sharp with the scent of pines. Shafts of sunlight slanted through the trees. Insects flitted through the hazy beams.

When Phil reached for a third sandwich, Rod asked, "How many did he pack?"

114

"There's four more. Bacon won't spoil and Jimmy knows my appetite."

His sarcastic murmur was larded with innuendo. "Does he?"

"It's not like that with me and Jimmy."

"Then why don't you tell me all about you and Jimmy."

Phil took a bite and finished chewing before she explained.

"Uncle Cal fell in love with Jimmy's mother when I was seven. It was the first summer I ever spent with Uncle Cal. It was supposed to be a few days of staying with him, while he checked out a medicine wheel and talked to the tribal historian, but it lasted all summer. Jimmy and I have been friends ever since."

"What happened with your uncle and Jimmy's mother?"

"She died. Diabetes."

"He never married?"

"Uncle Cal? No. He likes it here on the rez. It's where she grew up and used to live. He does what he can to stop the carnage."

"What do you mean?"

"Trying to keep out the mining companies and loggers."

"I thought you said this was reservation land."

"As long as there are politicians with holes in their pockets there'll be businesses ready to rape what's left on the reservations. The government holds the land in trust and hands it over whenever the bribe is fat enough. Let's talk about something else. This subject makes me crazy."

"Let's get back to you and Jimmy."

"Sorry. Didn't mean to get off track." She took another bite of sandwich and stared at the road between the mare's bobbing head and twitching ears. "Look at her. She's such an eavesdropper. She loves to listen."

Rod snorted. "Better than this guy. He hasn't relaxed his snarl since I got in the saddle. Jimmy says he doesn't shy, but I'm not so sure about that."

"Jimmy doesn't lie. He may not answer, but he never lies. And Jake the Snake can turn on a dime and give you change, as the old boys used to say."

"Back on task, Phil."

"To put it simply, Jimmy is the brother I never had. Are you a single child?"

Rod grimaced. "I have two older sisters from Mom's first marriage. She was in her teens when she had them."

"They weren't in that photograph on the plane."

"Away at college."

"Your mother doesn't look that old."

"Barb and Trina got accepted when they were fifteen and sixteen."

Phil swallowed the last bite and wiped her hand on her thigh. "I matriculated that young. It isn't easy being so much younger than all your classmates. What are they doing now?"

"Barb has her own law firm. Trina has her own menagerie—kids, dogs, horses, cats, chickens, turtles, ducks. If you can name it, Trina's got it in her back yard."

"What did your mother have to say about Trina not using her education?"

Rod shrugged a shoulder. "Mom just wanted her kids to have an education, not set the world on fire. And who's to say that Trina isn't using it? She's not dead."

"I most heartily agree and apologize. My question stemmed from my own mother's point of view. She was very serious about education—one's career being the priority and money insignificant. Publishing is high up there but mostly, she was keen on making use of one's education. She's the one who pushed me to publish. She wanted me to teach."

"What did your father have to say?"

"Dad doesn't care one way or the other. He isn't really here." She paused. "What I mean is that he isn't part of our world. He lives in whatever project he's working on. If I didn't feed him at night, he'd forget to eat. Most of the time, I'd find him asleep at his desk. When I moved out, I hired a live-in housekeeper and cook."

"Doesn't sound like much of a life for a kid. No wonder you glommed on to your uncle."

"There was a lot more to my relationship with Uncle Cal than that. I took to Uncle Cal the minute I met him. My parents scoffed at me for saying so, but I can clearly remember the first time he held me. It was my second birthday. He picked me up and held me on his lap and told me a story about a Maya princess."

"At two? The farthest back that I can remember is my first day of school."

"Nobody believed me. I had to prove that I did remember back that far by describing the room where it happened. It was at a house in Urbana when Dad was an associate professor. We moved to the Chicago campus when I was four."

"I've heard of early impressions leaving a mark but nothing that young. Perhaps nothing eventful happened to me. And I can't say that I've ever had that kind of instant connection to anyone. Except recently. I was really impressed that you were ready to slice my head off with a fertility mask Frisbee."

Phil laughed. "I know you like it rough, Chaucer, but decapitation seems a little extreme!"

Rod dropped his voice to its lowest register. "Got hanky-panky on your mind, doc? I wouldn't turn down a romp in the midst of Mother Nature. You could save the candy bar for a rainy day."

Phil's cheeks tingled. She touched her heels to the bay's sides, urging the mare into a lope. She called over her shoulder, "The cabin's about an hour from here. We get off the road a mile beyond this curve."

"Chicken," he hollered and tapped Jake's ribs to catch up with the bay.

They left the road and followed a footpath. The forest ended at a clearing, a broad meadow. At its center was an A-frame house built on rising ground.

"It's modular," Phil said. "Uncle Cal had a helicopter transport it here in pieces. Jimmy and his friends helped him put it together."

She pointed at an abandoned cabin, collapsing in decay on the other side of the meadow. Square-cut logs sagged, toppling to one side, like a child's neglected toy. "That was where Jimmy's great-grandparents spent the winter after they survived Sand Creek."

The passing wind whistled through the pine needles and riffled the tall grass in the meadow. A breeze lifted Rod's dark hair as he studied the peaceful scene.

"I didn't know that there were survivors."

"There's a lot of revisionist history from the whites' point of view. Uncle Cal prefers to believe tribal historians."

"What makes them better?"

Phil looked Rod in the eye. "They have no political agendas, nothing to lose, and nothing to hide."

Rod returned her look without blinking. Phil was impressed. If he was a liar, he was good at it. His smile was slow, conveying challenge and promise. He held her gaze, waiting for her to break contact.

Phil directed the mare into the glade before she succumbed to the impulse to fling herself at the Marlboro man by her side.

Why does he have to look so good on a horse?

When Phil halted in front of the porch, Rod's grip on her wrist stopped her from dismounting.

"It's too quiet. Wouldn't your uncle come out to meet us?"

Phil looked around. "If he's still here. He might have gone for a walk. There's an old burial site not far from here."

Rod relaxed and withdrew his hand. "Just be careful. What do we do with the horses?"

"They ground tie. Jimmy trained them, which means you could fire off a shotgun and they'd stay where you dropped the rein."

The A-frame's front wall was mainly glass. There was no sign of anyone in the great room. Phil opened the door, glanced around, and stepped inside.

"There are crystals here, even if no Uncle Cal."

She called his name and waited.

A door slammed at the back of the house. "Phil? Is that you? You got my note from the safe-deposit box!"

She was across the room and ready to fling herself at her uncle when he appeared in the hallway.

"Uncle Cal!"

Chapter 16

Calvin Hafeldt still looked fit enough to climb mountains. He had an air of ruggedness and arrogance that disappeared when he hugged his niece. He didn't release her when she started to step back.

"Just a minute, Philly."

She shoved free. "You know how I hate to be called that! Why haven't you answered my letters?"

"Calm down."

"Have you been in the field and just got back?"

"No. I've been up here over a year. Jimmy brought me your letters but I couldn't answer them."

"What's going on? Did you know that your lawyer thinks you're dead? Somebody sent him an urn full of ashes that were supposed to be yours."

"They're mine. In a way. I got them out of the fireplace."

"What?"

"The ashes. I took them from the fireplace and sent them."

"But why?"

"To find some peace and quiet to work. I knew you'd find me here. Who's this you've brought with you?"

Phil felt her body go still. She slowly turned and glared at Rod. "Why am I not surprised that you don't know your own bodyguard?"

Rod extended his hand. "Rod Chaucer."

Phil studied her uncle's frown. Rod looked distinctly uncomfortable. She wasn't going to help good old Not Bob out of this one.

Careful not to look at her, Rod asked, "Did you get my letter, Dr. Hafeldt?"

Releasing Rod's hand, her uncle said, "Sorry, but I never received your letter. As I told Phil, I don't get much mail when I'm up here. And my computer isn't online. Why did you write to me?"

"The truth is, I wanted an interview."

Before he could say another word, Phil punched Rod's arm. "So now you're pretending to be a reporter? You lying jerk!"

Rod rubbed his arm. "Sheesh! That hurt, Phil! And I'm not a reporter. I'm a writer."

"You're a stinking, lousy, lying creep, is what you are!"

"Gee, doc, you lose that hoity-toity way of talking pretty quick when you get mad."

"You're fired! And leave Jake here. You can walk back to your stinking plane. No, just marched yourself all the way back to your jet in Colorado, because I'm going to have the one at Jimmy's torched!"

Uncle Cal touched Phil's shoulder. "Hold on there, slugger. Before you leave, Rod, are you the same Chaucer as R.W. Chaucer?"

"Yes, sir."

Uncle Cal smiled. "Why, I think I do remember getting a letter from you, but I'm sorry to say that I can't remember what it was about."

Rod edged away from Phil, who looked like she was winding up to smack him again. "Research. I'm doing some research on crystals, especially the industrial applications aspect."

Uncle Cal stared at Rod. "Wait a minute. I know you. Your father is Paul Wakefield Gameson. I met him and your mother at a party in D.C. years ago."

Pointedly ignoring Phil's stunned expression, Rod said, "Yeah. That must have been around the time Dad decided to retire."

"I was under the impression that your mother was going to take over the business."

Rod said, "No. They sold it and she started one of her own, SilCon Limited. She got in on the ground floor of Silicon Valley."

Phil listened, her head bobbing back and forth, feeling as if she were following the bouncing ball at a tennis match. The men were wholly occupied with their conversation. It was as though she'd left the room.

Uncle Cal said, "She's a remarkable woman, your mother. How is your father?"

"Enjoying himself. Dr. Hafeldt, would you be willing to answer some questions?"

"Later, perhaps. I'm more interested in what you're doing teamed up with my niece."

"Uh, regarding that, I lied so that I could stay with her. At first I wanted to get to you, but now, I'm more interested in her."

"Excuse me," Phil interjected, "does it look like I've left the building?"

Ignoring her bristling outrage with a doting smile, Uncle Cal returned his attention to Rod. "I'm not at all surprised. I enjoy being with my niece, too. She's so intrepid and interested in everything."

"Yes, I noticed that right away. And she's very goal oriented."

"I would expect you to like that. Your mother is positively driven, but in the nicest way, of course. She reminds me of a science fiction tractor beam locking onto its target. She doesn't go to it. Her objective comes to her. She kept everyone at the party enthralled, as I remember, and she was talking mainly about you."

Rod was looking uncomfortable again. "She tends to go on and on about her kids."

"Nobody was bored, I can tell you that. Her children are interesting, too. I distinctly recall her saying that you published quite young, not commercial work, but an article on subatomic particles. That field is beyond me. Barely scraped through physics, but the interesting thing she said was that you changed fields and went with engineering."

Rod was beginning to perspire. "Yes, sir. About those questions—"

"And mentioned that you double-majored at MIT, did postgrad work at Berkley, and then chucked it all to go commercial. Now you write bestseller novels."

Phil stepped into the breach. She glared up at Rod. "How despicable can you get? You've been passing yourself off as a no-brain jock and have degrees in engineering and physics?"

His smile felt feeble. "Sorry. You're too easy, Phil. Couldn't resist teasing you a bit."

"Teasing? Let's count up the lies, Rod, Bud, Bob, Roddie, Buddy, Bobbio! By the way, what is your real name?"

"Roderick Wakefield Gameson. I swear it. And Chaucer is legal. It's my pen name."

"As if I'd believe anything you'd say. All you wanted was to get to Uncle Cal through me, so you can write another sleazy thriller."

That got him ticked off. "Hey, my thrillers aren't sleazy!"

Uncle Cal cleared his throat. "Uhm Phil, I can vouch for that. They're quite entertaining. Not in the least sordid or sleazy. Rather exciting in some parts."

They were interrupted by the sound of an approaching car. Fuming, Phil asked, "You expecting someone?"

"That's Mike. He drove down to town to pick up supplies."

Perplexed, Phil asked, "Mike? As in Mike Richardson? I thought you two had a falling out."

"He came a few days ago. Just showed up without an invitation. He wants to patch things up. I figured he must really want it to brave the logging trails to get all the way up here. I haven't encouraged him to stay."

"How'd he know you were here?" Phil asked.

"He must have guessed it. We used to be pretty close."

Phil watched Richardson step down from a dust-rimed, black SUV and come up the porch steps with his arms full of paper grocery bags. Rod opened the door.

Mike Richardson's face retained all of its boyish charm and animation. His facial youthfulness had been a point of fascination as far back as Phil could remember. His manner of speaking with a vague eastern seaboard accent had sounded odd and intriguing to a child of the Midwest. It wasn't until she achieved collegiate cynicism that she suspected that he affected the Kennedy family accent.

She later found out that Richardson did come from a wealthy family from Newport, but he studied at Stanford and the University of Illinois, neither campus anywhere near Massachusetts. Even though he hadn't lived on the East Coast since leaving prep school, the accent hadn't changed.

"Phil! What a pleasure it is to see you again. You were in your second year at the University of Chicago the last time I saw you."

Not forthcoming, Phil only said, "Hi, Mike."

Rod closed the door and shared a long look with Phil. She saw him register her disdain and discomfort with Richardson's presence. Rod crossed to stand beside her.

Phil inwardly smiled. Liar, con-artist, or suck-up, it didn't matter. There was something comforting about having Rod nearby.

Phil watched Richardson take the bags to the kitchen table and set them down. Paper bags crunched and crackled as he removed the items. He spoke over his shoulder. His round face glowed with a form of good humor that reminded her of panting puppy adoration.

"Phil, if you don't mind, I'll just put these away before meeting your friend. In the meantime, what brings you all the way to Wyoming?"

"I hadn't heard from Uncle Cal and wondered what he what he was doing. How are things at USC?"

"Oh, I haven't been there in years."

"Really. Where are you teaching?"

Richardson took a box of crackers to the cupboard and came back to the table for cans of vegetables and soup. "Teaching gets old. All that pressure to publish or perish and so little of interest to write when it comes to nonfiction. Students aren't what they used to be. Got tired of the tedium, one might say. I suppose some would call my career course a middle-aged life change."

Phil watched him reach deep into the bag and said, "Whatever it was, it had to be significant to make you quit after being tenured."

Richardson's back was to them as he felt around the bottom of the paper bag. He stilled when he found what he wanted. "Oh, I wasn't tenured."

When Richardson turned around, he held a pistol. "They got rid of me before that."

Chapter 17

Phil sensed Rod easing closer to her side. Uncle Cal took her hand. Her uncle's fingers squeezed, a warning to be quiet, to not move, and to hold on to her temper.

The smile centered in Richardson's round face was benign; its hidden menace was all the more frightening in a countenance that looked harmless. The pistol in his hand looked unreal, ludicrous. It didn't seem possible that jovial Mike Richardson knew what to do with a weapon.

"I'm sorry, Phil dear, but I must warn you to stay exactly where you are and not move even the slightest bit. Calvin has done a great deal of bragging about how competent you are in the martial arts. I remember when he signed you up for your first class in Tae Kwon Do. He was so proud."

Phil couldn't hold back the accusation. "You used to be best friends."

Richardson laughed silently. "Past tense in every way, my dear. He preferred his Indian girl to our friendship. What he saw in her I'll never know."

Uncle Cal said, "That's a strange remark, since you tried to take her from me."

"She wasn't worth the loss of our friendship, Calvin."

"You're lucky I never told Jimmy about that."

Richardson said, "I know you very well, Calvin. You would never risk embarrassing her in front of her son."

"Come on, Mike. Let Philadelphia and her friend go. They don't have anything to do with this."

"Wrong again, Calvin. She has everything to do with it. She has a crystal with her. Where is it, Phil?"

She looked up at her uncle. He nodded and she said, "In my briefcase."

"And where is that, my dear?"

"Tied to the saddle on the horse out front."

"Go and get it, Phil. Chaucer, you stay right where you are. Calvin, while your niece fetches the crystal, I want you to sit in that chair. Put your hands on the armrest. Go on, Phil. Get the crystal."

Phil went out and down the steps. She unfastened the briefcase from the saddle horn and brought it inside. She set it on a side table.

"There it is. Take it."

Richardson stayed in the kitchen area. "Remove the stone from the briefcase. Set it on the side table and back away. Chaucer, you back up, too."

Rod asked, "How do you know my name?"

Richardson stayed focused on his captives as he came forward to pick up the black crystal. He backed toward the kitchen table. "Everyone knows who you are, Chaucer. Three bestsellers in a row. The last one has your picture on the back."

Richardson looked at the rock he held and back at Phil. "This isn't one of the synthetic ones. Or did someone grind the glyphs off the base?"

Phil clenched her teeth. This was bad. He knew everything about the crystals. She hadn't known that Richardson and her uncle were that close.

"Sorry, Richardson, that's all I've got. There's only one other synthetic that I know of. The one on loan. You'll just have to trot off and find a way to steal it."

"No need to get snippy, Phil. It's not as if I want to hurt you or your friend, but I must have your help, you see. You'll just have to go back to Chicago and recheck the safe-deposit box."

Phil gasped. "You're the one? You had us followed? Uncle Cal, one of his goons tried to kill me! No, he was going to kill you. He shot up your apartment door."

Uncle Cal stood up. "That does it. Mike, I let you hang around because I felt sorry for you. You've never come up with anything on your own and never will."

Richardson's bland expression never changed. His reproof was gentle, pitying. "That's not kind, Calvin."

"I wasn't blind to the fact that you were using me. I didn't mind, but you should know me well enough by now that threatening Phil is not the way to get what you want from me."

Richardson's smooth face lit up with an angelic grin. "Then I'll have to use you as incentive. One would never suspect that Phil would require motivation but there it is." He looked at Phil. "I'll start with his knees. I've taken marksmanship lessons. This is small caliber, but even so, there won't be much left of your uncle's legs after I empty the clip."

Phil moved sideways—a single, protective step toward her uncle. She stopped when Richardson aimed the pistol at her uncle's knees.

"Richardson!" she cried. "Stop it! Can't you see that it's useless?"

Richardson's black button eyes blinked as he paused to consider. "I see nothing of the sort, my dear."

"The crystals in the safe-deposit box in Chicago are natural. The government confiscated the one on loan. It's probably at Langley."

"Then you'll have to find another one. Try Site Fifty-four."

Phil shouted over her uncle's immediate protest, "You know it's unstable!"

"Of course I do. That's why you're going in there, and I'm not."

Phil's mind whirled, scrambling for excuses. "It will take months to prepare."

Richardson's shoulders shook with a silent laugh. "Leave the preparations to me. Everything is in order."

"And what's going to happen to Uncle Cal for the weeks it takes to get there and back?"

"I haven't that much time, my dear. I want this over and done in a few days. And your uncle is my assurance that you'll go back inside Site Fifty-four. I must have a synthetic one, you see. I have a buyer waiting and a book deal about my discovery. Your uncle's discovery, of course, but that's neither here nor there. It's mine now."

Incredulous, Phil said, "Your family's been rich for generations. What could you or anyone do with so much?"

"Ah, as to that. A downturn in the market and other investments have proved sadly disappointing. Father and Mother chose unwisely when they put everything they had in one company."

Rod murmured, "Let me quess. The company started with an E."

"Exactly, Chaucer! They refused to listen to me and didn't place their money in offshore accounts. They weren't members of the board and didn't get the inside tip to sell their ENRON stock before it all collapsed. All I had left was rental property and a house that needs a great deal of upkeep. Unfortunately, the rental properties had to be sold to pay for this venture. The advance on the book deal was fortuitous."

Revulsion deepened Uncle Cal's voice. "You're enjoying this. You like the idea of watching your victims squirm. I always knew you were something of a worm but never thought you'd sink this low."

An unsightly expression rippled over Richardson's face—a brief view of ugliness underneath—before returning to its honeydew melon smoothness.

"It was always so easy for you, Calvin. You've never been among the professional have-nots. You had your niece to lead you to the most important discovery of the century. What about me? I worked hard. I paid my dues, and what did I get? I got to watch my dearest friend allow himself to be sidetracked from a major historic find by an ill-bred female and her grubby offspring."

Phil grabbed her uncle's arm before he lunged. Richardson jerked up the pistol and aimed it at Phil's chest.

"I'll shoot her if you come near me, Calvin."

When Richardson was satisfied that he had resumed complete control, he said, "That's all the time we'll waste chatting up the old days. Everyone has a job to do before nighty-night. Phil and I will be clearing out the storage closet for her and her friend. Before she starts, Calvin open the bedroom door. Stay in my field of vision. Find a backpack for your niece. She'll be gone a few days. Don't pack too much for going through the labyrinth. She'll only be in there five hours."

"That's not enough time," Phil said, "and you know it!"

"Nevertheless, it's all I'm going to allow. Chaucer, as soon as my assistant arrives, you will take the horses to the barn. We wouldn't want things to look out of place if Jimmy decides to join us. And thank you for providing transportation and a pilot, Chaucer. Your jet has international credentials. How convenient and you've saved me so much on overhead. Please extend my compliments and gratitude to Mrs. Gameson."

Straight-faced, Rod said, "You don't want to mess with my mother's toy. She might get impatient with you."

"Yes, I believe that I've met her. Cal and I were invited to a social event in D.C. some time ago."

Rod added, "She's not one to cross."

"Note taken. Phil, take a look inside that storage closet. You'll need to make room for you and the famous fiction writer to share it for the night."

He looked at Rod. "Chaucer, when you get back from the barn, we'll get you and Philly tucked in for the night, nice and snug."

Phil said, "There's not enough room in there for three people."

"Your uncle will be elsewhere. Ah, I believe I hear one of my assistants now."

A second vehicle came up the road. A car door slammed and footsteps squeaked the porch boards. The highlight of Phil's day peeked through the windows before coming through the door.

Phil smirked at The Weasel. He changed from the parking attendant garb to well-worn slacks and a short-sleeved shirt that would have been fashionable twenty years ago. Dark smudges encircled his eyes above the gauze bandage covering his broken nose. He looked like an anxious raccoon wielding a pistol.

The first words out of The Weasel's mouth were an adenoidal accusation. "She brope my nobe!"

Phil grabbed Rod's wrist and squeezed hard to help swallow a bubble of inappropriate nervous laughter. Dense nasal packing forced The Weasel to mouth-breathe, which significantly enhanced his resemblance to a rodent.

When Phil had the laugh under control, she said out of the corner of her mouth to her uncle, "At last, the comic relief has arrived."

Richardson's face darkened, "Reed, stay outside. Keep an eye on Chaucer while he puts the horses away. Phil, start on the closet. Calvin, until she's done, you're going to sit in that chair. Make it your friend. You two will be tied together for a long time."

When Chaucer hesitated to obey, Richardson turned, aimed the gun, and fired. Phil swallowed an outcry and watched blood seep through her uncle's fingers. He had immediately grabbed the wound on his left arm.

Richardson pointed the Beretta at Rod while looking expectantly at Phil. "Six rounds left, Philly. Anyone care to test my patience again?"

Phil struggled not to lunge. She concentrated all of her protective rage into her stare.

Her uncle said, "No, Phil. Don't take chances. He just creased me. Do as he says."

After a pause, she nodded and went into the closet. When she was sure Richardson wasn't looking, she rubbed the frustrated tears from her face with a sleeve and began to plot.

Chapter 18

Binky heard the clatter of a horse cantering across the tarmac. He slipped a bookmark between the pages, set the book aside, and went to the open hatch.

A teenage boy, riding bareback, stopped his buckskin horse at the base of the steps that descended from the cockpit door.

"Hey, you the pilot?" the boy called.

"Yes."

"I've got a letter for you."

Binky went down the steps and accepted the envelope, nodding his thanks to the boy before he rode away. Binky tore open the sealed message, scanned the contents, and looked up. He blasted a piercing whistle to call the boy back.

The buckskin slid to a halt, pivoted, and loped back to the steps.

Binky asked, "Who gave this to you?"

The kid smirked. "A *wasicun.*"

"In English."

"A white guy."

Binky tapped the message on his open palm. "Can you tell me more about him?"

The teenager squinted up at Binky. "Early thirties. In shape. Tattoos on his arms. Likes to think he's a big, bad man but didn't want to come all the way onto the rez."

"Where did you meet up with him?"

"Down the road. I've been watching him for a while. Came from town. Looks like he's driving a rental. Gave me a five to give the letter to you."

Binky gazed at the dirt road beyond the landing strip. Trees blocked the view. "What makes you think it was a rental?"

The kid shrugged. "They've all got that stripped-down look. And I know everybody's car."

Binky pulled a wad of cash from his pocket, peeled off a bill, and offered it.

The kid took it and incredulously said, "This is a fifty!"

Binky put on his fiercest drill instructor face. "You pumping me for more, kid?"

The horse took off at a run. Binky watched horse and rider fly away, his smile fading as he remembered the letter. He went up the steps and inside the cockpit to sit down and study the contents.

The writer of the note included a second sheet of instructions. Binky glanced over the flight plan before returning to the first page.

To the pilot of Mr. Chaucer's plane:

We are holding your employer hostage. Any attempt to contact the authorities will result in his immediate death. Prepare for flight. Your employer will be released to you unharmed when we reach our destination.

"Yeah, right," Binky murmured.

A thought occurred to him while booting up the plane's computer. He found the business card Rod gave him and rang the phone number. No answer, so he left his number on voice mail. Ten minutes later the call was returned.

"This is Estelle. Who the hell is calling me during my facial?"

"I apologize for the interruption, ma'am, but this is urgent. I'm calling in behalf of Mr. Roderick Gameson."

"Don't know who that is and don't care, now that I've heard your voice. You sound pretty good."

"He's the guy you met on your flight to West Palm."

"Oh, Stud Muffin! What about him?"

"He mentioned that you talked to the authorities."

"Yeah. Said just what I was told to say."

Binky prompted, "Which was?"

"That he and his girl were on their way to the Keys."

"Nothing else?"

"Nope. Hey. Do you look as good as he does?"

"Better. Did they ask for names, dates, or anything unusual?"

"They seemed to know names. Didn't ask about dates but never had much chance. My son's lawyers came and got me out of there just when it was beginning to get fun. They didn't even bother to do a strip search."

"Thank you for your help, ma'am. Take care. Gotta go."

Binky cut the connection before she could continue hitting on him. Rod had warned him about Estelle.

He gazed out the jet's front screen at the hangar. The place had been locked up after Rod and Phil flew off in the rented plane. Binky had watched through the open doors, noting that the mechanic in the hangar never got around to working on the torn-down plane.

He supposed there was nothing else to do but wait for whatever was going to happen next to happen.

"Don't move."

Mentally kicking himself for being so lax, Binky did as he was told. He smelled the intruder—gasoline, sweat, and the raw onions from a recent burger.

The intruder said, "I see you got my message. Turn around. Stay seated."

The teenager's description was dead-on, except for the fact that the guy needed a bath and plastic surgery. A serious problem with acne left him scarred and coarse looking. Tattoos decorated his arms. Amid the writhing snakes, knives, naked women, and crude words was the motto *semper fi.* Another well-known military emblem, a yellow eagle's head, was on his left forearm.

The intruder tossed a large manila envelope onto Binky's lap. "Read what's in there. Do what it says."

Binky removed the contents and scanned the information. He looked up. "Mexico? That's a different flight plan from what was with the letter."

"Things change. Just do what you're told and nobody gets hurt."

Binky started the prep for a flight south. While he fiddled and pretended to be busy, he cheerfully sang a cadence he'd learned at Coronado.

"I don't want a BAR. I just want a candy bar. Lead me to the pop machine. I'm a candy-assed Marine."

Out of the corner of his eye, Binky noted no response from his stinky guest. A few minutes later, he tried another taunt, this time sung to the tune of "Oh, My Darling Clementine."

"I'm a bastard, I'm a bastard, I'm a bastard dressed in green. But I'd rather be a bastard than a candy-assed Marine."

The guy pried his stare away from the view out the front window long enough to glance Binky's way but still said nothing. Pointedly disinterested, in fact.

Binky rearranged his smirk to a frown of pretended concentration. The intruder was definitely not a Marine. No self-respecting Jarhead would have let those insults to the Corp pass without some kind of comment or retaliation. To top it off, the guy had a tattoo of the Army's most famous airborne division pierced into his flesh—unless he got the tattoo before enlisting in the Marines and then got turned down. Or had a grudge against them.

Binky doubted any branch of the military would take this loser but it's always wise to do some intel on the capability of the opposition. The problem was that he couldn't think of a cadence about the Screaming Eagles. He mentally smiled. If he couldn't remember a derogatory tune about the airborne division, he could always invent one. It gave him something to think about until Rod and Dr. Hafeldt made an appearance, but it really wasn't necessary. Special forces never got tattooed unless told to do so. Insignia or identification of any kind was avoided in case of capture and interrogation.

Things were looking up. It wasn't going to be a boring day after all. He had a mouse to play with.

Chapter 19

Phil stared at the faint glow of firelight seeping under the storage closet door. Before herding Phil and Rod into the storage room, Richardson set a match to the fireplace logs, while Reed duct-taped her uncle to a chair. The crease wound stopped bleeding as soon as a bandage was wrapped tightly around her uncle's upper arm.

The storage room door was locked and something heavy shoved in front of it. They heard a chair being dragged across the floor to another room. There was no way to know what had been done to Uncle Cal after that. She hoped he didn't have to sleep in the chair all night.

Darkness and confinement intensified the smell of camphor, ammonia, and musty clothes. The largest boxes had been pushed into the great room area, giving them enough room to lie down. Rod pulled a coat from a hanger and spread it across the dust and dirt on the floor. They searched the room by feel but couldn't find anything to use as a weapon or to free themselves.

Rod pushed boots aside so he could lie with his back against the wall, facing the door. Exhausted, Phil stretched out on her side on the coat and used her folded arm for a pillow. After she settled, Rod startled Phil by hauling her back against his chest. Phil muffled a squeak when she realized where her bottom ended up—cupped in his lap with his knees tucked up behind hers. She had read about sleeping like spoons but had never experienced the startling intimacy of the position. Jeffrey always got up and left afterward, sometimes showered.

She wrapped her fingers around his forearm and tried to pry him free. "This is a bit too cozy, Chaucer."

His voice was warm against her ear. "You're better off back here. What if they open the door? They'd step right on your face."

"They won't open it any more tonight."

"They might, and you're keeping me warm."

"Try another one. You're as hot as a furnace. No comment on that, please." After a few minutes of trying to get the Elvis burning love tune out of her head, she said, "Since we're stuck here, we might as well take advantage of the situation."

Rod stilled. "Which one?"

"Not what you'd like. Let's sort things out one at a time. We can use this time to plot a course of action and maybe even get some rest. I also need to talk to you about where we're going. Chances are that we'll get separated at some point once we get inside Site Fifty-four. I have to explain in detail how to get out of the maze if separation occurs. Or if something happens to me."

"I won't go in or leave without you, doc."

"Let's just worry about surviving the maze. If I do the reconfiguration wrong, none of us will get out."

"You're telling me that the maze is set up like a mathematical puzzle?"

"Somewhat. It's not like the kind where you follow a single path through the maze to find the end. I learned that lesson the hard way. I got stuck in there once and had to find a way out. This time, I'm going to have to change the configuration on purpose to lose Richardson's goons."

"Let me get this straight. You're telling me that the entire labyrinth moves?"

"Yes. Incorrect movements within the maze usually trigger the changes. I think it was some sort of security thing. The maze has any number of physical riddles, depending on where you are standing in it."

"How did you figure this out?"

"When I got stuck, I was trapped behind a wall. There was plenty of time to figure out how certain corridors link up with others and that each configuration has its own signage. To find the way out, you have to follow the signs, but they were extremely tall, and I wasn't."

"Who's they?"

"The Atlanteans. My flashlight gave out, so I couldn't see the signs. When I moved anywhere in the maze, I had to leave markers to know if I was going in circles."

"How did you get out?"

"Uncle Cal took the crystal he had with him to the entrance and waited there. I followed the hum. Each have a distinctive vibration. The synthetic ones inside the labyrinth are louder than natural crystals. I liken it to listening under the radar."

She waited for him to remark about her ability to hear crystals, but his interest was firmly caught by her plight inside the maze. She preferred to keep his attention focused on that and not on a talent she considered deviant.

He asked, "How long did it take to find the way out?"

The traumatic memory stiffened her muscles. She forced her body to relax. "Nine hours."

His arms tightened around her. "How old were you when this happened?"

"Twelve."

His lips pressed against the side of her neck. "Poor baby. No wonder your uncle doesn't want you to go back there. Is there another crystal we could use as a substitute so you don't have to go back in that place?"

"No, and I'm thinking it might be better if you don't come inside the maze with me. You can wait outside with a global cell phone. If I don't get back out in time, you can call Richardson and stall him."

"I don't think so. I told you, doc, if you're going in there, I'll be with you all the way."

She rolled over and faced him. "Rod, I wish I could explain how serious this is. There's no way to describe what it's like in there. It's underground and darker than anything you can imagine. And the walls shift without warning. I'm not entirely sure what triggers it to move. It's neither predictable nor stationary."

"The entire maze moves around by itself?"

"I don't know if all of it does. Only part of it may move. I think I know how to change the configuration, but it's still just a guess."

"Why change it at all?"

"One thing I learned is that the configuration changes automatically whenever a vault is opened. If worse comes to worst, that's how I plan to get rid of Richardson's watchdogs. The less I have to worry about, the faster I'll get us out. Richardson said he'll give us five hours to get through the maze, find the crystal, and come out. Five hours is not enough time and he knows it."

"He's seriously into power trips."

"Amen and may the Lord save us from males who are penile challenged. One has to wonder what Estelle would have to say about Richardson."

Rod didn't respond, she noted, as men usually don't about the subject of penile inadequacies. Having seen Rod sans towel at the hotel, she doubted he had anything to worry about. Since she wasn't as obsessed about sex as Maddie, she concentrated on a more important issue.

"I might be able to do it in six hours. Rushing makes for mistakes, and we can't afford any. The way Richardson's mind works, he expects me to lead his goons to the crystal and get rid of us at that point. He'll have them leave a bright trail to X-marks-the-spot, just to prove he found the crystal, and then get rid of them, too."

"But you plan to get rid of the goons first."

"I'm going to trap them inside and let the maze do what it wants. There will be plenty of opportunities to lose them along the way. The place is riddled with traps."

"Is this the real reason why you pretended to hire me?"

"One of the reasons. Something told me Uncle Cal's disappearance was connected to Site Fifty-four. It's not wise to go into places like that alone."

"Why were you in there alone when you were a kid?"

"Uncle Cal didn't know I'd gone inside. He thought I was making a rubbing of a stele that's near the site. When we encountered the first trap the day before, he had me escorted out."

"What kind of traps are you talking about?"

"The unexpected kind, collapsing floors, knives coming out of nowhere. I've sprung most of the traps, but we can still use them as fear factors."

"Fear factors?"

"Richardson will undoubtedly send someone inside with us. I think I've got him figured out now. I'm willing to bet the farm that he doesn't know what to do when the configuration changes. He probably tried to explore the site himself—and being significantly gonad-challenged, he gave up and ran home to lick his wounds."

"So tell me, doc, how are you going to find the way in and out this time?"

"I'm working on it. If all else fails, I left markers the last time I was in there. Some plastic candy containers I jammed into the walls every time I found a link. If the configuration is the same, we can use them."

"What constitutes a link?"

"Places where the maze changes. I'll worry about that when we get there. At this point, I'm wondering about what's happening with Binky."

"He can take care of himself."

"That's patently obvious, even from a distance. No, I'm worried that he'll eat Richardson's goons for a snack. Binky may not realize that Uncle Cal's life is at stake."

Rod thought about that. He snuggled closer. "Don't worry. The Binkster might get bored and have some fun messing with their minds, but he'll stay with the plane and won't do anything until he hears from me."

"How long have you known Binky?"

"He was my present for my eighth birthday."

"Scary."

"You bet it was. But then, Mom keeps him on a short leash."

"Is he in love with her?"

"Binky? In love with my mother? I doubt it. There is some question of his lacking the essential organ, and I'm not talking procreation."

"He's not married?"

"He never said, and the Binkster is not the sort of guy one gets chummy with. He talked more to you than he ever has to me."

"You need to read the romantic writers of the nineteenth century. Then you'll have something to discuss."

"Doc, you don't get it. I'm not interested in a meaningful relationship with Binky."

She shrugged. "I like him."

"So do I, but I could care less about his love life. That's a chick thing. Hey, are you tired? Can we make-out or do some grope and grunt until the sun comes up?"

She groaned. "Chaucer, you epitomize every cliché that I have ever heard or read about libido-driven males."

"Yeah, but do you wanna neck?"

"Rod, *please!* We're in a bit of a pickle here."

"Just teasing, doc. It got your mind off the problem for a minute, didn't it? You need to rest. I got the feeling we're going to be tramping through a jungle by tomorrow night."

"I can tell you right now that I am not hiking through a tropical forest at night. Which reminds me, we've got to find some socks that fit you and stick them in plastic baggies. The insects are bad enough, but foot rot is the pits when you have to trudge for miles and miles."

"You should have talked about foot rot earlier. Works better than a cold shower for me. Did you pack an insecticide?"

"Useless. I've always suspected that Central American and Amazonian insects are attracted to it. But that gives me an idea."

"This is gonna be good. Your ideas would give a serial killer a headache."

"You should meet my friend, Maddie. If we're lucky, Richardson's goons won't know anything about the lay of the land."

"I get it. You're going to let them know what treats are in store. Maybe exaggerate a little?"

"No exaggeration needed. We'll pretend I'm giving you a crash course on what to look out for insect-wise. The really gruesome stuff."

"Did you get brain damaged from listening to slasher legends around campfires?"

"Heh-heh. I'll start off with a story about the fly that likes to burrow under the skin and lay eggs. The eggs grow and make welts the size of a walnut. When the insects hatch, they erupt out of the skin."

"Charming."

"I'm just getting started. Then there's the worm-type parasite, which we won't mention is actually found in Africa and not Central America, at least that I know of. It lives in water and incubates in the human body after it's ingested. It travels in the blood vessels and settles in the feet, usually the heel area under the ankle. A pustule forms and the worm crawls out after maturing, drops back into the water, lays eggs, the eggs get ingested, and the cycle begins again."

"OK, it's official. I'm turned off."

"You're such a wuss. So this will be your first time in a tropical forest?"

"No, doc, and no more talking. I've had enough bedtime stories for one night. Time for sleepy-nigh-nigh."

Phil chortled. "Don't worry, big guy. We won't see many mean bugs where we're going, but Richardson's goons don't need to know that."

She gave herself over to the decadence and novelty of cuddling with a bonafide hunk. It sure beat the last time she went out with a guy; a dismal evening wasted with a computer analyst, who was more interested in the library's cataloging system than his date.

Chapter 20

Phil woke to the startling and pleasant pressure of a man's hand where it shouldn't be. She stayed absolutely still and evaluated the experience.

So this is what it's like to wake up with someone. Cozy and safe. Protected and toasty warm.

She decided to pretend to be asleep for a few minutes more. Then she'd put on a display of feminine outrage.

Rod's voice, gritty from sleep, rasped against her ear. "I know you're awake."

"Something's poking me. It woke me up."

"The part of me that's not a banana is really glad to see you, too."

"I meant that I was laying on something har—"

When he suggestively growled and snuggled closer, she shoved away. "Oh, never mind. Does your decadently expensive watch happen to have glowing numbers?"

He sat up with a grunt of discomfort, slowly stood, and bumped his head. "Ow! Who put that shelf there? It's 4:30." Brisk head scratching sounded in the darkness. "I hope he lets us out soon. It's time to use the facilities."

Phil rubbed her face. "Past time. How about we bang on the door?"

"For want of banging anything else, why not? And I don't like the idea of being penned up in here with you without your morning infusion of caffeine. Hope you aren't growing hair on your palms."

Phil repressively said, "I'm not that bad."

Under his breath, he grumbled, "That's a subjective statement, if I've ever heard one."

"I heard that."

"Yeah, yeah. Do you have any of that monster chocolate bar left?"

"Dang! That was stupid of me. I tucked it into my backpack. It's out on the couch."

Rod inhaled for a jaw-cracking yawn. "Sorry. Didn't sleep that well. Do you think Professor Honeydew will let us have a snack before we invade Southern Mexico?"

Phil reacted to Rod's contagious yawn with one of her own. "Honeydew?"

"Yeah. Richardson reminds me of that moon-faced Muppet character."

"You're right. He does. The Weasel doesn't look much like Beaker, but he sounds a bit like him. Kind of squeaky and nasal."

"I assume you're responsible for Reed's pre-rhinoplasty work."

Since she was already sitting, she carefully stretched out the spinal kinks from sleeping on the floor. "I ran into him at the hotel before we had breakfast at the IHOP."

"And didn't bother to tell me about your little escapade with another man? There's been plenty of time since then to come clean. Sheesh! Come to think of it, that was only yesterday. We've been busy."

"You're talkative in the morning. Are you one of those annoying people who can wake up right away?"

"It's not all that difficult when you don't get to sleep in the first place. Wish I had your ability to drop off standing up."

"Not all the time. Couldn't get to sleep at Jimmy's for some reason."

"Hey, doc, you never did say how you knew for sure that your uncle was here."

"There was a note in the safe-deposit box. He also left some photos. Coordinates and information for a private plane to fly to Jimmy's airstrip. The note was in code to let me know that he's figured out a way to map Site Fifty-four's maze configurations. I know only the one pathway that got me out. That could have changed by now. Especially if Richardson has been down there nosing around."

"What if you can't figure out the configuration?"

"I'll use the key to make it change to one that I know."

"A key?"

"You saw it, the black crystal. It's actually a key when it's placed in the right hole. It was sitting in plain sight on the table last night. Richardson doesn't know what it is."

Rod grunted and thought for a moment. "That means we've got to create a distraction to swipe it."

"If it's still there. It's still in the house. That much I know. Can you feel around for my other boot?" A moment later, she said, "Rod, my left breast in no way resembles a shoe. Look on the floor."

"Oops! Got carried away. I guess the only words my brain felt like processing were *'feel'* and *'around'*."

"For heaven's sake, Chaucer, do you have to be so predictable?"

Phil put her hands on the wall and felt her way to a standing position. Her fingers found the doorknob.

She warned, "I'm going to start pounding on the door. It's time for the little girl's room."

"I'll help as long as you promise me that I'm next in line."

They hammered on the door until they heard the heavy object in front of it shoved out of the way. A sleepy Reed opened the door. The bandage was off and his naked, swollen nose was exposed to the world. He held a gun—a fashion accessory that worked with the hair on his head that stood on end. He scuttled backward when Phil stepped out of the closet.

Phil was in no mood for pleasantries. "I've got to pee-pee."

Reed cupped a protective hand over his mangled nose. "You dough where-ah da bafwoob id."

Phil smirked before heading toward relief. It only took a minute of searching to discover that the bathroom had been stripped of everything that could be used as a weapon. She washed quickly and vacated.

The glow of daybreak peered through the bank of floor-to-ceiling windows, filling the room with a buttery haze. Dawn bloomed on the horizon, golden and pink. She passed Rod, who looked disreputable and more than a little frightening sporting an aggressive crop of morning bristles. She headed for the backpack on the couch until Reed stopped her.

"Dough, you don', gir-wie."

Phil huffed an exasperated sigh. "I just want my things from my backpack."

Reed used the pistol to wave her away from the couch. "Dough way. Moob-it ober dere."

Peripherally, she noted that the crystal wasn't anywhere in sight. She settled for snagging a seat cushion as she passed by the easy chair. Obviously fearing that any object in her hands deserved respect, he aimed the pistol and backed away.

Phil shook her head with disgust and tossed the cushion onto the closet floor. She sat on it and glared at her pathetic captor through the open door.

The muted sound of an electric shaver buzzed behind the bathroom door.

That's too bad. The hairy and dangerous look sort of worked for me.

She glanced around the closet, now lit by the steadily intensifying morning light. There was nothing left more intimidating than a muffler. The seat cushion would make a lousy Frisbee.

Rod was more successful in the food department. He conned Reed out of a carton of orange juice and a box of dry cereal.

Phil took the juice carton and savored a long swallow. "Yum, calcium enriched. How did you get him to give you this?"

Rod dug into the box of cereal. "Gee, I don't know. Maybe, by not breaking his nose? By the way, when he wasn't looking, I checked out your briefcase. The crystal's inside."

"That's odd. I wonder why they put it back. Maybe Richardson knows it's a key. He could have guessed that by looking at the photographs."

"Or he's a neat freak. Hey, let's play a game. The one who can sound the most like Reed wins." He popped a handful of cereal and munched.

"Knowing the direction your mind runs, let's not. I don't want to think about what I'd have to forfeit if I lost."

"You're no fun, doc."

"One thing I do know is that I can't take any more adenoidal whining without caffeine." She paused and lifted her nose. "Do you smell that? Oh, Lord, thank you, thank you! The Weasel's making coffee. It smells so good! Get me some. Please, *please,* Rod!"

"Oh, so now it's *please, please, Rod* when you want something." He leaned forward to get a better view of the kitchen counter. "Almost done. Only see one cup, though. Looks like Reed's gonna be stingy. Best to make do with what we got and hit on him to share after he's had a cup."

Rod shoved his hand back into the cereal box. "Sheesh, I love this frosted stuff. Never thought your uncle was the type to go for cereal that's ninety-nine percent sugar. I see him as more of a granola kind of guy. It sounds like the coffee is done."

"Praise be!" She snatched the box. "Hey, save me some! You know this is my favorite. I said so at the IHOP when they didn't have it and I had to order pancakes instead."

Rod cocked his head to one side. She swallowed and said, "You look perplexed."

"Something just occurred to me. Why would Richardson buy your favorite? He took this out of the grocery bag yesterday."

Phil stopped chewing. She withdrew her hand from the cereal container. "Was the box open when you took it from the cupboard?"

"Yep."

They exchanged a long, meaningful stare. Rod said, "Maybe he's just messing with our heads."

Phil set the box aside and wiped her hand on her pant leg. "I didn't eat much of it. We'll know soon enough if he put anything on it. Was the orange juice container open, too?"

Rod nodded. "Sorry, babe. I should have thought of it."

"Don't worry. We didn't have that much."

The grogginess started minutes later.

Chapter 21

They woke up in the cargo hold of a plane with their hands duct-taped behind their backs. Phil struggled to sit up. She nudged Rod with her foot until he stirred.

He blinked and sat up. One side of his face was pockmarked from the skid-proof rubber mat. She had been on her back and suffered the unreachable itch of the mat's indentations in the flesh along her spine and across her shoulder blades.

Rod blearily looked around. "How long have we been out?"

Her throat felt dry and scratchy. She wasn't surprised by the hoarse sound of her voice. "I'd say at least eight to ten hours from the look of your beard."

Rod yawned. "Well, at least we know where we're going and where we are."

She struggled to sit and then stand. "I'll bite. Where are we?"

"The hold of the Kitty."

Phil didn't bother to hide her disgust. "That's not the name written in gold on the nose."

"Naming it that was my dad's idea. He has a weird sense of humor."

"Now I know where you get yours. But all is not lost. If this is your mom's plane, that means Binky is flying. Right?"

"I'd say you're right about that. Unless he didn't wait to kill Richardson's hired help until we get to Mexico. In that case, who knows who's flying."

Rod paused. "Don't worry, Phil. I was just joking. Binky would wait to find out what was going on before doing serious damage. He might break a few bones, though."

"That might be enough to set off Richardson. I don't think it would take much for him to shoot Uncle Cal. Just a phone call."

"He'd be killing his insurance."

"There's no way to know if Uncle Cal is all right, now that we're miles away. If Richardson's been able to hide his true feelings this successfully over the years, we can't trust anything he tells us. How can people live with all that ugliness inside? I knew he was jealous but never suspected his hatred of Uncle Cal. I think I've got to cry now. Can you get this tape off?"

"Sure." He got to his knees and stood up. He placed his right boot on the cabin wall level with the height of her hips. "Turn around. Feel down the side of my boot for a knife handle. It's hidden down the inside."

Phil backed into his boot. Following his directions, she felt around until she located the slender handle. The stiletto was tucked into a sleeve sewn into the ankle of his boot.

"One of Binky's better ideas," he explained.

Focusing on the task, she wriggled it free. "Why didn't you use this to get us out of the closet?"

"It wouldn't have been much help with getting the chiffonier moved away from the front of the door."

"You know what I mean."

"After seeing your uncle shot, I wasn't going to push any more panic buttons. Give me the knife. Lean against the wall so we move at the same time with the plane. Let's hope Binky keeps this a smooth ride."

Rod cut away the tape around her wrists in gradual increments, stopping whenever he felt the plane dip into turbulence. "While you were sleeping last night, I listened."

Worried for good reason, Phil said, "Careful with what you're doing back there. Are you sure you can cut and talk at the same time?"

"Yeah. And I can do that thing where you pat your head and rub your tummy and chew gum, too."

"I'm impressed. So what did you hear?"

"They have your uncle tied to a bed in the loft. Richardson stayed with him all last night and left Reed downstairs to watch us. Professor Honeydew was on the phone most of the time, making arrangements to commandeer this plane."

"Why would Binky let them do that?"

"Maybe Richardson said he was holding me hostage. In that case, the Binkster would play with their heads until he knew I was safe."

Phil said, "I wish I had half of Binky's patience. Did Richardson say where we'll be landing?"

"We fly into Cancun first. Then drive to the harbor. There's a boat waiting to take us down the eastern Yucatan coast to the border of Belize."

"That leaves lots of opportunities to get away."

Rod said, "I don't think it's worth the risk. Richardson is staying with your uncle. All his men have satellite phones and will be keeping in contact."

"We can work the phones to our advantage. Anyway, they're useless once we get inside the maze.

Those walls are underground and thick enough to survive a nuclear blast. There's also the possibility that they might not work anywhere close to the site. Something about the maze makes gauges go haywire."

"How are we going to tell the time?"

The tape around Phil's wrists snapped free after a final slice. She said, "It doesn't do anything to wrist watches. Just gauges or directional devices."

She ripped the strips off, tearing away flesh and fine hairs. She peered at her abused skin. "I'll have to remember duct tape if I ever want a wax job. That danged stuff tore off meat almost down to the muscle. Is there a first-aid kit anywhere back here? I want this cleaned up and dried out before we go into the jungle."

"It's on the wall by the door. What about me? Aren't you going to cut me free?"

Phil stopped. She turned away from the door and stared at Rod. The unshaven, dangerous look was back. His shirt was partially undone, his clothes wrinkled, hair nicely tousled. Even though he held an open switchblade behind his back, he was securely tied, helpless.

First aid kit forgotten, Phil sauntered across the black rubber mat to Rod. Binky's excellent flying skills allowed for a slinky stroll and not a clumsy stagger. She liked the feel of the wicked smile on her lips. Payback was such fun.

His eyes widened when she slid her open palm across the front of his shirt and up over the bared top half of his chest. Her fingers curled around his neck. She watched his lips part in anticipation and glided her other hand down his arm. She stopped at his wrist and slowly removed the knife from his relaxed fingers. She folded it and slid it into the waistband of her jeans.

Placing her left hand in the center of his chest, she directed him backward with steady pressure until he was flat against the cabin wall.

Phil lowered her voice to a husky purr. "You're all tied up, big boy, and I'm remembering some of the not very nice things you did to me. And said to me. It's retribution time, Chaucer."

He closed his eyes. His head fell back against the wall in defeated submission.

"Please, Phil."

"Begging won't help you now, tough guy. I could break your knees for starters. Maybe carve a few initials on your chest. What do think, Chaucer? Naughty words or just Mommy loves me best?"

She watched him swallow. His face was taut and strained. Victory stretched her lips into a smile. Then he opened his eyes.

"Do me, baby. I've fantasized about this so many times. Me strapped down and at your mercy."

Phil glanced down and saw the evidence straining against the buttons of his jeans. He was so not afraid.

She clenched her teeth and curbed the surging need to punch him, but she'd seen his iron belly. It would take an energetic working over to hurt this guy, and she couldn't afford to maim her only ally. Quasi-ally.

And someone had to be with her in order to make it through the maze. She couldn't do it alone. Never mind that she couldn't bring herself to hurt the smug rat. That realization made her furious, frantic to lash out in frustration. But she would keep her cool. She would be a lady, dignified in a crisis.

"You're a scum-sucking pig, Chaucer."

His broad grin renewed the urge to whack him. "And I love the way your speech deteriorates when you get mad."

She opened her mouth to tell him off, stopped herself in time, and went to the first-aid kit.

Rod sneaked up behind her and leaned over her shoulder to whisper in her ear. "Don't you want to play doctor, doc? How about a little of the rough stuff? I bet we got time before we land."

Phil slammed the kit's lid shut. "That does it. Turn around."

She grasped the rounded hardness of his forearm to use as a brace and sawed through the tape. She strove to ignore Rod's exaggerated groan of disappointment.

"Aw, doc, you're no fun anymore!"

"You said that before, and I'd say it depends on one's definition of *fun*."

Rod elected to do a slow peel of the tape rather than Phil's rougher all-at-once maneuver. "I bet you were the life of the party as a kid, doc, lording your IQ over the lesser beings and forcing everyone to listen to you recite declensions."

Phil clenched her teeth. It wasn't quite like that but close enough, propelling her back on the defensive, which was exactly what he wanted. And that made her angrier and unable to hide the hurt in her reply. "While you bored them to tears with nonstop techno-babble?"

She looked up when he didn't respond. He studied her with a softness in his eyes that she'd never seen before. Something inside, just under her heart, turned over. The smile on his mouth matched the warmth of his steady gaze.

"You know, Philadelphia Casca Hafeldt, we're a lot alike."

She quickly looked away and fumbled with an impossible-to-open packet of ointment. Rod gently took it from her trembling fingers, ripped off one end, and used the tips of his fingers to tenderly smooth a thin application over her wrists.

He said nothing as he wrapped the gauze around her raw flesh and taped the bandage in place. She gave him back his knife and worked really hard to pretend he didn't exist. And that her heart hadn't turned to mush.

Chapter 22

Her instincts were right on target about Binky's flying skills. His landing was smooth and as light as down. No one came back to check on them. She and Rod looked out the cargo hold's small window, agreed that they had landed in Cancun, and waited for someone to let them out.

Hours after their arrival, they finally received clearance. Binky taxied the jet to the end of the airport, far away from the main terminal. The rear cargo door opened with a screech and a clunk.

Phil squinted to block out the sunlight and took the hand Rod offered to help her step down the ramp. Heat rippled up from the tarmac. She recognized the climate and smell of Mexico, even though she was a child when she last saw Cancun. The airport and surrounding area had changed a great deal. Or she and her memory of it had.

Reed and two Hispanic tough-guy types waited at the bottom of the ramp. Two more guards escorted Binky from the front of the plane. He sauntered ahead of the men, a power play that forced them to walk slower. His guards looked nervous, even though they carried weapons.

Binky grinned at Rod and Phil as he joined them at the bottom of the cargo ramp. "Enjoy the flight?"

Rod said, "The food was rotten and you've taken us a bit out of our way."

Phil added, "Think nothing of it, Binky. Nobody—who is anybody—goes to the Bahamas at this time of year."

A car backfired. The guards flinched and turned to the sound. They watched an antique VW van approach.

Phil expected to see a trail of metal bits and pieces bouncing in the van's wake, but the vehicle held together and rolled to a squeaking halt next to the plane. The rusted door opened with a shriek of protest. The driver stepped out.

Rod nudged Phil with his elbow. "Ain't this a hoot? The people you run into in diverse places."

Phil smirked. "The Tattoo Guy cometh."

The removal of the nasal packing allowed for a distinct improvement in Reed's speech. He yelled a greeting at the van driver, "Hey, Schulz, you're late!"

Reflector sunglasses hid Schulz's eyes. Smug disdain for the world, with the exception of himself, was relayed via an arrogant and cocky posture.

"So what, rat boy? I'm here now. Let's load up the Spics and the losers." He lowered the sunglasses to peer at Phil over the silver lenses. "Hey, sweet thing, long time, no see. Get the door fixed?"

"Before you ran out of the building with your tail between your legs."

"Aw, are we having a bad day? Too bad I had to leave before showing you a fine time. Miss me, Philly baby?"

"Don't call me Philly, and some things are easier to miss than others, Tattoo Boy. I doubt that I would have noticed you occupying any form of space—within or without my person."

Under his breath, Binky laughed and murmured, "Hoo-yah. A set-down to make Georgette Heyer proud, Dr. Hafeldt."

Phil sent him her coyest smile. "You are too kind, dear sir. One has to keep the peasants in their places. Can't have the riffraff getting above themselves."

A sudden, rampant display of meanness didn't help Schulz's life-ravaged face. He broke out in red splotches, opened his mouth to spew a nasty comeback, but swallowed whatever he was going to say when Binky only said, "Shut up."

Phil marveled at the authority in Binky's delivery. She tried to memorize the inflection and demeanor. Women often required an authoritative tone to get their point across. Binky's delivery was perfection. She wondered if she could duplicate his razor sharp glare.

Her distraction ended when Schulz covered his lapse of bravado with retributive acting out. He rammed a pistol point into Binky's temple.

"Shut up yourself, old man. Turn around."

Binky calmly did as he was told. Plastic handcuffs were attached to his wrists behind his back. Rod's were also cuffed, but Phil was allowed to keep her bound hands in front.

Reed said, "Hey, Schulz! You don't want to get too close to her. She's got a nasty sucker punch."

"Shut your face, Reed. She's just a girl."

Schulz missed the smirking, visual exchange between Rod and Binky, and stalked to the rear of the van to open the squeaky back doors.

Rod grinned at Binky. "This is going to be fun. Nothing like having a few idiots on the opposing team."

"Let us not forget the comic relief." Binky glanced at the rodent-faced Reed, who scuttled backwards out of range.

Rod sent Phil a playful leer and wriggled his eyebrows. "Hey, doc, there's supposed to be a nude beach somewhere around here. Think there's any chance of us stopping for a peek?"

"Why am I not surprised that you asked? Especially since I've just met your tattooed twin—the epitome of arrested development in reflector sunglasses."

"Ouch, doc! That was a low blow."

Schulz yelled for them to stop talking and ordered Reed and the guards to bring the hostages to the rear of the van.

The ride in the back of the ancient Volkswagen became the trip to hell. The floors were filthy, the interior smelled of unwashed bodies and old urine. The orange shag carpet on the interior walls sealed in the heat and stench. Worn shocks intensified the jarring passage over potholes and rough roads.

Their handcuffs were tied to metal rings on the floor, leaving no opportunity for mischief. Binky slept through the entire trip, while Phil concentrated on not throwing up. Rod sat quietly, snoozing on and off. Phil almost wept when the van doors were opened and the refreshing tang of an ocean breeze rushed into the back of the van.

Binky woke up and yawned. "Here already?"

Stiff and aching, Phil unfurled her locked knees and waited to be untied from the floor. She slid on her bottom to the end of the van and dropped down onto hot sand.

A beach graced with waving palms and frothy surf made up for the hellish ride. Sea air ruffled her clothes, sweeping away the stench. She lifted her face to the sun and smiled. This was what a vacation was all about.

A shove ruined the blissful moment.

Reed had learned how to stay out of her reach. "Welcome to the Yucatan Peninsula, girlie. Sorry about the accommodations."

Phil ignored him and stepped out of the way. Rod had been uncuffed and put to work unloading cases and baggage. She moved to stand beside Binky, who leaned against the side of the van. Relaxed and unconcerned, he braced the back of his shoulders and head on the van and watched the seabirds whirl overhead. Palm leaves swayed and clacked against each other in the shifting breeze. Gulls called and the surf bubbled up and slid away from the shore.

Phil inhaled the tangy air deep into her lungs and glanced up at Binky. "You look contented, considering the situation."

"I love the beach. It's where I feel at home."

Phil looked around to see who was within earshot before asking, "In Colorado, did you see anyone at the hangar? A guy named Bill?"

"There was somebody pretending to be working on a Cherokee, but he left not long after you and Rod took off. Never talked to him."

"I'm curious as to how Schulzie, the Tattooed Wonder, got the plane from you."

"His boss sent a letter. Said he had Rod. He called later and told me he'd send pieces of Rod to his parents if I didn't fly the plane to Cancun. I wasn't worried about Rod. He'd get himself free, if and when he wanted. I was concerned that the head man...Richardson?"

Phil nodded, and Binky continued, "I was worried Richardson would contact Mr.and Mrs.Gameson. What can you tell me about what's going on? Is there a ransom?"

"No ransom. This has nothing to do with Rod. My uncle's former friend and colleague is holding my Uncle Cal hostage until I locate an artifact. He thinks it will make him rich and famous. I'm sorry that you've been caught up in this."

Binky gazed at the frothy breakers. "Don't worry about it. Life with Roddie was getting predictable. There's not much for me to do, now that he can take care of himself. By the way, a boat is coming this direction from the north. It's staying close to the coastline."

"How do you know?"

"You should be able to see it any minute now. There it is, coming around the curve of the beach."

As Binky predicted, an inboard pleasure craft appeared around the graceful bend of the shoreline. He didn't pay it any attention and watched the sea birds.

Phil squinted up at Binky. "You didn't tell me how you knew about the boat."

His eyes never left the soaring birds. A faint smile lifted his thin lips. "I believe a guy should preserve an aura of mystique, don't you?"

Phil snorted a laugh, and Binky said, "You're all right, Dr. Hafeldt."

When Phil grinned her appreciation of his compliment, he asked, "So where is the artifact?"

"Inland, south of here, near the border of Belize and Guatemala. It's a bit of a hike to get to it. There are no roads."

"They couldn't find it themselves?"

"The entrance to the site is almost entirely overtaken by the forest."

"Camouflaged, huh? How did it get discovered?"

"That's a long story for another day. I wouldn't be surprised if that boat is coming to take us down the coast. We could drive most of the way there, but there's a lot of tourist activity in this part of the world. Less tourism than north of here, but I suspect that Richardson doesn't want us noticed."

"The roads aren't that great. Boat's a better way to go."

"He'll have us go by water as far south as possible, then drive inland as deep as the terrain will allow. Then we'll hike through the bush for a couple of days. Anyway, that's what I would do."

"Richardson's the guy holding your uncle?"

"Former best friend, no less."

Rod came around the side of the van. Schulz followed but stayed far enough away from Rod to avoid a conflict. Using the pistol as a pointer, Schulz directed Rod to join Phil and Binky against the side of the van.

Schulz stepped back into the shade of a cluster of palms. The pale skin around his tattoos was beginning to burn. He lit a cigarette and pulled out a cell phone. Phil recognized the cell phone Bill had given her and worked not to react. Schulz misunderstood her expression, smirked, and flipped the cell open

Phil bowed her head and made designs in the sand with the toe of her boot to hide her relief.

Schulz watched his captives as he talked. "Hey, boss, we're here. The boat's on time, just like you said....No, it was smooth all the way....We should be on board in about twenty minutes....I'll check in when we get there, and I want a decent vehicle waiting....I don't care what you planned. I'm not camping out in the jungle for three nights. I know what we agreed, but now I'm telling you what I want. I've got your girl and that means I've got some leverage. Get us a four-wheel drive and we'll get as close as we can. And it better come loaded with supplies....Don't worry about that. Nobody's tailing us....I said I'll check in....When? When I feel like it. Later."

Schulz shut the phone, slid it into a zippered pocket of his vest, and turned his attention to the meager collection of provisions sitting on the sand.

Phil wondered what they'd brought along for equipment. She could get along in the jungle with only a knife. She hoped that Binky had taught Rod survival skills and figured that Richardson's flunkies wouldn't have a clue. The nationals looked city bred and wouldn't know a salamander from a viper.

She evaluated the small stack of supplies that would have to be walked through the surf to the boat. They needed a lot more. A tent was mandatory. She wouldn't mind lugging the extra weight if it meant keeping the insects and reptiles at bay throughout the night.

"Yoo-hoo, Tattoo Guy."

Schulz took a final, deep drag and glared at Phil. "What?"

"If you expect me to find what Richardson wants, you better have my briefcase in that pile."

Schulz eyed her for moment. He flicked the cigarette away and shouted, "Hey, Reed!"

Reed and four other men came around the side of the truck. Phil covered her surprise when she recognized one of the hired men. The four that met them when the plane landed were nowhere in sight. She wondered if they stayed to trash the jet or sell it.

The Mexicans flanking Reed flaunted standard hoodlum accessories—bulging ammunition vests, automatic weapons, and surly attitudes.

Reed, acting cocky and reckless, made the most of his second in command role. He held his pistol in a loose grip by his side and snapped off orders that were ignored, since the hired thugs didn't understand English.

"What's up?" Reed asked.

Schulz gestured with his head at the supplies. "Did you see a briefcase in that pile of crap?"

"Yeah. Hers is at the bottom."

"Keep it someplace where it won't get wet. I want to go through it before we give it to her."

"The boss went through it already. What'd he say when you called?"

Schulz stuck a toothpick in his mouth and rolled it around before answering. "He wants a call before we get on the road. He still thinks we're being tailed."

"Taking a boat ride will solve that. Should we start loading?"

When Schulz nodded, Reed looked at Rod. "You and the old guy start hauling this stuff."

Schulz said, "Leave the cuffs on the big guy, and he stays where he is. I don't want him let loose."

Reed made use of his bad-guy sneer. "He's no sweat. If he tries anything, I'll shoot him."

Rod shook his head. "I wouldn't do that. You might piss him off."

Reed thought about that. His sneer turned ugly. "Maybe I'll do him right now. We don't need a pilot anymore."

Schulz said, "Give it a rest, Reed. Just get the boat loaded."

Chapter 23

The weather stayed balmy. The wind abated and the sea settled down to a slight chop. Phil, Rod, and Binky sat aft on the deck's polished boards, using their flotation pads as cushions. The cruiser skimmed across the water beyond the breakers, spewing a tangy spray from the bow.

Phil licked the moisture from her lips and watched the sun dry the seawater from her soggy pant legs. She was grateful that the goons had allowed Rod to remove her boots before going into the water.

She wriggled her toes, wishing she had taken time to have a pedicure. A girl should never show up on the beach without her toenails polished. Just another sign of how she'd let herself go the last years.

She muttered to herself, "At least things aren't boring any more."

Rod leaned closer. "What did you say?"

"Nothing important. Just wishing I'd kept a pedicure appointment."

"I never noticed it before, but you've got pretty feet, doc."

"I always thought I did. My feet are a bit wide from going barefoot so much as a kid, but the toes aren't bad. Not crooked or anything. How are yours, Binky?"

"My toes? Never thought about'em."

Phil puffed out a disgusted sigh. "If that isn't just like a guy." She bowed her head and whispered, "I know the guy standing next to Schulz. He used to work as a guide. Aztec descent. I asked him what he's doing with this trash."

Binky shifted his weight. The move was meant to look like an attempt to find a more comfortable position. His casual repositioning had more to do with angling his immense shoulders to block the sunlight from Phil's face.

"Thanks, Binky. Is my nose turning red? My face feels tight, so I know I'm starting to burn."

Rod peered at her nose. "We'll be calling you Rudolph anytime now."

She grimaced. "I hate it when I peel. It always feels like I'm in molt." She bowed her head. "Are they looking this way?"

"Uh-uh," Rod replied.

Phil carefully murmured, "The Aztec calls himself Rico. The other one's name is Carlos. He says his wife is ill. He needs money for her treatment. They promised him a thousand to guard us."

"Liars," Rod muttered. "He won't get a peso."

"I told him that, and that you'd pay him five thousand to help us."

"You're pretty free with my money, doc."

Binky's deep bass whispered, "Don't worry about the five grand, Dr. Hafeldt. He's loaded. What did you tell the other guy?"

"Nothing. He doesn't know the dialect I was using. Rico said he'll pretend to go along with Richardson's goons until we tell him otherwise."

Binky asked, "You're sure you can trust him?"

"More than I trust the other ones."

Rod asked, "Isn't it a bit too coincidental that you know this guy?"

"Not really. People who work as guides and know this area are limited. Liken it to the way we belong to unions and specialize. Everybody knows everybody or is related to them."

A pair of tattered running shoes stepped onto the deck by Phil's feet. She looked up at Rico.

"We can trust this guy," she said. "Before we spoke, he didn't know where we were headed. Now that he does, he doesn't want anything to do with it."

Rod asked, "You mean Site Fifty-four?"

"That's what Uncle Cal named it. Rico and his people have known about it for centuries. They call the place 'The Well of the Eater of Souls'."

Rod groaned. "I thought you said your life was boring."

"I guess I spoke too soon. Oh-oh, here comes Tattoo Guy."

Schulz tossed her briefcase onto the deck. With her hands still hooked together in front, Phil did what she could to brush away the strands of hair whipping around her face. She pulled the case forward and looked inside.

Everything was in a jumble from being searched. She tried to open the case wider and still couldn't find the black crystal.

Hiding her disappointment, she glared up at Schulz. "Who took my Berry Bright lipstick?"

"Probably one of the Spics. They'll steal anything that's not nailed down."

On his return to the bow, Schulz snagged a beer from one of the coolers. While he snapped it open and drank, Phil made visual contact with Rico, who slowly unwrapped his fingers from the barrel of his Uzi. He folded back the top flap pocket of his vest and exposed the tip of the crystal. Phil nodded slightly and pretended to be interested in searching through the contents of the briefcase.

The sun was beginning to set when they anchored in the shallows near the coast road. Phil heard Rico ask to stay on board with the prisoners, saying he wanted to have fun with the woman.

Reed, Schulz, the boat pilot, and the local help disembarked for the beach, where Schulz disappeared into the jungle. The other men made a fire and began to chug the contents from one of the coolers they'd taken ashore.

Darkness settled over the water. Rico waited for the men on the beach to pass out before removing the handcuffs. Phil ran for the head the second she was free where she refused to confront the mirror. The scream evoked from looking at her hair and glowing nose would surely wake the drunks on the beach.

The cooler that was left on the boat held bottled water, tortillas, green chilies, and pottery jars of refried beans. Phil looked longingly at the outline of the monster chocolate bar poking out the sides of her backpack. She submitted to an inner voice that cautioned her to save it for emergency consumption. Stressful times lay ahead. No telling when a girl would need her chocolate fix.

Binky guzzled an entire bottle of water with precision. He took only one tortilla from the stack wrapped in a cloth and nothing else.

Rod watched as Phil and Rico smeared beans on tortillas laid flat on their palms. They dropped chilies on top, and rolled them up. He copied them, omitting the chilies.

Rod reached for a third tortilla. "These don't taste like the gluey ones you get at the store."

Phil licked bean sauce from her thumb. "These are homemade. Manuel, one of the guys on shore, bought them. He stopped at a vendor on the way to the beach."

"Ask Rico how he heard about this job."

Phil relayed the question. "He says that his cousin Manuel lives in the apartment across the hall. He knew that Rico had lost his job and that his wife was sick. Manuel's brother-in-law was ready to take the job, but he got scared and backed out. Rico jumped at the chance to make some money."

Rod asked, "How much does he need for his wife?"

Phil relayed Rod's question. Rico studied Rod for a few moments before replying.

Phil said, "He isn't sure. She hasn't seen a doctor in a long time. If he can get her to a hospital, she might live out the month. She hasn't been eating. They've been saving the food for the children. This is the first time he's eaten in three days."

Rod returned the last tortilla to the cloth they'd been wrapped in and rubbed his palms on his thighs. Phil picked up the tortilla and scraped the last of the beans from the earthenware jar. She scooped up the remaining chilies, rolled up the tortilla, and handed it to Rico, who murmured his thanks and accepted it without hesitation.

Rod looked out over the water. "Binky, do you still have your wallet?"

"Left it in the plane's safe. I've got some cash on me."

Rod opened his wallet, slid his thumb along one edge, and popped open a secret compartment. He tugged out the bills folded inside.

Binky stretched out his right leg and shoved his fingers into the side pocket of his tight jeans. They had four hundred dollars in cash between them. Phil added forty-three dollars rummaged from the bottom of the briefcase. She hadn't expected to find the envelope of cash left untouched. The envelope was still there but the money was gone. She kept a folded hundred dollar bill tucked inside the left cup of her bra, but she wasn't going to reach for that in front of three men.

Rod extended the money to Rico. "Tell him to write down his address and give it to Binky. We'll cover the hospital tab."

Phil rubbed away tears with the back of her wrist. "You guys are so nice."

Binky memorized the address Rico gave him before tearing it up and flipping the pieces over the side of the boat. "Don't get too impressed, Dr. Hafeldt. That wasn't much for Roddie. Not even lunch money. Tell Rico that Señora Gameson will contact him in a few days."

Phil thought for a minute before relaying the message to Rico, who bowed his head and whispered a reply.

"Rico says thanks. I told him to get away from these men as soon as we get on land and go back to his wife. He knows where we're going and will pray for us."

Rod said, "One less to deal with. That leaves Mutt and Jeff and the drunks on the beach."

Binky rubbed his jaw as he scanned the beach. "Two less. One of the dumb and dumber team went into the jungle. The one with the tattoos."

Rod leaned back and propped his elbows on the port-side gunnel. He belatedly realized what he was doing, glanced at the beach, and slowly lowered his arms.

"If he hasn't come back by now, we know it isn't a potty break."

She said, "He must be connecting with someone for a vehicle. The coast road isn't far from here. Very bad road, though."

Rod watched Phil finger comb her hair. When she saw him watching, she stopped.

Binky leaned across, unzipped a pocket on Rod's vest, and pulled out a comb. "How would you gauge the risk factor if we get rid of these guys now and fly back to get your uncle?"

"I wish it could be that easy, but Richardson's keeping close tabs by phone. The only time we could safely do anything is when he thinks we're inside the maze and out of contact."

Binky asked, "Have you thought about reporting it to a government agency?"

"There's one that already knows. For some reason, they want to keep a low profile. Anyway, I don't want to take a chance. Richardson has more on his agenda than just getting a crystal. His hatred runs pretty deep."

"Tell Binky something about where we're going."

Phil explained Site Fifty-four's background until Rod interrupted. "You should hear some of her stories. She knows everything about that Atlantis stuff. Hey, doc, will we be finding any skulls in that maze?"

"Not the crystal kind."

Chapter 24

Phil, Rod, and Binky marched along the narrow strip of shoreline. The wet sand was littered with tidal backwash. Dawn was a pink and gray affair that gradually improved to rosy gold as the sun rose above the treetops.

Silent and severely hung over, their captors trudged behind them. The Weasel, last in line, herded the group from the rear. They walked over a mile on the sand, hiking parallel to the road, until they spied a newer model SUV in the distance.

The black vehicle was parked on the verge of the north and south road that followed the eastern coastline. A vague outline of the driver showed through the vehicle's smoked glass. A small, covered trailer was hitched to the back.

Phil sat on a bleached rock beside the road. Rod joined her, and Binky stood by them, facing the sea. Dawn's sun glowed on his closely trimmed silver-blond hair.

Their captors maintained a respectful distance from Binky. They eyed him with wariness and perplexity, as if he were a tamed beast capable of mayhem at any moment.

Schulz stepped out of the SUV, wearing the sunglasses that seemed a permanent fixture on his blade thin nose. "Aren't we a cheery crew this morning?"

Phil looked out to sea. The last thing she needed was to face Tattoo Guy in the morning without a cup of coffee to soften the blow.

Reed, who had been trailing the group in sullen silence, plodded through the sand and up onto the firmer ground of the roadside.

"We didn't get to sleep in a hotel, like *some* people," The Weasel whined, swiping at his nose with a sleeve. "And you didn't have to walk a million miles in the middle of the night."

"Told you not to drink the tequila. And this spy-chase stuff is Richardson's idea, not mine." Schulz's amusement dimmed. "Where's the other two Spics?"

"They walked off sometime during the night. The one that stayed on the boat kept the Uzi."

Schulz snorted and pulled a pack of cigarettes from his shirt pocket. Around the act of lighting up, he muttered, "Thieving Mexicans."

Phil stood. She'd had about all she could take. "Hey, Schulz, I'd make some derogatory remarks about how people who deface their bodies with tattooing are looked down upon as social inferiors but prejudice is the easiest way to identify an idiot."

Schulz slowly lowered the hands he had cupped around the flame. "You wouldn't be calling me an idiot, would you, Philly girl?"

Philadelphia tamped down a flare of temper and forced her body to relax. She'd thrown down the gauntlet; now it was time to see what happened.

Schulz threw away the cigarette and advanced. Phil kept her ground and glared up, never breaking eye contact, even when Schulz crowded her space. Another inch and his chest would be against hers.

"Well, little Miss Smart Mouth, how about we take a walk in the woods?"

Phil was disappointed he hadn't come up with something better. Like a slap or a punch she could make him pay for. She used her mouth instead, since she was limited, but not completely hampered by plastic cuffs.

"What's the matter, Tattoo Guy? Afraid to go take a pee by yourself?"

Before Schulz could react, Rod resurrected a high school football move and rammed his shoulder into Schulz's. They landed on the sand.

Even though his hands were behind his back, Rod was up in an instant. Schulz wallowed in the sand for a few seconds before leaping up. Surprised and embarrassed by Phil's hoot of laughter, Schulz fisted his hands and headed for Phil.

Rod stepped in front of her. "Back off, Schulz, or next time I'll let her take you apart."

Schulz shuddered with rage. He rammed his pistol into the side of Rod's neck. "And why am I letting you live?"

Phil answered with a calmness she didn't feel, "Because my uncle told him the codes to the maze."

Schulz's breath whistled through his gritted teeth. "What's that got to do with anything?"

"Without him, we can't get into the vault." She paused, and then began to enunciate, as if explaining to a particularly dim-witted child. "Do you get what I'm saying, Schulz? No vault, no crystal—no crystal, no money. See how that works?"

Phil thought it prudent to leave off the "bonehead" part. She figured it might be a bit over the top and pushing Schulzie's limit.

Schulz stepped back, his face dark with frustrated anger and his stare murderous. True to form, he took out his frustration on someone weaker.

"Reed, load this clown into the back of the SUV! She sits in front with me. We'll get as far as we can before sundown."

Reed asked, "What about the old man?"

"He goes back to the boat with the Spics. You're coming with me."

"But they aren't going to like walking all the way back there, Schulz!"

"Tell them what I said. And if they and the guy with the boat want to get paid, they better be waiting right here to pick us up four days from now."

Phil stood by the passenger side of the SUV. She'd just learned why an incompetent like Reed was teamed up with a hardnose like Schulz. The Weasel had a rudimentary understanding of Spanish. Schulz had none.

She refused to budge when Schulz opened the door and gestured for her to get inside with a jerk of his head.

When he reached for his gun, she said, "Excuse me, but perhaps you haven't noticed that I'm wearing a backpack. I can't take it off until you remove these cuffs."

He shoved her at the seat. "Excuse *me*, girlie, but you're not taking them off. The backpack stays where it is for that crack you made."

Phil chastised herself for aggravating Schulz and sinking to his level. The satisfaction gleaned from her nasty remark was momentary. Brief gratification wasn't worth long-term discomfort. Wearing a backpack meant that she had to lean forward the entire drive and risk losing her front teeth if a deep rut slammed her mouth into the dash.

By the time they left the main road, turned inland, and entered tropical forest country, Phil's back muscles were tight from the strain. To bide the time and keep the pain and her temper under control, Phil began to catalog a list of Schulz's meanness and past insults to her and others. She added the way he took the roughest route to aggravate her discomfort.

It was obvious that Schulz had been given detailed instructions where to go, which would end soon, when the forest became too dense to drive through. The SUV would be left behind, and then she would lead the way.

Schulz parked the SUV behind a stand of brush and covered it with a dull green tarp. Rod became the expedition's human mule. Schulz loaded two packs on Rod's back and refused to allow his hands to be unbound. Reed was warned to watch Rod's every step.

Schulz removed Phil's cuffs. She eased the backpack straps down her arms and clenched her teeth to the point of pain to conceal her relief from Schulz. She looked at Rod as she rolled her shoulders and rubbed circulation back into her wrists. The sun's heat bore down from overhead.

Phil searched for her uncle's folded fedora in the backpack she had filled at his cabin. She rooted deeper for a spare cap. When she found it, she plunked it on Rod's head.

"Helps keep off more than the sun," she murmured.

Reed, whose attention to Rod never wavered, asked, "Whoa! Are there ticks?"

Phil concentrated on keeping her face expressionless to hide her glee. "The forest is full of them. They drop down from the trees, but that's the least of your worries."

Anxiety narrowed Reed's eyes into a feral squint. "If not the ticks, what should I be looking for?"

"Lots of spiders, mosquitoes, all kinds of flies, but what really hurts are the centipedes."

Reed scratched his cheek and arm. He glanced at the wall of tropical forest looming up from the savanna floor. The various screams and shrieks of birds and creatures filtered through the brush and tree trunks.

A light rain began to fall. Phil checked her backpack to assure herself that everything would be kept dry. The black crystal was still tucked safely in the zippered pocket where Rico had hidden it. She buttoned her sleeves and adjusted her hat and backpack. She chugged half a bottle of water and helped Rod drink the rest.

She asked under her breath, "You going to be all right carrying a double load?"

"This isn't heavy. Binky made me run seven miles every day carrying more."

"No bravado, please. Maybe I can talk them into letting you out of the cuffs."

"I doubt it. At least it's easier now that the cuffs are in front. And thanks for the hat, Mommy."

She looked over at Reed, who was still eyeing the forest and thoughtlessly scratching. "He's sweating. Mosquitoes love that."

"I heard you priming the pump, doc. You got him thinking."

"Wait till you hear the rest of the stories. I'll pretend to be giving you a crash course while I give those two some food for thought."

Rod hitched the packs into a more comfortable position. "Like the one about parasites that pop out from under the skin?"

"I don't think that kind is around here, but they don't need to know that. Wait till you hear about the snakes. Snakes are the challenge in this part of the peninsula."

"Oh, goody."

"Look at Schulz. He doesn't even bother to wear a hat. I hope he heard the bit about ticks."

Rod said, "Binky always wears a hat when he's in the sun. Never thought about ticks. Reminds me of monkeys grooming each other. Sort of fits with Schulz and Reed."

"The idea is to keep them sleepless all night. I'll need your help. Time to polish up your acting skills."

Phil started on made-up horror tales by the time they were huddled around a campfire. The forest got in on the act and seemed to hover over and around them—a lurking, watchful presence. Night creatures made unsettling noises, sometimes clicking or screaming. Phil wove nature's helpful special effects into the exaggerations she was telling Reed.

She squatted at the edge of the fire to poke the coals. Heat seared and tightened the flesh of her face. She felt awash with a contentment she had no right to feel in the middle of a hostage situation. But the forest, the night, the sounds, and the fire brought back so many memories of her youth, camping out in some godforsaken bush. Excitement zinged along her veins. It was old home week. She shook off the twinge of guilt for feeling so happy when her uncle's life was at risk.

She tore open the top of a BAR packet and squeezed out a chicken concoction that actually tasted good. Or maybe it was that thing about everything tasting wonderful when eaten around a campfire. Whatever. She slurped up the stuff oozing out of the end of the plastic tube, thinking that the present day Army had it pretty good compared to the rations the servicemen had during World War II.

Phil knew the grisly stories were getting to Schulz, even though he pretended not to be listening. She'd told most of the stories to prime Reed. The time had come to scare the wits out of The Weasel with Rod's crash course in rain forest travel.

"This is breeding season for pitvipers, you know, so be prepared for a lot of aggressive activity. Be careful where you step. They have a defensive posture if you startle or threaten them. First, they draw back, or coil up, and open their mouths. It provides a few seconds to get out of their way. All of them are lethal. Takes a few hours of pain to get to the point where you're happy to die. I brought some antivenin but most of it doesn't work."

Reed nervously checked his pistol. "Stir up those coals a bit, girlie. Will they stay away from the fire?"

"Depends. Sometimes the heat draws them. The fire is better for keeping the jungle cats away."

Reed pinched his lips together. "There's big predators?"

"A variety of felines. This is Maya country. They revered the jaguar. We'll be coming up on a Maya stele tomorrow that has a jaguar on it."

Reed asked, "What's a stele?"

"Think of a totem pole. Like that, but made of carved stone. The one I need to find tomorrow is a marker for a city that hasn't been excavated yet. There's another one outside the city ruins near the site."

"You mean we'll be seeing, like, one of those pyramids up north, where they chopped off people's heads?"

"Similar to that, but what Richardson wants is outside the city ruins. Underground."

Reed thought about that. "Are there snakes down there?"

"I doubt it. You should carry a walking stick in the forest, Reed, like I do. Helps with the snakes, but a stick won't help when it comes to the jumping snakes. Keep a close watch for the Jumping Pitviper. People around here say they've seen them leap out of the brush as far as five feet."

Reed rubbed his mouth with the back of his wrist. "Poisonous, huh?"

"Lethal. And zip up your sleeping bag. They'll be drawn to your body warmth at night."

Phil finished her dinner in a pouch and tossed the packet into the fire. She watched the plastic twist and melt and worked not to glare at Rod.

His merriment of Reed's discomfort was too obvious. While they had waited in Cancun for the plane to get clearance, Phil specifically warned Rod about the real danger, the beautiful and deadly Terciopelo, the most poisonous of the Central American vipers. She'd aso told him about other creatures to avoid. Having heard the unvarnished version, Rod was having too much fun witnessing city-boy Reed's mounting distress. Her exaggerations had reduced Reed to a shifty eyed wreck.

A rustling in the brush beyond the firelight caused Reed to emit a muffled shriek of surprise. Schulz stepped into the light, glanced over the scene, and scowled at his cohort.

"Reed, you must have a brain the size of a pea. Can't you see that she's jerking you around?"

"But, she said—"

"Get a grip, you wienie. This is the jungle. There's going to be snakes and bugs and other crap. We're only going to be here a few days, so get used to it. In just a couple days, we'll be outta here. We knock off the Spics, take the rock to Richardson, and collect our three hundred thou."

"If he let's you live that long," Phil muttered loud enough for Reed to hear.

Schulz stepped closer to the fire. "You got somethin' you want to share with the rest of the group?"

Phil stood. "I said, if we live that long."

Schulz snorted. "Tell your bedtime stories to someone else, Philly girl. Now, get out of the way."

Schulz pulled out his gun. He aimed it at Rod, but said to Phil. "Put your hand over the front of the barrel. Don't grab it. Just place your palm over the opening."

Phil hesitated and then complied, knowing it was a waste of time to argue. Experience had taught her that the easiest path around Schulz's kind of personality was to placate him. She would give Schulz what he wanted now in order to get what she wanted later.

Schulz said, "Time for beddy-bye, boys and girl. Reed, get those cuffs off him. He's going to set up the tents."

After freeing Rod of the plastic cuffs, Reed confronted Schulz. "I don't want to sleep on the ground."

"Now what's your problem?"

Reed glanced around. "Too many snakes. There's a hammock in one of the packs."

"Why are you telling me? Do I look like I care? Get the mule to hang it for you when he's done with the tents. And pull yourself together."

Feeling a twinge of guilt for picking on Reed, which was like pulling wings from flies, Phil said, "Maybe he's the smart one, Schulz."

Schulz huffed a silent, mocking laugh. "Ooo, now I'm really scared! How about it, Philly? Want to share my tent and some quality time with my snake?"

She knew he was bluffing. "Let me think. Should I eat dirt and die, open a vein, or expire from laughing at the sight of you at your most vulnerable?"

"There are lots of ways, Philly. We could make you do whatever I want. If you don't get on your knees, I could chop off your rich boyfriend's fingers one by one."

"Who says he's my boyfriend? And I thought you were more creative than that. You disappoint me, Tattoo Guy. I would have thought you understood that I hate men in general, not just you in particular."

Schulz lost interest with her lack of response to his intimidation. He smoked non-stop and watched Rod finish putting up the tents. When the camp was set up, he told Reed to reapply the cuffs and ordered Phil and Rod inside the narrow tent. There was just enough room if they stretched out on their sides, facing each other. Their legs were taped together and the tent zipped shut.

Chapter 25

Rod and Phil were squished face to face in the narrow confines of a tent made for one.

He whispered, "This isn't exactly what I had in mind when I fantasized about getting tied up and sleeping with you. We're lucky that you're kind of small."

"I'm not small."

"OK. Petite."

"I'm not petite. I'm average."

"Doc, you are the most *un*-average woman I've ever met."

"What's that supposed to mean?"

"Don't get your hackles up. I meant it in the nicest way. You're extraordinary, doc. Really. You are."

Something about his tone of voice made her insides go soft. She'd been acting tough for so long, and it wasn't fair that he was being nice. She pinched her lips together to stop the gushing feelings. *You can't cry now!*

"Hey, Phil, are you OK?"

She couldn't answer. If she opened her mouth, she might start to blubber. She pinched her lips tighter and wished he would stop acting so nice.

His lips grazed her brow. "It's going to work out, honey. Don't worry. Breathe. That's it. You're just tired. Lean against me and get some rest."

Her muscles screamed with relief when she allowed her body to rest against his. The thin foam pad inserted

190

between the tent's floor and the ground provided a meager layer of comfort. She didn't like the caustic smell of the new tent but putting up with the smell was worth knowing that there were no split seams or holes that would let in insects or reptiles.

"Move back just a little," he whispered.

Rod maneuvered his hands, which had been cuffed in front, up over his head. "Sorry about the lack of shower, but if I loop my hands over your head, you can use my arm for a pillow."

"Don't worry about the bathing thing. I'm used to roughing it and could use a bath myself. There's a waterfall not far from here. Tomorrow, we can use Mother Nature for a shower. If you listen, you can hear it in the distance."

"I heard it earlier. Doc, promise me you'll stop baiting these guys. They're under a lot of stress and could get unpredictable."

"Does this mean I can't tell them stories about cannibals and headhunters?"

He thought about that. "Are there any around here?"

"I don't think so. There certainly are in Peru, because they're the only thing stopping Uncle Cal from going there instead of Brazil."

"It seems impossible that tribes like that exist in this day and age."

"Technology can be as isolating as the rain forests. We all know people who live with their faces glued to computer screens. They never see anything they can't control or change. They're just as isolated."

"I guess so." He paused. "Come to think of it, I have some friends who never watch anything but sports. Never vote or watch the news."

"Or people who only read what reinforces their opinions."

Moments later, he asked, "Feel better?"

"Actually, I do. And I'll try to keep my mouth shut. I guess I've been taking out my anger at Richardson on these two idiots."

After a moment, he said, "Reed is barely functional, but don't be too quick to dismiss Schulz. My grandma Wakefield would call that guy crookeder than a bucket of guts."

Phil pressed her face into his chest to smother a laugh. She stilled when she realized what she was doing. Rod's body stiffened against hers and she lifted her head.

"Sorry," she whispered.

"Don't be."

The rough sound of his voice sent a thrill skittering down her spine. His lips glided along her cheek and settled on her mouth. For a moment, the world stopped. They didn't move, startled by the contact. An instant later, she was pulled underneath him. Aches and pains were gone. Liquid fire slid through her veins. She opened her mouth and let him in, soaring on a wave of dizzy bliss, distantly horrified by her lack of control.

She knew that he meant to use his arms to protect her from the ground, but the solid muscle of his forearms pressed into her back, crushing her against his chest. His bound hands cupped the back of her head, holding her still. She wished she could get closer. Her arms were trapped between their bodies. Then she felt the evidence of his excitement pushing rhythmically against her bound hands. The wildness of his response and the way he savored her snapped the leash of her fears. Answering passion urged her to move. She spread her fingers wide for him to thrust into her touch. A moan from deep in her chest slipped out, and hearing herself, she was shocked by the primal sound. Phil jerked her mouth free and turned her head away.

Minutes passed as they listened to the sounds of their breathing and forced the shudders to subside.

Rod pressed his lips to her ear. "I'm sorry, honey. Did I hurt you?"

"No. Get off me."

He paused before moving. In his hesitation she sensed that he was as surprised and unsettled as she was by the vehemence of the brief passion they'd shared. Never mind that she wanted those wildly passionate moments back. She would remember that sudden, frantic interlude for the rest of her life. Before this, she never understood how people could lose themselves in a physical relationship.

He rolled them onto their sides. "Sorry, Phil. I didn't realize what I was doing. Are you all right?"

"I'm fine."

"You don't sound fine."

"I'll get over it, Chaucer. Go to sleep."

She could feel him mulling over what had happened in the dark quiet.

"Phil, you've got to stop thinking that I'm like the other men you've known."

"I don't want to talk about it."

He tightened his hold when she tried to pull back. "Stop that. You can't go anywhere. I'm not your father, Phil. I won't ignore you."

"I love my father. Don't talk about him like that."

"I'm not bad-mouthing him, honey. I'm just repeating what you told me. And I'm not like your uncle. I won't push you away when times get tough."

"Leave him out of this."

"He's part of this. He's one of the reasons why you won't trust me."

"Trust you? Who are you, anyway, Chaucer? Rod, the Relentless? Buddy, the Saint and Confessor? I've got news for you, Bobbio. You've never been honest with me from the start. You've never given me a reason to trust you, so why should I now?"

"Let's see. Because I'm all you've got at the moment?"

"That's a comforting thought, slick, but you're going to have to do better than that."

"Because I lo—"

"Don't go there. Don't even *think* about that one."

She was *not* going to cry. Not now. Maybe a week from now, but not when Rod was around. What a low trick—using the "l" word when they'd only met three days ago! Her brain stopped.

Three days ago? It's only been three days?

He reacted to her sudden stillness. "What's the matter?"

"It just came to me. We've only known each other a few days. How dare you use that word. You don't even know me!"

"Easy, doc. Don't go ballistic on me when we're inside a confined area. And Dad fell for Mom when he saw her covered in mud."

"Mud?"

Her single word reply blared the warning that his answer better be good.

"They were at a spa. She was fixed up like a mummy. All he could see were her eyes. The rest of her was wrapped in cloth and drying green slime."

194

"You're lying."

"Ask them. He saw her cleaned up the next day and didn't recognize her until she took off her sunglasses."

Unable to stop herself, she asked, "And she recognized him?"

"She recognized his hair. Hers had been wrapped in a towel. They both knew right away. It can happen. It happened to them in a second."

Phil heaved a sigh. "I don't want to argue any more. I'm going to sleep now."

"Good idea. Tomorrow sounds like a busy day."

A few minutes later, he asked, "How long will it take us to hike to Site Fifty-four?"

"Two hours at most. We'll lose a few hours cutting our way through. It'll take six to eight hours to get in and out of the maze."

"That's a full day. Rest, doc. I'll stop talking."

She couldn't stop the smile from forming when he used his nose to brush back her hair to clear a spot on her temple for a goodnight kiss. She closed her eyes and sank into oblivion.

Chapter 26

Their wake-up call was a scream—a panicked shriek that ended with a thump on the ground. Next came the sound of frantic rustling amid the forest floor debris. The crack of a gun silenced all jungle noise.

Phil yawned and said, "That reminds me, I forgot to tell Reed about tree snakes."

A furious Schulz unzipped the tent. He sliced a box-cutter through the tape around their ankles and stood back as Phil worked her way out of the tent first.

Rumpled and shaking, Reed stood by his hammock, pointing his pistol at the ground. His gaze flitted across the damp forest floor in a frenzied search. The instant Phil stepped out of the tent The Weasel was ready with an accusation.

"You didn't tell me about snakes falling out of trees!"

Phil tested stiff muscles before stretching. Half-awake and distracted by the holy image of a steaming cup of cappuccino, she mumbled, "Constrictors aren't poisonous."

Reed yelled, "The thing could have eaten me!"

Phil blearily watched Rod extract himself from the tent's narrow opening. "You didn't have anything to worry about. Constrictors that large would be more likely to go after a goat." She scratched her nose with the back of her wrist. "Although, there have been some stories of anacondas swallowing humans."

Reed glared at Schulz. "See? What did I tell you? You said this was an easy deal, and I told you this could get tricky. Three hundred thousand isn't worth anything if I end up dead."

"If you don't shut up, I'm going to tranq you and leave you behind. We're leaving. Now."

Reed whined, "But what about breakfast?"

Schulz turned on him. "Do you see any restaurants around here? Grab a BAR. And get her out of those cuffs. Philly girl, you get to clean up the camp. Leave the tents. After a pit stop, we're outta here. It's already too damn hot and the sun's just come up."

Phil took advantage of the privacy when the men disappeared into the brush. She was surprised when she got back to the campsite before them. She chuckled and smiled at the thought of Reed trying to find a safe spot to squat in the forest.

Phil packed up the tents and sorted through the supplies in her backpack. She lightened the load in Rod's packs and kicked wet dirt over the fire by the time the men returned.

They headed for the distant sound of the waterfall. Phil hadn't argued with Schulz about starting out early, knowing that the temperature would continue to rise.

Steam issued up from the forest floor. Sunlight slanted through the trees, creating bars of golden light that illuminated the rising vapors. The air was thick with the scent of decomposing vegetation and new growth.

The humidity in the air increased as they neared the river. Reed complained that it was like walking through water. They broke through the trees and stood at the bottom of the waterfall.

Talking was impossible in the continuous roar of cascading water. The river's onslaught filled the air with a rushing sound and thundering power. A soothing dew of cool moisture hovered above the foaming pool. The air shimmered with sparkling rainbows.

Phil pointed to the opposite side of the river and then at the falls. An outcropping of flat stones formed a natural shelf to cross underneath the river. The rock ledge under the watercourse was their way across.

Phil led the way under the pouring wall of water to the other side, where she set down her pack. She dropped her hat on the backpack as the men came from under the waterfall.

She stepped directly under the less forceful rush of water at the river's edge. Rod was allowed to remove his pack and do the same. Reed joined them while Schulz sullenly watched.

Phil wrung out her hair, refreshed. She preferred to be wet and dripping from a shower rather than sweat-drenched. The cold water was a too-brief respite from the constant itch caused by relentless heat and humidity. Steam rose from their saturated clothes as they stood in the sunlight to dry.

Water, clear and sparkling, had collected in a natural rock bowl at the river's edge. Phil said nothing when Reed knelt to drink. Rod shared a speaking glance with Phil, while Schulz was preoccupied with trying to light a soggy cigarette.

Phil waited for Reed to drink his fill. She pointed west, indicating the increased density of the jungle growth. Schulz gestured that he wanted Reed to take the first turn with the machete.

Getting through the denser undergrowth near the river slowed them down. Phil didn't remember it taking so long but it had been more than a decade. And Reed wasn't making efficient use of the machete.

She stopped and looked back at Schulz, who was last in line, and called, "You might consider giving Reed a break. This is a lot thicker than I remembered."

Schulz came to the front of the line. "How much longer till we get there?"

"We'll be another hour of hacking through this stuff before we get to the perimeter of the city ruins. The underground site is beyond it—about a twenty minute walk from the center of the plaza."

Schulz yanked the machete from Reed's sweaty hand and began to chop, grousing all the while. Phil watched Reed rub his belly as he passed by to take Schulz's place at the rear. She smiled and turned to follow Schulz.

A few minutes later, she heard Reed groan and throw up. Schulz refused to stop. Reed continued to retch and frequently escaped into the brush. Phil figured he was too sick to worry about snakes.

The forest ended abruptly when they encountered a row of squat, carved figures. Vines and foliage nearly enshrouded the low, stone barrier. A stele sprouted up from the ground next to an opening in the wall. All four sides of the rectangular obelisk were covered in swirling designs and toad-like faces.

Phil led the way through and walked into a broad clearing. The plaza, paved with massive stones, was losing its battle with the ever-encroaching forest. She estimated that in another hundred years the entire site would be swallowed up and covered over.

A huge mound spiked with trees rose up directly ahead, a minor mountain in the middle of an expanse of bleached dirt and spindly weeds. Clumps of hillocks surrounded the immense hill. Smaller mounds, sprouting hackles of tiny trees and brush, were scattered about the perimeter. Some were entirely engulfed by the encroaching forest.

Schulz lit another cigarette. "This is the ruins?"

She pointed. "That central mound is the pyramid. The smaller hills around it are lesser buildings."

Schulz squinted through cigarette smoke. "Any gold in these ruins?"

"Probably not. Most of the ruins were looted centuries ago. Even if you did find something, you'd have to have a helicopter to take it out. Thieves only take what they can carry."

Schulz flipped the cigarette into the forest, smirking when Rod stepped into the brush to crush the glowing tip. "There's a good Boy Scout. Let's keep moving. You lead the way, Philly."

She couldn't hide her annoyance any longer and sent him a mean glare. Schulz was the type to grind salt into the tiniest wound. She fantasized the ways she was going to make him pay for calling her the hated nickname.

Phil stepped out into the sunlit plaza. The ruins looked the same, as if the area had waited in a holding pattern for her return. Green shoots were still working up through the paving stones. The majestic sprawl of the walled square—what had once been the center of a thriving community—was layered with powdery dirt. The tropical sun bleached the surface, its heat pulverizing the soil. Their tramping boots disturbed the fine dust, creating puffs with each step as they moved across the plaza.

A haunting silence hovered over the long-forgotten city. The feeling of shrinking in size and significance intensified as they neared the gigantic mound at the plaza's center.

She turned to check on Reed, who had stopped retching and now looked overwhelmed by his surroundings. The half- finished bottle of water he carried testified that he paid attention to her advice. Guilt had prompted her to advise him to take only sips until the nausea passed.

Phil reveled in the familiar sensation of being surrounded by time and history. Much had happened at this abandoned site in ancient times, everything from markets to sacrifices. She recalled the hours of listening to her uncle and his colleagues speculate why the Maya left their cities, leaving behind their monuments to be overrun by the jungle's unstoppable sprawl. She tended to side with her uncle's opinion that it was most likely due to successive years of relentless drought. No water for the irrigation systems would kill off an agrarian culture in a few years. The thought saddened her.

Before they reached the central pyramid, she turned east and headed for the forest. Before she entered, Schulz grabbed her arm.

"Why are we going this way?"

"Because the maze is on the eastern edge of the city."

"We're standing on the edge right now."

Phil searched for patience. "More than half of the city has been overtaken by forest. This is just the central plaza. The city itself stretches out for acres in every direction."

Schulz mulled over the information. "All right, but you better not be lying to me."

Phil shook her head and stepped into the shade. She pulled a compass from her vest pocket, keeping an eye on the wobbling needle, while being mindful of the tree roots writhing across the leaf-littered ground.

The truth was that she wasn't paying attention to the compass. She followed the low thrum of crystal song that increased with each step. Her heart began to thump. Memories she'd rather not think about pushed at the door of her mental closet. She had to suppress the fear, concentrate, and most of all, not think about the fact that Uncle Cal's life was at stake.

Chapter 27

She saw the stele through the trees, a towering block of carved stone shrouded in vines. She stopped in front of the ancient column, tilting her head back, remembering. Then she put her fears and memories away. It was too late for making wishes.

Phil yanked the foliage from the stele's base and revealed the face of a grimacing gap-toothed demon. Behind her, she felt the men staring at the ancient work. Rod was fascinated. Schulz kept a wary eye on the surrounding forest. Reed was bug-eyed and mouth-breathing, and Phil gave him marks for being the wisest of the three. What they were about to do deserved a large measure of awed respect.

Reed cautiously approached and touched the age-roughened stone. "They sure liked polka dots."

Phil tossed away a handful of vines. "Dots are part of the Maya numbering system. This sequence means that something happened at this site twenty-three thousand years ago."

Schulz said, "Skip the history lesson. Where's the crystal?"

Phil gestured at a rock-strewn descent into a shallow ravine. "Down there. We're standing above the entrance."

Schulz went ahead and Reed followed. Rod took Phil's arm and asked under his breath, "Are you OK? You look worried."

"Not worried. It's the crystals. They're making my head ache."

"A headache?"

"Didn't I tell you? I have this thing with crystals."

"Thing?"

"I can hear them." She waited for the usual reaction.

"Hear them? Sounds kind of kinky. Get it? *Sounds* kinky?" When she didn't respond, he said, "Sheesh, Phil. It's a joke, not the end of the world."

Something tight inside her chest eased and melted. A thread of hope reached for the impossible. She swallowed and asked, "You don't think that's sort of weird?"

"Weird? Sure. But I like weird. Can you do any other tricks?"

She struggled not to laugh out loud or smack him. It was hard to stay focused when handed the precious and unexpected gift of unconditional acceptance. She had no time to savor the exquisite relief of knowing that he didn't think she was scary. She wasn't sure what she thought about his liking her freaky connection to rocks.

Schulz and Reed waited at the bottom of the gentle slope. They looked around, Schulz skeptical and Reed perplexed.

When she reached the bottom, Phil said, "Hey, Tattoo Guy, I've got to have Rod out of the cuffs."

Schulz stared at her as if she hadn't said anything.

Phil put away the compass. She didn't want them to know that it was useless this close to the maze. The wildly spinning needle would stop altogether once they were inside.

She asked, "Do either of you know how to rappel? And you better smoke now, because you can't once we're in there."

Schulz tapped a cigarette from a pack and lit up. "I don't see an entrance."

Phil nodded her head at a fissure in the bank. "When we clear away that brush, you'll see an opening between the rocks big enough for us to get through. The Maya who lived here found this place and did some excavating a few thousand years ago."

"I told you I wasn't interested in a history lesson. Why can't I smoke in there?"

"I'm allergic to smoke. A cough or a sneeze could set something off."

Phil started to remove some of Rod's heavy load. She left a small pack on his back and looked pointedly at Schulz.

Schulz yelled, "OK. Reed! Take his cuffs off. And you better not try anything, Chaucer. I'll do the girl first."

Phil was grateful when Rod didn't respond to Schulz's bluster. She had no patience left for male posturing.

Rod said, "Then you might as well shoot me now, cause if you do it in there, you won't be able to find your way out. That is, if you survive the traps."

Schulz took a long pull on the cigarette, squinting through the smoke at the gap between the rocks. "What kind of traps still work after so long?"

Phil readjusted her hat. "The kind that I don't want to disturb. You might want to wrap that cell phone in plastic and leave it out here. It won't work underground and certainly not in there. It might burn up its wiring."

Pasty and scared, Reed peered into the fissure. "Is that, like, some kinda tomb in there?"

Phil lied, "This is King Palanque's burial site. His priests invoked a curse on anybody who violates his rest."

Schulz said, "Enough with the kiddie scare tactics. I want to know what sort of traps we're talking about."

"Floors that collapse under your weight. Or sometimes disappear after you cross over them, leaving you with no way out. But the floor problems come later. Getting through the blades is the trickiest part."

Schulz squinted at her. "OK, I'll bite. What kind of blades?"

This time she answered truthfully. "Big ones. Then later on, little ones. Make that phone call to Richardson. He's going to want to know that we've arrived, and I need to know how much time he's going to give me to get in and out."

Reed pointed and screamed, "A snake!"

Phil and Rod stepped back when Schulz pulled out his gun and emptied a clip into the ground. Phil decided not to point out that he'd just blown into mushy bits a harmless salamander.

Phil said, "If you're done with your impromptu killing spree, I need to talk to Richardson."

Schulz dialed the number and said, "Voice mail."

He left a message to call and lit another cigarette while they waited. When Richardson called back, Schulz handed the phone to Phil.

Her stomach lurched hearing Richardson's voice—his smug glee sounded magnified without his cherubic face to soften the underlying rancor. The connection was poor, riddled with static, and fading in and out.

"We're at the entrance, Richardson."

"I can tell. The connection is breaking up."

"I want to talk to Uncle Cal before we go inside. I need to know he's all right."

"He's a bit tied up at the moment, my dear."

"I am so *not* amused. Put him on the phone."

"Impossible. I've just activated a security blanket, so to speak. He's been attached to an ingenious bomb that Schulz devised. I haven't set the timer. Yet."

"You've hooked him up to a time bomb? You liar—"

"Before you lose your temper, you need to know that I won't trigger the timer, as long as you call me back in six hours with the crystal."

"I've got to have seven."

"It started out at five hours, then you demanded six. If I give you any more, you'll use all that spare time for figuring out a way to rescue your uncle."

"Have *all* your brain screws come undone? I'm thousands of miles away. What possible harm can I do from here?"

"Perhaps I might feel more sporting about the whole thing if you had told Schulz that your phone was equipped with a tracking device. How am I to know who is listening in on this conversation?"

Phil's heart thumped to a full stop. "Tracking device? What are you talking about?"

"You never could lie, and it was very unwise of you to forget how resourceful I can be. You were too young to realize that I was the one who did all the research, while your uncle took all the acclaim. But now we have the wonderful world of cyberspace, where it's hard to tell a lie and easier to track one down."

Phil struggled to jump-start her brain. One thought kept repeating itself inside her head: Richardson knew that they were being tracked. Nothing else happened inside her head. Her brain refused to move beyond that thought. She couldn't even shut her gaping mouth and didn't know what to say next. Her silence gave Richardson all the power.

It didn't seem possible, but Richardson sounded more smug that usual. "What's the matter? Still stunned? Didn't think I'd find you out, did you, Philly?"

The nickname jarred her back to life. She didn't have to admit that she knew about the tracking device. "That phone was given to me. How was I supposed to know it was bugged? I'm a librarian, not an engineer."

"And a clever girl, Philly. You knew."

"How are we going to make the drop? I want assurances that Uncle Cal is OK."

"You'll just have to trust me. Mark the time. And because you've always been special to me, even though obnoxious and arrogant, I've decided to be generous and give you seven hours. Call me when you're out and we'll set up a contact point. And Philadelphia, leave the black crystal on the ledge when you exit."

The connection broke off. She couldn't tell whether it was on purpose or not.

Phil closed the cell phone. Richardson knew a lot more than she thought. Terror wrapped icy fingers around her heart. She didn't even know if her uncle still lived. She had no time to decide what to do. She needed every second and the countdown had started.

When Phil handed the phone back to Schulz, he said, "Richardson says that we're supposed to keep it outside."

Phil dug into her backpack. She took a clean pair of socks from a plastic bag and wrapped the socks around the phone. She tucked the bundle inside the plastic before shoving the bag behind a cascade of vines and scattered dead leaves around the area.

She looked at Rod. "Take note of the time. We've got to be back out in seven hours."

She looked at the fissure. The last thing she wanted to do was go back in there. Even though more than a decade had passed, the black terror of the past still chilled the blood in her veins and eroded her confidence. She closed her eyes and said a prayer, resolved to do what had to be done, because in her heart, she knew that Uncle Cal lived.

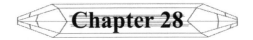

Chapter 28

Phil pulled on a pair of gloves and tugged at the vines that obscured the opening. The twining growths crawled across the hillside like needy green tentacles.

"I need two backpacks emptied out and filled with rocks. They each should weigh at least fifty pounds."

Schulz asked, "What for?"

"To spring traps and test the floors."

Rod helped her tug vines away from the gap between the rocks. Dirt clods and pebbles landed on her boots. They kicked the mess out of the way. Phil clicked on her flashlight, pointed the beam into the opening, and peered through the breach.

Rough-hewn stone steps led downward until the light would penetrate no farther. Leaves and decaying debris had collected on the steps. The entryway was clear—no collapses or dangling tree roots blocked the descent.

She started down the steps. Her nose wrinkled, rejecting the acrid smell of moldering stones and decomposing vegetation.

The beams from four flashlights offered plenty of light, allowing her to check the condition of the passage. She stopped the men at the bottom of the steps. Twenty paces ahead was a portal to a hallway of smooth gray granite speckled with sparkling flecks of black.

She turned to the three men. It struck her again how very different they were. Rod was calmly vigilant. Schulz was sullen and impatient. Reed was beginning to sweat. She suspected that Reed might have trouble with confined spaces, which could work to her advantage very shortly. She had to get rid of Reed and Schulz. There was no way she was going to allow them to see what the maze protected.

Schulz reached for the cigarettes in his breast pocket. He connected with her glare and dropped his hand. Caught in the act, his tone was defensive. "Why are we stopping?"

"Because I have to know that you'll do what I say while we're inside here. One wrong step, and we all die. Whoever designed this place meant for it to be used by people who knew the maze and how to immobilize the traps. You put your foot on the wrong spot and the floor will slide open."

Reed asked, "What do you mean?"

"The floor retracts into the walls, disappears from under your feet. If it happens, expect to find a lot of bones wherever you land. It can happen at any time. And there are traps everywhere. The only obvious ones are the blades and The Well of the Eater of Souls."

Reed glared at Schulz. "Why do we have to go with her? Can't we just let her get the thing and bring it out?"

"Richardson said there might be another exit besides this one. So we stick with her."

Twenty feet into the maze the corridor branched out into seven hallways. Phil went straight. At the next turning, she took off her hat and handed it to Rod.

"There should be a ledge up there. Put the hat on it."

"A marker?"

"Yes, and I don't want to lose it inside. If you end up coming out alone—"

"I won't be. Put the hat back on."

"Rod, I need to do this just in case. If I know you can find the right hallway, it's one less thing for me to think about. I have no idea what kind of noise I'll run into once we're on top of the crystals."

The expression on his face told her that he understood her cryptic remark. They weren't close to where the crystals were stored and already the humming inside her head was loud, discordant, and distracting.

She shined the light at the ceiling and watched as Rod stretched to slide the hat onto a ledge that was almost undetectable.

"Doc, have you thought about the size of these granite blocks? Some of them are over twenty feet long and almost that high."

Phil started walking. "Thirty feet long and ten feet high."

Nervy and jerky, Reed said, "It's creepy the way there's no dirt anywhere."

For fun, Phil said, "Ancient kings killed and buried their servants with them. There must be active spirits too bored to rest, keeping the place picked up."

She heard the click of Reed's nervous gulp from the end of the line and smiled.

After ten minutes of walking and following turns, she brought them to a halt. Ahead, the gray stone ended, replaced by streaked green. The memory of her uncle running his hand over the smooth surface bloomed in her mind. She was glad she'd left his lucky hat behind. The going from this point on was going to be rough. Uncle Cal's hat, like combination old friend and good luck charm, gave her hope. It was comforting to know the worn fedora was waiting for her when this was over.

Phil extended a hand. "I need one of the weighted packs. Rod, run your hands along the wall about shoulder height. Feel for bumps."

"Found some," he said a few moments later.

She took the pack from Schulz, asking, "Explain what you feel."

Rod paused. "Two dots and a line."

"Is the line vertical or horizontal?"

"Horizontal."

"Where are the dots—before, after, or above?"

He paused. "Two dots in front of the line."

"Take my flashlight."

Phil walked seven steps and halted. She carefully swung the pack in a gentle arc and lofted it into the air. It landed a few feet ahead.

Immense metal blades slammed down from the ceiling, skewering the pack to the floor and severing the stones inside.

Phil stuck out her hand for the flashlight. "Now we slide through the gaps between the blades. Don't get near an edge. They're still sharp. At least the poison's worn off."

Maneuvering through the blades took thirty minutes. When they were on the other side, exactly seven feet away, the blades silently retracted into the ceiling.

"Coming up on another trap," she said, stopping the line. "I need another weighted pack."

Rod asked, "Do you want me to check the walls?"

"That won't work this time." She dropped the pack on the floor every few feet until the floor slid back and the pack disappeared into the void. She waited ten seconds for the distant sound of the pack's muffled landing.

Schulz peered over the edge and flashed light into the empty black below. "Can't see the bottom."

"It's quite a ways down."

Rod asked, "Now what?"

She took off her pack. "Next comes the small blades, but before that, we have to check out the floor on the other side."

Angry and impatient, Schulz demanded, "How do we get over there?"

"Jump," Phil said, throwing her backpack across. "Rod, throw yours. At least another foot beyond."

The instant his pack landed, thin blades shot across the hallway into holes on the other side.

"Time to jump," Phil said, preparing to leap.

Schulz grabbed her arm. "What's stopping those blades from shooting across?"

"No time to argue. The floor is about to retract."

She grabbed Rod's hand, and they sprang across the breach. Behind them, the gap in the floor began to widen. Reed shrieked and stumbled backward. Schulz hollered at him and backed up. The farther he went backwards, the more the floor retracted until there was a thirty foot span.

Furious, Schulz started to pull out his gun. Phil grabbed her pack and called over her shoulder, "Don't!" she hollered, knowing he would.

She pulled Rod around a corner. The gun's report barreled along the hallways. The walls immediately began to move. The maze floor shifted under their feet.

Phil clutched her pack and Rod's arm, yelling, "Point your flashlight at the floor! Watch the color of the granite. We want red!"

The granite blocks began to glide, soundless and slow, narrowing the corridor. Phil flicked on her flashlight, pointed the beam at the floor, and sidled along the wall.

She shouted, "There! It's red on that side!"

She tugged on the backpack and stepped onto the different colored granite, staying with the dull red portion as the stone slid. Rod joined her as the hallway narrowed and closed in around them.

Rod grabbed her hand. "Phil, it's down to six feet! It's wider down that way."

"Don't go there. Just stay here on the red!"

Rod extended his arms and locked his elbows. He flattened his palms on the granite block that was sliding nearer, closing them in like a tomb. "Five feet!"

His arms buckled and bent. He wrapped them around Phil and held her tight, chest to chest. Phil dropped her flashlight and threw her arms around his neck. The blocks closed in, touching their backpacks, pressing them even closer, and stopped.

Phil felt Rod's heart pounding in rhythm with her own. She eased her arms from around his neck and looked down over her right shoulder. The flashlight beamed a line on the floor, illuminating black-streaked ruddy granite.

Phil sighed. "We did it."

"Uh, doc, we're sandwiched between a couple of stone blocks thirty feet deep. The gaps on the ends don't look big enough for me to get my hand through."

"I can get us out."

"What's that noise?"

Phil stopped squirming to listen. Brushing, scrambling sounds whispered in the darkness, like thousands of clicking dried leaves blown across pavement. The frantic noise increased.

Phil flinched and froze in horror as a river of scrambling insects sped over and around them, streaming away from the maze's interior. Tiny feet scampered over her bare face and the backs of her hands, skittered along her neck and through her hair. The creatures swarmed by in a frenetic race until the throng ended with a few confused stragglers.

Rod shivered. "That wasn't pleasant."

She looked down and saw a last tarantula scuttle through the flashlight beam. "Tarantulas. Wonder what caused the stampede."

"I swerved to avoid one on the road last month. When I looked back, it hadn't missed a step. If a moving car doesn't bother a lone tarantula, I can't imagine what scared an army of them."

Phil pressed her brow into his chin. "You know, Bobbio, I really don't like spiders. Or anything else that resembles an arachnid. I think I hate them just about as much as I hate snakes."

"Can't blame you. The ones in the herd that just ran over us were huge. I don't think I want to know what spiders that big are afraid of."

"We'll deal with it when we get there, because we have to go in the direction they came from."

"I was afraid you were going to say that."

"Just keep in mind that this will be over in another seven hours. Try to lean back as far as you can. I need to get the crystal from my vest pocket. You didn't happen to bring any smaller bars of chocolate with you, did you?"

"You know, doc, if you got laid once in a while you might not be so addicted to chocolate. I'd break off a piece of the big one but you'll need all of it."

"If you don't give me your chocolate, I'm going to smack you so hard you won't be able to make a smart aleck remark for a month."

"Gee, doc, if you're gonna sweet talk me like that, maybe I'll keep it for an appetizer."

His chuckle reverberated against her chest. Lust shimmered along her veins and tingled low in her belly. She called herself a fool for slavering after a guy when she should be concentrating on getting out of the maze alive.

"Last warning, Chaucer."

"OK. Just give me a minute to figure out how to get to it. Since it's two pounds worth, I switched it to my pack."

"Then you do have it. Thank you, Lord. I thought I'd lost it somewhere along the way. I didn't mind the extra weight. It was worth lugging it around just to have it in reserve. And stop moving like that."

All innocence, he asked, "Like what?"

"That thing you're doing with your hips. Stop it."

"How am I supposed to get to the chocolate without moving? You having any luck with the crystal?"

"I need to get lower. Can you pull off my backpack?"

"Put your arms straight up. If we both exhale at the same time, I'll try yanking it off."

Phil inhaled a deep breath the instant the backpack was freed from between her back and the wall. Rod squirmed out of his. Without the packs, there was enough room to sidle to one side and slowly turn around.

Phil said, "I've changed my mind about the chocolate. Let's look for markers on the wall. Tell me if you feel anything. I'm looking for a hole for the crystal."

"You mean like a keyhole?"

"That's right. The black crystal is a passkey, what the Amazonians call a set-free stone."

"What did these guys call it?"

"Haven't the foggiest. You know that ledge where I left Uncle Cal's hat?"

"Yeah."

"That's where I found this crystal. I was almost out of the maze but didn't know it."

Rod stopped searching. "You've got to be kidding me. Somebody stuck it up there a few thousand years ago, like leaving a key on the backdoor lintel?"

"Exactly. I heard it humming."

"You were a kid. How did you reach it?"

"I had a stick with me. Uncle Cal always made me carry a staff or a stick in case of snakes. The edge of the crystal was sticking out and I fiddled with it until it fell. Keep looking for that keyhole."

"What's the real reason you left your hat back there? As a marker?"

"For that reason and it holds too many memories to get lost and left in here. It won't be there when Mutt and Jeff go looking for it. The maze has shifted so they'll take a wrong turn, but we'll see it on the way out."

"Hey, doc, what if the configuration squishes us the next time it moves?"

"We can only hope it doesn't. There's no way to know for sure. I have the feeling that most of the corridors don't close any narrower than this one. But that's just an assumption."

They searched in silence until Rod said, "What's that spot by your foot?"

She leaned over and felt around. "This is it. They put the release on the floor this time. Get the flashlights.

We can't have them crushed if the wall moves in another direction."

She slid the crystal into the hole. "The trick is to turn it in the opposite direction."

"You mean no righty-tighty, lefty-loosey?"

"Exactly. Uncle Cal thinks their script reads the same way, from right to left."

"Like Chinese?"

"Yes. Are you ready?"

"Which way do we go?"

Phil turned the crystal key. "In the direction the spiders came from."

She heard Rod mumble something not very nice under his breath as the walls began to move slightly inward before retracting. When the walls spread wide and stopped, they were surrounded by red granite.

Phil tucked the crystal into her vest, picked up her pack, and started walking. "What time is it?"

"Almost two hours since we came inside. How come my watch works and the cell phones and compass won't?"

"You're the one with the engineering degree. I barely got through the math courses."

Rod asked, "How are we doing with the time issue?"

"Not bad but we can't slow down. Rats! I think I see trouble ahead."

Chapter 29

Phil stopped him by holding up her hand. Rod looked where she was pointing the flashlight's beam. There was a hole he judged to be seven to eight feet across and the width of the walls.

He peered over her shoulder. "That's quite a drop. So this is the Well of the Eater of Souls?"

"No. That's out in the plaza. I just said it was in here to scare Reed and tick off Schulz."

"That's quite a drop."

"We don't know how deep it is. This is where we stopped the last time. Uncle Cal said we couldn't go across when he couldn't estimate the depth of the hole."

"So we don't know if there are mutant turtles or pungi sticks at the bottom?"

Phil said, "No bottom, as far as we could tell. We lit a torch and tossed it in. The light disappeared. We threw in the heaviest object we had and never heard it land."

"Sheesh. That can't be good."

Phil took off her backpack and set it down. She knelt. The noise of the pack being unzipped sounded alien and strangely magnified in the murky dark. "What's more unsettling to me is the way the granite walls end here and don't start up again until the other side."

Rod touched the bulge of crumbling earth between the gap in the granite slabs. "It looks as if this section was shoved into this hallway, like an afterthought. Maybe the soil extruded through the wall after an earthquake."

"Could an earthquake create a hole that wide this deep underground?"

Rod scratched the whiskers along his jaw. "I don't know. I was never interested in geology, other than what I needed to know to pass a test. This is definitely local soil and rock, but this red granite isn't from around here. Are you sure we're going the right way?"

"The hum is getting louder, so we're getting closer."

Phil pulled out what looked like a flare gun. She inserted a dart-shaped projectile in the muzzle and clipped a high-density cord, the kind the military used for rappelling, onto the end of the dart. She pulled on a pair of gloves and replaced the backpack.

Rod asked, "Now what?"

"We're going across to the other side."

"How do you know it's safe footing over there?"

"That's one of the reasons we're using this gadget." She coiled the rappelling line, tested the knots, and checked the metal clips. "You're right to question the possibility of a boobytrap on the other side. That's what this hole was, but after so many years, the fake flooring has disintegrated."

"Or was broken off by people falling off a crumbling edge. The edges don't look safe."

"This whole area is unsafe. It was meant to catch the uninvited. This breach in the wall made it worse."

She released the gun's safety switch. "Point the light up there, please. I'm looking for a ledge or slight overhang."

"Why?"

"This dart turns into a grappling hook once it's fired. It's also supposed to embed itself like a pylon. I'd rather have something under it for a brace in case it slips."

Rod moved the light across the stone, stopping when she touched his arm.

"Go back a little to the right. There. That lip under the ceiling. What do you think?"

"Go for it."

She aimed, slowly inhaled, exhaled, and fired. The hook thumped into the wall. They both waited for the maze to react. When nothing happened, they relaxed.

Phil tested the line with her weight. "You said that you've done some rappelling."

"The basics. Do you want me to go first?"

She shook her head, swiftly adjusted the line and was moving across the rough wall above the hole seconds later. An avalanche of dust and small rocks dislodged by her boots tumbled down into the gaping void.

Rod's heart pounded with fear. He released the air he hadn't realized he'd been holding when she finally reached the opposite side. She tested the cave floor before standing.

He watched her wrap and tie the gun to the end of the line to act as a weight. She threw the gun across while holding onto the slack.

Rod caught the gun and unfastened the line. He tucked the gun into a vest pocket and tossed her the flashlight. She lit the way as he moved across the wall. The surface crumbled away from under his boots. Phil had made the treacherous crossing look easy. She beamed a smile of relief when he arrived safely on the other side.

He unwrapped the makeshift rappelling line and handed her the gun. "You weren't worried about me, were you, doc?"

Caught caring, she scowled. "Let's keep moving. Something about that hole gives me the creeps."

He directed the flashlight beam on her pack as she shoved the gun inside and zipped it shut. While she pulled the pack into place on her back, he flicked the light over the tunnel ahead.

A dull cracking sound echoed along the corridor. The floor under his feet shifted.

Rod heard the faint sound of Phil's startled exhalation. He whipped around in time to grab her out flung hand as she groped for the rappelling line dangling from the ceiling. A section of floor collapsed under her feet. The grip she had on his shirt slipped through her fingers.

In the next instant, Rod was on his stomach. His right hand caught Phil by the arm just above her wrist. She swung above the yawning void. All he could see was the flashlight beam whirling down through the black. It disappeared, leaving them in total darkness. The only sound was the harsh gasps of their breathing.

Rod's rapid heartbeat pounded inside his head. The floor under his chest was collapsing by degrees, falling away from his weight. He couldn't move backward, fearing that any movement would dislodge more of the flooring. He kept his left hand splayed—anchored to the floor by his hip. He crushed the toes of his boots into the smooth stone, trying for anything to create more friction. He focused all of his concentration on his grip, which was slipping. She was sliding through his fingers, now encircling her wrist.

He couldn't hold her full weight much longer. He considered pulling her up, but further movement might displace more of the crumbling floor. He had to remove some of the pressure from the edge before it gave way entirely.

"Phil, grab something. The wall. Anything!"

The fear she was battling rippled up his arm. His joints screamed from the strain of her swinging weight. A moment later, the pressure eased.

Her shaky voice said, "I've found a grip with my fingers and right toe. Can you get my other hand nearer to the wall?"

Rod didn't answer. He focused all his being on maintaining his grip and getting Phil closer to the wall. Exquisite relief oozed along his arm when the weight tearing at his ligaments lessened. She'd found a secure grip.

"I'm going to pull you up. Have to do it quick. Ready?"

"Just a second. OK."

Still holding fast to her wrist, he leaned forward and used his other hand to reach down and grab the tough material of her vest. Bits of the rock wall crumbled. Rod inhaled and pulled.

Together, they maneuvered up and over the edge. They scrambled away from the rim and sat on the floor, chests heaving for air.

Sudden understanding came with the rush of relief that washed through him. He reached out to grab her and clutch her close. He reveled in the feel of her solid and safe against him. "Don't do that again!"

Chapter 30

After a shaky laugh, Phil hoarsely replied, "I guess there was a little of that fake floor left on this side."

She couldn't hold back her grateful response. He flinched, surprised, when she hugged him back.

She quickly withdrew. "Let's check out your arm. I'll get the other flashlight from my pack. How's your shoulder?"

"Numb, at the moment."

"Is it still in the socket?"

He paused. "Can't tell."

Phil groped around inside the backpack until her fingers found the plastic cylindrical shape. She pulled out the flashlight, clicked on the light, and immediately reached for his shoulder. Her fingertips gently searched. She sat back on her heels with a shiver of release and exhaled the breath she'd been holding

"Thank God, it wasn't dislocated. Can you lift it?"

"Not much, but it'll come around in a few minutes."

She began to massage his shoulder, telling herself it was all about gratitude. He stilled, and she could feel his concentration settling where she rubbed his sore muscles.

Pleasure purred in his voice, "I'll give you a year to stop that."

"It doesn't hurt?"

"Not any more."

Because she could use gratefulness as a reason, she threw her arms around him. Her mouth found his and settled.

Rod captured her head to hold her in place. Phil was too busy to notice the miraculous healing of his shoulder. Passion roared through her body, a validation of life and celebration of survival. He started to withdraw. She clutched his shirt collar to hold him in place, but he was only shifting so he could crush her closer.

The fact that they had no time for this seemed unimportant. Being in the most unromantic spot in the world didn't even cross her mind. The constant drive to save her uncle had been replaced by insatiable hunger.

She almost laughed, recalling her scorn whenever she read about passionate encounters like this. She never believed this kind of thrilling wildness existed. Reckless desire was suddenly possible, ferocious, and exhilarating.

Rod was yanking open the front snaps of her vest. She was gripping the hair on his head to hold him against her mouth, rising up on her knees to shove him down, dying to crawl all over him. Runaway desire was happening now, spinning them both out of control. She was no longer frightened. Liberated from all reservations, she reveled in the ferocity of passion's impulse. Nothing was going to get in the way of this.

A scrabbling noise sounded in the hole. A whirring hiss slithered along the dark corridors. Sprawled on the floor, they froze.

Rod lifted Phil off him. He jumped up and grabbed her hand, hauling her away from the edge as a huge, hairy spider leg appeared.

Phil whispered, "Now we know what scared the tarantulas."

"No fair, doc," he whispered, taking her hand to draw her behind him. "You never said that anything in this place was still alive."

"That's because I didn't know. Oh, rats. Rod is that what I think it is?"

Phil gaped at the furry head. Six beady eyes glittered, watching. The lidless stare froze her limbs. Terror fixed her feet to the floor.

Rod grabbed the flashlight and shined it at the creature. The spider ducked its head and body down inside the hole, but its legs stayed in the light. Curved spurs anchored the spider's weight in place. It had no intention of leaving, only moving to avoid the glare.

Rod kept the light pointed at the hole, flashing the beam as a distraction. "Get the dart gun! Do we have anything else?"

Phil came to life. She dropped to her knees. Hands shaking, she undid her backpack's zipper and groped inside. She found the gun and handed it to Rod.

She jerked the bag opening wider and began a frenzied exploration. "I can't find the darts!"

"Give me something to throw."

She slapped a full bottle of water into his open palm. When the spider's head began to creep up, Rod cocked his arm and waited until the last moment. He threw an overhand pitch. The bottle clunked into the spider's head.

"I got one of its eyes. Give me something else."

Phil continued to rummage. She ran her fingers over the backpack's zippered exterior pockets. "I don't have anything else! Throw the gun!"

He threw the dart gun as soon the head reappeared. It connected with a dull thud. The whirring sound became louder, more agitated, joining with the noise of clicking teeth.

"OK, doc, this isn't working. I think I'm making it mad."

Rod tried moving the light quickly, flashing the beam into the beady eyes. He stopped when the mouth opened, a warning display. Teeth glinted between the clacking mandibles. A warning hiss issued out of the open jaws.

Frantic, Phil dumped the contents of the pack onto the floor. "I need light!"

Rod shifted the beam to the floor. He grabbed the pack with his free hand and tested the weight. Items in the zippered pockets made it heavy enough to throw.

He heard Phil searching through the mess on the floor while he kept his attention on the spider. He jerked the beam from the floor when he discerned movement by the hole.

He dashed light into the spider's eyes, and when the jaws opened wider in a renewed threat, he threw the pack.

The spider caught it, held it a moment, and spit it out.

Phil stood and yanked on his arm to pull him out of her way. She shouted for him to stay back and flung something sideways. An object whirled at the open mandibles. Something dark hit the mouth, which snapped shut.

They held their breath. The creature didn't move for a second and then disappeared down the hole.

Chapter 31

The flashlight beam showed an empty hallway. No sound came from the hole. Phil squinted when he shifted the light to her face. She lifted a hand to block the beam.

"Phil, what did you do?"

"I gave it that big chocolate bar."

Rod paused to look thoughtfully back at the hole. He lowered the beam. "Must be a girl spider."

She punched his arm, and they laughed off the adrenaline aftermath. They quickly sifted through the remaining backpack contents and stuck a few items in their vest pockets.

Rod said, "Did we lose anything important in the backpack?"

"We're not eaten, and I consider that more important. I'd rather make do than be wrapped in a cocoon awaiting the novel experience of having my vital fluids sucked from my body."

"Now that you put it that way, I'm not going to feel guilty about the loss of a compass."

He flicked the light at his watch. "We're running low on time. Which way?"

"Give me the flashlight." She grabbed his hand and began to move quickly along the corridor. "We'll follow the hum from here on."

"Not so fast, doc. We'll make a wrong turn. You're the one who said rushing around in here made for mistakes."

"I don't care. I just want to get away from that thing. If I had a rocket launcher, I'd blow it up for forcing me to give up that bar."

Rod's husky laugh sounded darkly inviting. "Now what are you going to do for a substitute?"

"You wish, Chaucer."

"If you're going to get snippy about it, I feel compelled to remind you that you're the one who said we didn't need bug repellant."

"Ha-ha. And you accused me of sounding pretentious! Look up ahead. We're coming to another link."

They halted before stepping onto the white marble. Phil flashed the light on the floor. "I've never seen white before."

"How's the hum?"

"Louder." She retreated a few steps, tilting and turning her head. "It's not that way. We have to go back the way we came."

Rod followed her as she slowly walked backwards. She stopped. Phil closed her eyes and pressed her hand flat against the red stone. "It's behind here. Something strong but dormant. The frequency is gigantic. I bet if we tapped the walls we could hear the change."

"How do we get on the other side?"

"There'll be a device somewhere. I've got the gismo to open it, if the black crystal will fit the keyhole for this. If it doesn't, we'll have to improvise."

Rod propped the flashlight on the floor to dimly illuminate the gray stone above the rosy granite.

"Phil, did you notice the change in the granite?"

"It doesn't have any black streaks. It's solid red now."

He placed his hands on the wall as high as he could reach. "What am I looking for?"

"A ridge or indentation, something that feels like the stone has been carved or altered. I'll check the walls at my height."

They searched for what seemed like hours, up and down the corridor. Rod tapped walls and strained to compare the change in the report. Phil stopped walking and retraced her steps when the waning frequency told her she was moving out of range.

After thirty minutes, Rod said, "I've checked this whole section. Nothing sounds hollow. Could we be looking in the wrong place?"

Phil ran the back of her wrist over her brow. "It's here! Behind this wall. I can feel it."

"Could what we're looking for be on the floor?"

"Yes! Oh, yes, Rod, that's it! Not it, exactly. But what we're doing wrong is not looking high enough. It must be on the ceiling—the only place we haven't looked!"

Phil looked up at the shadows overhead. "Shine the light up there!"

Nothing was etched into the stones overhead. Phil refused to be discouraged and continued to search the wall near the ceiling. She held the flashlight and Rod followed the beam with his fingertips.

Minutes later, Rod stopped. He was stretching as far as his fingers could reach. "There's some writing up here. How did they do all this in the dark?"

"They quite obviously didn't." She stepped closer and peered up. "There are early Egyptian etchings that show the use of what looks like a huge light bulb. Batteries have been found. Some still work, with a little fiddling. I can't see what you're touching. What's the etching feel like?"

"Pinwheel-shaped. The circles get smaller moving to the left."

"Bingo! Follow them until you feel something different."

He sidled along the wall. "Got it. It's a hole. Hexagonal in shape. The edges are too perfect for it to be erosion. Damn, I'm feeling this with my fingertips. Were they giants?"

"That's what Uncle Cal thinks." She unzipped a vest pocket and pulled out the black crystal. "And that they had greater brain capacity. Did your friend ever tell you about that huge, elongated skull that was found in Central America?"

"Elongated heads? For real? I gotta hear this."

"I'll tell you later." She tugged on his arm. "Lift me up. I'm going to try Uncle Cal's handy passkey."

Rod squatted, tucked a shoulder under her bottom, and wrapped an arm around her thighs. When he carefully stood up, Phil didn't have far to reach to slide the passkey into the hole.

The massive stone glided inward. Rod staggered backward out of the way. They bumped into the opposite wall. He broke Phil's fall by sliding her down his body. She grabbed his shoulders to stay upright.

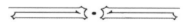

Phil stared at the black void on the other side of the corridor. Excitement made her fearless. She concentrated on what might be revealed in the dark chamber and resisted the throbbing hum that verged on pain.

Her lips felt stiff when she tried to smile gamely at Rod. "This could be it."

Rod stared into the secretive black, his expression one of appreciation and profound awe. "Phil, that stone block is the same shape as the others but it revolved without projecting out into the hallway. That's not possible."

Phil picked up the flashlight and pointed the beam into the darkness ahead. "I have the feeling we're about to see things a bit more amazing than that. Look dead ahead. The dark inside the vault absorbs the flashlight beam."

She edged a toe across the threshold, extending the tip of her boot cautiously over the stone floor. Rod curled his fingers over the top of her shoulder and followed.

Nothing happened until they were between the stone wall and on the verge of entering the vault. The mammoth stone started to re-close, revolving without a sound. They had no choice but to step forward into the void, or be carried along with it and crushed between the stone blocks. They sprang forward and out of the way.

Light flared to life when the door sealed. The chamber was splashed with a ruddy glow. Narrow blue beams sprang cross the ceiling and walls. A grid crisscrossed the room, an unmistakable pattern. The blue lines delineated where they were allowed to walk and what could not be touched. They stared until Phil cautiously advanced one step. Another wall slid open at the back of the chamber.

Phil doubled over. She grabbed her head and pressed her fingers into her temples. Rod threw his arms around her before she collapsed.

"Phil, what is it?"

Hunched over in pain, she whispered, "Can't you hear it?"

He brushed the hair back from her face. "I don't hear anything. Open your eyes. You've got to see this."

Phil straightened up from the painful hunch, took a deep breath, and dropped her hands. She opened her eyes and gasped. "Oh, my!"

"How's your head now?"

Stunned and disbelieving, she whispered, "The pain's gone. It went away the second I opened my eyes. Even the caffeine withdrawal is gone. Oh, Rod, isn't this incredible?"

Phil did a slow turn of her head to see what she could without moving. Polished copper reflected blue laser light. Glossy walls were strewn with swirling designs and dancing glyphs. Transparent coating protected the writing etched into the burnished metal, creating a sparkling sheen.

Directly ahead, a huge diamond-shaped gem stood poised on its point, braced by two silver hands reaching up from the floor. Rainbow colors flickered within the crimson facets.

Rod took her hand. "Do you have any ideas about this place?"

"I think it's as simple as a storage room. The directions of how to use that gem must be the writing on the walls. Look how clean everything is!"

"Not the floor. Look at the size of those footprints!"

"They could be painted on. Let's not go in any deeper. I don't think this room is booby trapped, but I don't want to take any chances."

"Good idea. And, doc, that's not a diamond. I'm willing to bet it's a ruby, but it's gigantic. Is that what Richardson wants?"

"It could be. But he's not going to get it. There's no way that we can drag that thing out of here and I'm not going to touch it."

"Do you think it's some kind of power source?"

Phil shook her head slightly, belatedly recalling a need to be careful, but there was no pain, not even a hint of the numbness that always followed a synthetic crystal headache.

"Perhaps. I'm still thinking that there's a lot more to this whole place than this room."

"Is that rock synthetic?"

She shook her head. "I can't get a fix on anything inside this room. Only outside. Is your watch working?"

"Yeah. You know, they've been creating hexagonal crystals for laser use for some time, but I can't imagine what it would take to make one that size."

"Don't put anything past researchers. I'm going to guess that this one is man-made. This might be what the Feds are after."

"Perhaps some kind of military application. Even so, selling a rock that big would bring enough to fund decades of wasteful government projects and a century of political pork. We could balance the dang budget for the next century."

"Rod, I don't have a good feeling about this. I'm thinking it's not just the crystal they want. Doesn't merely finding a single stone seem too simple?"

"What if they want to know how Atlanteans used lasers? No, come to think of it, can't be that. There's too many studies done. The death ray thing was figured out decades ago. It's got to be something else."

"Rod, what you just said made me think of a possibility. What if the Feds or the utility companies want to understand the Atlanteans' use of magnetics?"

He frowned. "Magnetic power?"

"Uncle Cal says that all major ancient sites are built on invisible magnetic lines. Like the Nasca drawings in Peru."

"We're talking something bigger than superconductors?"

Phil watched him soak up every bit of information. She could see him weighing the possibilities and embedding theoretical arguments into his memory.

"Rod, I don't want the wrong people to find this place."

He glanced over the swirling glyphs. "You're right. And don't worry. I can keep it to myself. I wouldn't want to see this place become a second Roswell."

"Perhaps a covert government agency could keep it intact and protected while they figured out the technology."

"Wrong, doc. They'd tear it to shreds. But that's an argument for another day, babe. Getting out of here is a bigger worry. And we need to find something synthetic to barter for your uncle. Do you see anything in here—feel any kind of stone—besides this huge mother that we can't get near?"

"There's nothing synthetic in here but there must be some outside this room. Somewhere. My fear is that in order to get to it we'll need to manipulate the configuration."

"I'm still trying to figure out how we can enter and exit the same place and yet go in different directions from unconnected routes. And let's not forget the cute revolving door trick. It boggles the mind."

"Don't give yourself a migraine trying to figure it out.. Wait for Uncle Cal to show you his map of the maze.

236

Turn around. I'm going to use your back as a brace and jot down some of these glyphs for him. A few have script underneath."

Phil pulled the stub of a pencil and the photos she'd taken from the safe-deposit box from a vest pocket. She scribbled glyph shapes on the back of the photos and passed them to Rod.

She started on the back of the last photo. "Did you notice the change in the tracking beams?"

"Yeah. When I turned around, some of the beams disappeared."

"I'm not going to try it, but I think that the closer one gets to the crystal, the number of beams in the field increases. A warning and protective device."

"But what powers it?"

"If we looked around long enough, we'd find a mirror or some sort of vent that lets in the sunlight. Or maybe this place is connected to others. I'm writing on an aerial photograph of this site. There are two other mounds close by, all in the Orion configuration, like the pyramids at Giza. That's how Uncle Cal figured out there was something important buried under all the vegetation."

"I never would have seen the entrance to the maze if you hadn't shown me."

"Without a directional hum from a crystal, I wouldn't have found it either."

"Are you about done?"

"I've run out of things to write on. Don't turn around. We're going to both face the exit at the same time. I think the door will automatically open if we get close enough."

Rod scoffed, "Can't be that easy."

"Oh, yes it can. The idea was to have a key to get in. I'm willing to bet that they don't care if we leave."

As she predicted, the massive stone wall revolved as they approached. Phil dared a glance over her shoulder—a last look at the wonders of the past to impress into her memory. Blue beams were shutting off, one by one, until the immense ruby stood alone, seemingly unguarded and vulnerable.

The light inside the vault went out the instant they stepped into the corridor. They heard the stone slide into place. Phil tugged the flashlight from her belt and flicked it on. She inhaled sharply.

Rod asked, "What's wrong?"

"The configuration's changed."

Chapter 32

"Rod, don't move. Watch where I put the light. Look for markings."

She ran the beam across the walls, a methodical sweep that started at the top and worked down. "I don't see anything."

"Shine it on the floor, doc. I don't think the stone floor looks the same as the walls."

"You're right. Let's look for signage. What's that?"

"In the corner? Something that looks like it doesn't belong in here. Do you want me to check it out?"

Phil hesitated. "We've got to move sometime. Try a few steps but remember where you were standing."

Rod moved. Nothing happened. He followed the beam of light to the object in the shadows. "Move the light to your left."

Rod squatted and picked up the object. He came back and placed a purple plastic Pez dispenser in her palm. "No fair. You ate all the candy."

Phil breathed a laugh. "We're close to a link. We have to backtrack."

"But this is a different hallway. Shouldn't we move forward?"

She pointed the light at the floor and they started walking. "Don't let your logic trip you up. Backtracking is actually going toward the exit. These were all shortcuts. The chambers revolve and stop at the point where the visitor is offered the shortest way out. One doesn't have to take the quickest way to the exit."

"So you're thinking that since the configuration has changed, the synthetic crystals are going to be near the exit."

"Or entrance."

"Whatever. Do you have any chocolate left?"

"If I did, I'd be eating it. Why?"

He pulled a Hershey bar from a vest pocket and handed it to her. Phil snatched it from his hand. "You've been holding out on me!"

"And glad I did. There's a big hole directly ahead."

Phil stopped. She started to mutter under her breath. Rod didn't interrupt her train of thought and kept a wary eye on the looming void. A rustling noise floated up from deep inside the hole.

"Phil, I think we've got company."

"Oh, rats, not again! I *hate* spiders!"

Her heart stopped and then turned over when Rod reached for his boot. Reflected light glanced off the knife blade when he flicked it open.

"Phil, I want you to run as fast as you can to the next link. I'll meet you there, but don't wait. If you hear anything but my running boots, keep going."

"But we've got only one flashlight!"

"Keep it. Flash the beam into the spider's eyes before you run."

"I can't leave you here!"

"Do it, Phil. Here it comes. You and your chocolate. Don't worry. That's not big enough to stop it this time. I think we've created a monster."

"But we could try," she protested, reaching into a vest pocket.

A hairy leg tentatively touched the corridor floor. Another was placed on the opposite wall. A third leg touched higher and remained on the other side of the hole. The head and broad mandible appeared with the next legs. The glittering beads of its eyes reflected the flashlight beam. The spider retreated slightly from the light and lowered its body, readying to spring.

Rod held the knife in his left hand and started to remove his vest, yanking the snaps free. The spider stilled and watched the rapid movements.

Rod shrugged off the vest and held it in his right hand, poised to throw it. He shouted, "Run when I distract it with my vest."

"No. Move out of the light!"

"Run, Phil!"

"No! Move aside."

Rod hesitated then stepped to one side. A beam of red shot by his shoulder. A sizzle and crackling snap evoked a shriek from the spider, and it scuttled down the hole.

The streaking red line bounced off the corridor walls and finally buried itself in the granite wall.

Rod stood up from an instinctive crouch. Stunned, he slowly put on the vest. "OK, so what was that?"

Phil swallowed and tried to relax her eyes that felt permanently stretched wide in fright. She realized that her mouth was still hanging open and snapped it shut. She had to clear her throat before she could speak.

"It came from this." She showed him the black crystal.

"What do you mean? You just pointed it—aimed like a gun—and it went off?"

"No. Something told me to shine the flashlight beam through it and aim it at the spider. I thought it would magnify the light and blind it. Never expected a laser beam to come shooting out."

"What a piece of luck. Look. You got one of its legs."

Phil couldn't stop staring at the result of her spontaneous reaction. The stench of the fried hairs on the spider's leg wafted up from its scorched limb. The dismembered leg writhed at the edge of the hole. She couldn't release her stare from its bizarre contortions.

Rod gave her arm a shake. "Hey, earth to doc. How'd you come up with that idea?"

"Um, that laser beam grid in the ruby vault. It made me think that a really bright light reflected into the spider's eyes might scare it away."

"You scared it, all right! I think I'll take that leg with us, because nobody is going to believe this."

Phil tucked the crystal into her vest pocket and zipped it shut. "I don't think you should touch it. There's no way to know if its limbs are venomous. Let's keep going. There's a ledge on the perimeter of this hole that we can use to get on the other side."

They avoided the dismembered spider leg. It finally stopped moving and rested in threatening stillness. The intense odor of burnt spider hairs was beginning to fade.

Rod pointed the flashlight as they crept along the narrow edge above the hole, using the corridor wall for support and balance. The going was slow. The width of the ledge was less than the length of Rod's boots.

On the other side, they hurried ahead. Phil kept watching over her shoulder for the spider to return until they rounded a corner.

She touched Rod's arm and he stopped. "I need to get oriented. There's so much humming everywhere in this hallway. Give me a minute to find the way."

He waited, shining the light around the corridor, until Phil asked, "What's up ahead?"

"It splits off into two branches. Both are red. No holes in the floor. Something's hanging from the ceiling on the right side. I think it's a web."

"Let's not talk about webs."

Phil closed her eyes. The hum reverberated loudest from behind, coming from the ruby vault. A gentle thrumming melody came from the left.

She pointed to the hallway that held the melodic humming. "We go that way. Stop when we reach the fork."

When they came to where the corridor split into three different directions, Phil asked Rod to check for signage while she rested her head on her arms. Caffeine withdrawal thumped a painful demand, its complaint muffled by the call of the crystals.

"Phil, are you all right? Do you want to sit for a while?"

"Can't. Running out of time. What does your watch say?"

"We've got forty minutes left."

"Let's keep going. What signage did you find?"

"Up there." He shined the beam near the roof. "See it? A fat circle with two indentations and a gash underneath. Think Pillsbury Doughboy's face."

She laughed softly. "Count on you to give a girl a good time, Chaucer."

"News flash, doc. It'll be more than a good time after we're out of here and get your uncle taken care of, you saucy vixen. We're due for some shared sacktime.

Hold on a minute, sports fans. There's another one of the signs ahead, and guess what?"

"You tell me. I can't look. My head's killing me."

"There's something sticking out of the wall."

He pulled her along the corridor and stopped to pry an object from a crevice in the wall. "Lookie here, doc. Another Pez dispenser."

"Can you tell what color it is?"

"Looks like green."

Relief relaxed the tightness across her shoulders. She sagged against the cool granite. "Praise be, you've found it! Search for the keyhole."

She held the flashlight while he reached high and ran his fingers across the wall. He inserted the crystal and nothing happened.

Phil exhaled a weary sigh. "No, don't tell me. Just try again. Are you turning the correct way?"

"Yep. Nothing's happening. I'll try the other way, just in case."

Two more attempts and the wall remained unmoved. The sting of gathering tears prickled inside her nose. She pinched her lips and tried to think through the weariness and noise in her head.

Rod came up with the solution. "I think you have to do it."

"What?"

"Phil, it's you. You're the key as much as this crystal is. I'm going to lift you up."

He propped the flashlight so the beam glowed on the keyhole. He wrapped his arms around her waist and hoisted her up. She slid the stone into place and turned it. The wall began to move.

Rod was waiting for the shift this time and allowed Phil to drop to the floor as he pulled her back. Copper light sprang through the opening and into the hallway, igniting sparkling reflections off the red granite walls.

When they started to step inside the chamber, Phil grabbed her head and retreated into the hallway. "You'll have to do it. I can't take the pressure. I'm going to wait outside."

"Phil, wait!" He caught her before she got all the way out and hauled her back. "The door might close and change the configuration. You'll be out there, and I'll be stuck in another corridor when I leave."

She nodded, hunched over from the pain and pressure. She tried to straighten up and subdue the pain. Rod took her by the shoulders.

"Open your eyes, Phil. It worked the last time."

The pressure gradually eased after she opened her eyes and looked around. The room was half the size of the ruby chamber. The walls were made of the same red copper metal, but there were no inscriptions.

Tubes had been embedded into the smooth metal. Crystals were nestled in the tubular containers. Each tube had a clear lid protruding from the top of the container, enough of a lip to grasp and open the tube.

Phil asked, "Do you see anything that resembles a security device? Beams or anything? My eyesight is starting to blur."

Rod shook his head. "Nothing. We probably won't know until we make a move. How do you know which one to take?"

"By the sound." She leaned against the wall. The slick metal was warm, unlike the cool blocks of granite that formed the maze.

"What about the one over there?" he asked.

She peered up and looked where he pointed. A milky-colored, round stone hung between two blocks of granite. Metal hands protruded from the granite to cup a stone that looked like a huge opal.

"No. Don't touch that one. Try the ones in the green tubes. Bring them to me. There's so much noise in here that I'll have to touch them to know if it's synthetic."

He brought the crystals to her one at a time and returned them, securing the lids carefully. "We're down to ten minutes."

"Start on the blue tubes."

He brought her a sapphire spike, and after touching it, she said, "The blue's have it. Let's go."

Phil wrapped her shaking fingers around the crystal as Rod took her arm. Her limp arms and rubbery legs were heavy, slow to respond. The stone doorway opened when they stopped in front of it, and they went out into the hall.

Rod flicked on the flashlight. Gray, black speckled granite, similar to the stone at the entrance, replaced the red.

Phil tucked the pale blue crystal into Rod's breast pocket. "You take it. Just follow the signage to the exit. Call Richardson. I can't take another step."

"We're almost out of here. Come on, doc. You can do it."

"Can't. My head's about to fall off. I've got to rest here."

"No, you're not."

He handed her the flashlight and picked her up. "Which way is out?"

She weakly pointed and he said, "Prop the flashlight so I can see ahead."

When he started walking, she mumbled, "Go around two corners. Always to the left. You'll see light in a few minutes."

"No more talking."

That was fine with her. The pain was out of control, making her nauseated. Her stomach rolled and writhed. She gave up and tried to relax into the pain.

She had always wondered what it would be like to be carried. She rested her pounding head on his shoulder and closed her eyes.

This is nice. Romantic. Prince Not So Charming to the rescue. I could do this for the rest of my life.

Chapter 33

The pressure inside her head eased as natural light brightened the corridor. She brushed away tears of relief as he neared the steps leading up to the entrance.

Underneath her legs and back, she could feel the strain of carrying her in the stiffness of Rod's arms. The longer he held her, the tighter his grip became, letting her know his body was being pushed to the limit, especially after the strain of breaking her fall into the spider hole.

She was sorry the ride was over when they arrived at the narrow entrance to the steps. She savored the last moments before he allowed her to stand.

Rod walked out into twilight. Phil followed, stepping gingerly. Inside the crystal storage area, even the slightest move evoked a wave of nausea. The pain and pressure relented the instant she cleared the entrance.

She lifted her head to the fading light. The ground felt alien under her feet but the piercing headache had eased to the point of a mere throbbing aftermath of its former onslaught.

Rod reached in, grabbed the phone from behind the vines, and unsealed the plastic bag. He flipped the phone open and hit the redial.

"Richardson? We've got the crystal." He listened and then extended the phone. "He wants to talk to you."

But I don't want to talk to you or ever see you again, you slimy jerk.

"Tell him I'm sick and need a few minutes."

Rod relayed her message and listened. "He wants to keep the line open and wait."

Phil breathed deeply, trying to clear her mind. The light and fresh air worked like a miracle cure.

She nodded and stuck out her hand for the phone. She gestured with hand signals, asking Rod to go back inside the maze and get her uncle's hat from the ledge. She waited until Rod returned to speak to Richardson.

"I'm here."

"Philly, this is Dr. Richardson. So you've got a crystal for me?"

"It's synthetic. Definitely hexagonal. I want to talk to Uncle Cal."

"In a moment, my dear. There's been a change of plan."

Her temper roared to life, flushing searing heat into her face. The sudden gush of outrage washed away the residual head and body numbness. Fury and energy zinged along her veins.

"You better not have hurt him, Richardson, or you'll never see this crystal or a day of rest. I'll hunt you down and—"

"Calm yourself, child. Your uncle is well. He spent most of the time you've been gone in bed. We've got him up in a chair now. He's refused food but has been taking water regularly. Not to worry. He's fine."

Something was wrong with this set-up. She ran through the possibilities from the adversary's angle. There were too many gaps in Richardson's plan, too many opportunities for error. He had to gather up the loose ends and cover up his dirty work. He couldn't leave people alive to tattle. The easiest way to fix the mess would be to kill everyone involved. If his two goons survived and were still in the maze, she didn't care what Richardson had in mind for Schulz and Reed. Knowing Richardson's tidy mindset, she figured he'd try to wrap it up all at once, in one shot.

She looked into Rod's eyes, hoping for direction. His level gaze told her that she was right to be worried.

Testing the water, she said into the phone, "I'm not giving you this crystal until I see my uncle."

"That may not be possible."

"You told me he was unharmed!"

"He is, my dear, but I'm not with him. He's still at the cabin under guard. I'm in Campeche. You're going to bring the crystal to me. Once it's in my hand, I'll call off my dogs and tell you how to save your uncle's life."

"How can I do anything with that kind of threat held over my head?"

"You're such a resourceful girl. You'll figure it out."

She didn't trust herself to say anything. She worked to control her breathing—to clear her mind of all the things she wanted to do to the miserable rat.

First, she might try that trick with the flashlight and the black crystal, burn off some appendages. Or cover him in chocolate and toss him down The Hole.

Richardson would probably give the spider indigestion.

Rod touched her arm and whispered, "Uh, you aren't planning to swallow that thing, are you? You're looking at it as if you're going to take a bite out if it, and it's the only phone we've got left."

Phil slanted him an evil glare. Headache and weariness forgotten, she growled into the phone, "Give me the directions."

She listened, snapped the phone shut, and handed it to Rod. The next few minutes were taken up with her repeatedly abusing a fallen tree until a final kick resulted in a cracked trunk.

Rod, who was wise enough to wait for her temper to expend itself, said, "I take it Richardson double-crossed us."

Her chest heaved as she sucked in air. "Big time."

"You shouldn't be surprised."

"I'm not surprised. I'm mad."

"I noticed. Have you ever tried that primal scream thing?"

"It's too undignified."

Rod glanced at the shattered tree trunk. He hesitated before suggesting, "Why don't we try to get as far as we can before nightfall?"

She nodded. "Let's head for the nearest road. Maybe we can hitch a ride with a tourist bus in the morning."

"Why not hike to the SUV?"

"We have the problem of the keys being somewhere inside that maze with Tattoo Guy, and I'm not going back in there."

"Doc, I can hotwire a car. If we move at a good clip, we can be there in a few hours. The path is cut. Easy to follow."

She blinked, tantrum dissolved. "Good idea. We might be able to make it to the beach by late morning. Once we hook up with Binky, we'll head up to Campeche."

"What's in Campeche?"

"Richardson. He left Uncle Cal at the cabin with some goons. He says he'll tell them to release Uncle Cal after I turn over the crystal. I know this is just another wild goose chase that leads to another double cross, but we'll follow it until I can think of something else."

"Let's find Binky. He can arrange for anything, if he's got a communication hookup, and there's still life left in this phone."

Phil tugged on her uncle's lucky hat and started walking. "The guy who gave it to me said it didn't need recharging but I don't know about how long its battery will last in this moisture."

"If it doesn't need recharging, it probably doesn't have a battery. I'd love to take that thing apart and see what makes it tick."

"You can have it when we're done. So what do you think? Could Binky get us some extra help? Maybe hire an out-of-work gang of insurrectionists?"

"Won't need mercenaries with the Binkster on our side. Don't worry, babe. Once I let Binky off his leash, Richardson is toast."

As they passed the machete Reed had stabbed into the ground, Rod yanked it free.

Phil said, "You won't need that. We can use the trail we made coming here."

"You got it wrong, doc. This is for snakes, spiders, and temperamental librarians."

Phil smiled and reached over to withdraw the blue crystal from his vest pocket. She snuggled it next to the black one in her vest as they headed into the jungle. She'd eat bugs and listen to talk radio before leaving behind the key to the kingdom for Richardson.

The two crystals got along very well together, humming a pleasant tune. No jangling noise, like the raging of sounds inside the maze. This was comforting, almost soothing, which didn't help the nagging exhaustion.

Darkness came quickly near the equator. Ignoring her protests, Rod insisted they stop to rest. Phil unfolded a thin sheet of plastic. They huddled under a tree sitting on a portion of the protective sheet and using the rest to shield them from the constant drips falling from the leaves.

Phil unwrapped the cell phone and checked for a dial tone. "Rod, I'm calling somebody I think can help us."

"Who?"

"I met him at the hangar in Colorado. I didn't tell you about it."

"That's OK, doc. I knew you weren't telling me everything."

"Isn't it tiresome, being so nice all the time?"

"Thanks for the backhanded compliment. So who's this guy you're calling? Should I be worried?"

"I'm fairly certain that he can be trusted."

"That's not what I meant, babe. I was fishing around to see if I was going to have to beat him up."

"Silly man. I do my own beating up. This guy's got federal employee written all over him. I haven't asked, but I'm willing to bet he's with one of those clandestine government agencies. I can't keep track of all of the acronyms."

Using the cell phone's faint green readout, she fiddled with the keypad until she figured out how to program Richardson's number into memory then dialed the number she had memorized. A second later a computerized female voice asked who she wanted.

"Bill."

The line rang and a man's voice asked, "Dr. Hafeldt?"

"Bill?"

"We've been waiting for your call. You're finally moving into range. We couldn't get a fix on where you were the last nine hours."

"I'll explain that later. Do you know where we landed in Wyoming?"

"Yes. We lost you for a while. You left the phone on the plane."

"That's another story. I'm calling because my uncle is in trouble and I'm not going to be able to get to him in time."

"How can we help?"

"There's an old logging road north of where we landed. Take it to a fork. Go south. Take the road going straight up the mountain. My uncle's cabin is at the end. Mike Richardson is holding him hostage at the cabin. The place has been rigged with a bomb. Can you go to him?"

"Hold on." She heard him talking. A moment later, he said, "A team will be there shortly. We've been using the hangar as a base."

Phil hesitated. "My uncle is that important?"

"Yes. We're not the only ones who want him. What can we do to help you?"

"I'll let you know later. Take care of Uncle Cal first. Don't go barging in to rescue him unless you have to. The men holding him are in direct communication with Richardson, the kidnapper."

"We know who Richardson is. We believe he's left the country."

"He's in Campeche. He's told me to meet up with him there to exchange a ransom. Wait a minute. Can this phone be traced or tapped?"

"Only by us."

She exhaled a relieved sigh. "In that case, you can help by providing transport in the morning. We'll call you when we get to the coast. I'd ask for help now, but we have to pick up someone else."

"Do you mean Captain Binkerman?"

Phil paused before asking, "Binkerman?"

She wished she could see Rod's expression. There was no light under the trees and plastic, not even a glint from his eyes from the faint light of the cell phone readout pressed to her cheek.

Phil slid her hand over the mouthpiece. "Am I correct in supposing that our Binky is also known as Captain Binkerman?"

"You knew he was in the Navy."

She took her hand from the phone. "What about Captain Binkerman?"

"He has a helicopter standing by."

Phil rolled her eyes in the darkness. *I should have known.*

"Where?"

"He'll come to you. We've got a fix on your location. Call us when you get to the nearest clearing."

"I'm concerned about the batteries in this phone, Bill."

"Don't be. It doesn't have any."

Phil was too tired to be intrigued by the technology she was holding in her hand. "We'll contact you in the morning."

Rod unexpectedly asked, "Want a drink?"

Phil tucked the phone into a dry vest pocket. "Where have you been hiding water?"

"I've been waiting for the drips to clean the plastic sheeting. I have a leaf folded to catch the runoff. It takes a while, but we have water."

She gratefully slurped the water from the leaf cone, past caring if the vegetation was toxic. Quenching her thirst seemed more important than waking up in the morning swollen up like a blimp from an allergic reaction.

"Hey, Chaucer, how about we splurge and share a square of chocolate?"

"You know, doc, that's the nicest thing you've ever said to me. You must like me if you're willing to share your chocolate. Let's do half-zies and I'll give you the complimentary chocolates from the hotel pillows. I saved them for an emergency."

Phil reverently unwrapped the chocolate. "You are a font of chocolate, a source of endless delight. Let's make the trade."

He handed her four squares encased in foil. "Careful. They're soft."

Phil set her unwrapped portion on her thigh and handed him his half. The rest of the complimentary treats were reverently swathed in tissue and tucked away.

She went for the whole thing at once, allowing the flavor to lie on her tongue and melt into glorious puddles inside her mouth.

"Phil, you're moaning."

She swallowed. "Can't help it. I'm starved and it's *so good!*"

"Yeah, but it's no fair making noises like that."

Forest night sounds surrounded them, secretive and primal. The roar of the waterfall came from a distance, filtered by the trees. Something primitive and ageless seeped underneath the plastic sheeting and invaded their snug cocoon. Jane and Tarzan descended from the trees, she thought, suppressing a nervous giggle.

His arm tightened around her shoulders but never moved from holding the edge of the sheeting to keep her dry. His solid chest warmed and comforted her cheek. Never in her life had she experienced so much overwhelming masculinity.

Essence of man. Eau de virility.

The urge to fling off the restraints and hold on tight took over. A purely primitive need to bite down on tough, male muscle seared through her veins and writhed along her limbs. She clenched her fists to quell the impulse before she made a fool of herself.

This is ridiculous. Why is it so easy for him to do this to me?

"Phil? Go to sleep. You need your rest. Tomorrow is a big day. You've got your uncle to save."

Disappointment reigned for a moment and then the crazies faded. If he wasn't interested then she certainly wasn't.

Her body sagged and she melted against his chest, grateful that tonight was not the night, no matter how much she wanted it to be. In a moment, she was asleep.

Chapter 34

They started walking as soon as dawn provided enough light to follow the path. The sun was still beneath the tree line when they reached the waterfall.

Phil took off her vest and set it on a dry rock. "After a night spent sweltering under a sheet of plastic, I've got to have a shower before we go another step."

She ducked under the gentler cascade at the edge of the river. The shock of the cool water took her breath. She stretched her hands up over her head and pressed her palms into the pulsing flow.

She vaguely sensed Rod's presence when he joined her. The caressing surge of the river held her attention. She slowly turned in a circle under the chilling downpour, wishing she could stay under the deluge. But there was her uncle to save.

Phil stepped out of the water and ran directly into Rod's chest. Water dripped from her eyelashes. His hair and clothes were plastered to his body. The look on his face told her that the time was now.

Shivers of excitement skittered across her skin under her wet clothes. Prickles of nervous anticipation sang in her veins. Suddenly there wasn't enough air.

His stare told her that she had to make the first move. His gaze never wavered from hers when she reached for the buttons of her blouse and peeled away the cloth. When her clothes were a sopping heap on a nearby rock, he looked down and made a lingering survey.

Her flesh tightened under his stare. The chocolate warmth of his eyes heated to black. The stern cast of his face was unrecognizable, a little scary.

She flinched when he yanked off his belt, tearing it from the loops. He threw his shirt onto the boulder by her hand, pointed at it, and reached for the front of his jeans.

It never crossed her mind not to obey his silent, terse command. Desperate for what he had to give, she turned and spread his shirt over the boulder's ash gray surface.

Her heart thumped and her breath stopped when the tingling touch of his fingers glided down her spine. His fingertips skimmed upward and under her arm to trace the underside of her breast. His fingers slid down her arm and encircled her wrist. He held her still, while his free hand explored. Her head fell forward, succumbing to the gush of unbearable sensations. She held out against the onslaught until her knees buckled. He grabbed her shoulders and tugged her around to face him.

The contained violence within his expression caused a fleeting moment of anxiety. The tender grip of his hands surrounding her waist washed away all hesitation.

He lifted her onto the boulder. The heat of the rock bled through the wet denim of his shirt and seared her bottom. She reached up and grasped a tree root that had worked its way through the rocks, knowing she was going to need an anchor. This was not going to be a sweetly pastoral encounter.

The waterfall thundered, pouring out a constant barrage of sound. Any attempt to speak would be drowned in the roar, but words weren't needed. She read what he was asking with his level stare, knew exactly what he wanted and how. The raw exposure of his hunger thrilled and terrified, but she was ready. More than ready. It seemed she'd been waiting forever. This was a fantasy come true. She wanted and needed it more than the next breath.

His guiding hands slid under her thighs, lifting and positioning. She released a sob of anticipation and was glad the coursing river covered the pleading sound. Waiting had pushed them too far, and she was too needy to smother the primal whine working its way up her throat. She wrapped her fingers around the root and pressed down the urgency to scream at him to hurry. She was already on the brink. She ground the tree bark into the tender center of her palm and waited.

He wasn't gentle when he entered. She was glad and surged into his thrust, shocked by the impact and the immediate clenching of her body. The instant release left her gasping and crying out with each luxuriant streak of sensation. Every ramming stroke sent her higher. The relief screaming along her nerve endings didn't stop until he did.

His arms supported her, wrapping her close when she sagged. His body shuddered against hers. The sounds of his completion came from his open mouth pressed high on her neck, under her ear.

She allowed her head to fall back and she looked up. An impossibly blue sky reigned above the vivid green of the treetops. Tears trickled from her eyes. She was too limp to wipe them away but not too spent to suffer embarrassment.

She struggled to sit upright on her own, praying that Rod wouldn't notice the wet streaming down her cheeks. She hoped it looked like condensation from the spray of the cascading river. Or perspiration. Anything but the blatant, humiliating excess of her release. The needy, dopey librarian finally gets laid.

His fingers raised her chin. The worry clouding his searching gaze surprised her. She was too fragile for truth at the moment. She smiled broadly to let him know that she was fine. More than fine.

When he leaned down to kiss her, she quickly looked away. Now that the initial lassitude had passed, she was horrified to feel her body greedily clamoring for another round. She was scarcely capable of handling the rubbery-legged aftermath of one miracle and couldn't imagine surviving another one so soon. And she absolutely had to put some space between them before her out of control body latched onto his and demanded more.

Next came the awkward business of getting dressed. Her clothes felt clammy but clean. She decided to carry her vest until the blouse dried, although getting it completely dry was impossible in the stifling humidity. She headed under the waterfall's natural bridge ahead of him, refusing to look back.

They hiked in silence under the falls and into the bush. Phil dreaded the near future, when the noise of the waterfall would fade. She didn't think he'd want to talk about what happened. Hoped he wouldn't. The handful of men she knew and dated didn't have a discussion gene between them. Avoidance of talking about any form of tender feelings seemed to be programmed directly into male DNA.

But she forgot about Rod's twisted sense of humor and weird sense of timing.

"Hey, doc, does the saying about going off like a firecracker ring any bells?"

She wouldn't punch him. She stomped onward without answering until he snagged her arm. She jerked free and kept walking with her head down to hide her flaming face.

Rod hustled ahead and stood in the trail in front of her to make her stop. She refused to look up. He stepped in her way again when she tried to continue. She stood still, smoldering, barely hanging onto her pride and temper.

His touch was cautious and gentle when he took her hand. "Phil, this is serious. We just did something really dumb. Well, maybe dumb isn't the right word, but it was reckless. Some meaningful dialogue is in order."

She unclenched her teeth. "I don't have any diseases."

"Babe, a disease wouldn't even consider coming within a block of you. I didn't mean that. There's that pesky little challenge of the timeless attraction of the sperm to the egg."

She hated being forced to admit what she had to tell him and dredged up her most evil glare. "I'm on the pill, so you're off the hook."

He grinned. She jerked her hand free and resumed the tramping down of all forms of vegetation in her path. Each footfall was a stomp placed on the smirking image of his conniving face.

She would eat bugs, listen to talk radio, AND swear off chocolate forever before she told him the real reason she used birth control. The truth was that she took the pills to lessen monthly discomfort and had taken them since she was fourteen. He was smart enough to leave her alone while she was riled up, but she could feel him thinking and watching her.

When they arrived at the clearing, there was no SUV.

Phil stomped to where she thought they had left the vehicle. Tire tracks showed where it had been parked. Disgusted, she kicked the toe of her boot at the dirt.

Rod said, "Mutt and Jeff must have found a way out of the maze. Don't worry about them, doc. Get the Feds on the horn and have them tell Binky where we are."

She made the call, connected with Bill, and snapped the phone shut. "He'll call us back with an ETA. The team has the cabin surrounded. There's a bomb expert with them."

"That means your uncle is safe. We can wrap this up today and make a stopover at Cancun before going home."

"But I'm not quitting just yet. I want Richardson to pay for what he did."

"Bill or whoever you're talking to will get him. That's their job. Your job is to save your uncle and take the vacation you're supposed to be enjoying right now."

The phone rang. "This is Phil."

"Dr. Hafeldt, we've run into a glitch."

Her heart sank. "Is he all right? The bomb didn't—"

"He's not at the cabin."

Phil tamped down her anger. Tears of frustration burned behind her eyes. She struggled to control a fresh wash of fear and outrage.

She was glad her voice sounded normal. "Then Richardson still has him."

"Do you have any idea where they might be?"

"He said Campeche, but I don't believe him."

"Give it some thought. I'll check it out on this end. Captain Binkerman should be at your LZ in a few minutes. Call if you come up with anything."

"Was there a bomb?"

"Yes. Rudimentary and easily disarmed."

She felt Rod's shared anger as he watched her put the phone away. His tone was sharp when he asked, "So what's going on?"

"Uncle Cal isn't at the cabin. They don't know where he is."

"Did Richardson give you any clue as to where he wants to meet to pick up the crystal?"

"He made some cryptic remark about me knowing where. I'm too angry to think."

"Then let's think backwards and walk through what might have happened. If I remember correctly, Richardson was pretty happy about the fact that Mom's plane has international credentials. That gives him leeway to go where he wants once he gets the crystal. He may be planning to use it to get out of the country, but he'll find out quick enough that Binky has the computer locked down. Binky's the only one, other than me, who knows the password. Even if Richardson has figured all this out, he's got to have some sort of backup plan."

Phil asked, "But what if he doesn't?"

"OK. That's a thought. Let's suppose he's improvising as he goes along, which is taking a chance. But doing it that way also makes it harder to catch him, since he's unpredictable."

"I know that Richardson can fly but I don't know if he's licensed for jets. He's a computer genius, capable of hacking into anything. Let's go back and rethink this again, starting in Colorado with the rented plane."

Phil stopped to sort through her thoughts. "Richardson drugs us and tells Binky you're his hostage. He uses your rented plane to fly wherever he's got Schulz standing by with your mom's hijacked plane and from there fly us all out of the country."

"That would explain how they got your cell phone."

"It could also mean that Uncle Cal was on the plane with us the whole time. He was never left behind at the cabin tied up to a bomb."

The pulsing sound of an approaching helicopter thumped in the distance. The distinctive sound made it easily identifiable as a Huey.

Rod looked toward the coast. "That'll be our ride. But where is Richardson now? He'll want someplace off the beaten path to meet."

A thought froze her in the act of lifting her hand to take off her hat. She yelled, "I know where he is! Richardson's taken Uncle Cal to the ruins! Signal Binky to land. We have to talk."

The helicopter noise intensified. Phil turned away as the turbulence blew across the clearing, kicking up whirling pieces of sticks and grass.

The rotor blades were still moving as Binky slipped off his headset and stepped down from the helicopter. He strolled across the grass to where they waited.

Rod called, "Where'd you find this worn-out crate?"

"Where there's drugs, there's transport. And I called in a few favors."

Rod stuck out his hand to shake Binky's and haul him close for a manly hug. Binky stepped back to look them over. He stood with his thumbs anchored in his jean pockets and his weight cocked to one side.

"You two look like you've just survived hell week."

In contrast, Binky wore well-washed jeans, a spotless white T-shirt, and an air of rested relaxation. Phil didn't need a mirror to know what she looked like. Her eyes would be sunken and dark-circled from sleep deprivation and stress. Her clothes were wrinkled and smelly, her fingernails ragged and rimed in dirt.

Rod looked worse. His smile was still killer—movie star in overdrive, but he looked rough. His laugh was still carefree. "Grandma Wakefield would say we looked like we were rode hard and put away wet."

Phil wiped at her clothes. "I'm heading for a spa when this is over. We expected you to arrive with an entourage. Where's the luxury cruiser and five star staff?"

"You mean the wanna-be bad boys? I left them on the beach."

She couldn't stop from asking, "Alive?"

Binky half-smiled. "Sort of. Where do we go from here?"

"I think Richardson is at Site Fifty-four."

"That must be the spot the Feds can't lock onto. There's some sort of magnetic disturbance that's screwing up the directionals."

"That doesn't surprise me," Phil said, "after what we found at the site. I'm pretty sure Richardson's taken Uncle Cal there. What he really wants is for me to lead him through the site."

Rod asked, "Then why didn't he just come with us?"

"He wanted a synthetic crystal first. The proverbial bird in the hand, but then I think he got greedy, knowing there must be more important finds inside."

Binky asked, "Like what?"

"Most likely one of the fabled Atlantean libraries. Their Hall of Records."

Binky put on a questioning scowl. Before he could say anything, Rod said, "No. There's no money in that. I think he's going for something bigger, like that ruby that's the size of a Volkswagen."

Phil rubbed her brow. "I agree that something like that would attract him, but there're other artifacts inside that site far more precious than the ruby. The travesty is what Richardson would do with the synthetic crystals, or even the big ruby, if he could bring the thing out. The possibilities make me sick. As you said, military applications."

Rod asked, "Is there a way to close up the place?"

"Uncle Cal might know how, but I can't go back inside there. My head still feels like I have mush for brains."

Binky crossed his arms. "Looks like we'll have to retrieve your uncle before doing anything else."

Famished, Phil despondently asked, "Do you have anything to eat?"

"Sure. How about coffee and a croissant?"

Phil didn't know what was watering more—her mouth or her eyes. She followed Binky to the helicopter, drooling like a besotted junkie. She hovered and danced with impatient excitement while he reached into the cargo bay for a wicker basket.

Rod laughed when he saw an assortment of chocolates wrapped in gold foil. He slapped Phil's wrist when she lunged for her favorite. "Not until you've had your breakfast!"

"Nazi."

"I heard that, doc."

They sat with their legs hanging out of the cargo bay. After chugging bottled water, Phil made eager noises as Rod unloaded the goodies. She reverently hunched over an empty cup and groaned with anticipation when Binky poured steaming coffee from a thermos. She sipped and sighed. The rich, gritty taste of caffeine coated her tongue and the roof of her mouth. Relief.

After two more sips, just to assure herself that this was real and she wasn't dreaming, she stared into the basket. She tenderly selected and lifted a flaky croissant to her mouth. The fact that her hands were grimy never caused a twinge or a moment's hesitation. She sank her teeth through the delicate crust and filled her mouth with the buttery flavor.

"Oh, my stars," she whispered, near tears, "I think I'm coming."

The men, distinctly uncomfortable, glanced away. She chortled and munched with grateful relish. She thought it hilarious that tough guys could be made uncomfortable so easily. She would have to remember that guys didn't mind talk involving crude body functions, but anything resembling a feminine sexual response must not be verbalized. They'd preen, if they were successful lovers, but Lord above, let's not go into verbal detail about it!

Two cups of coffee, three croissants, and four squares of milk chocolate later, Phil judged herself fit and girded for war. She wiped her mouth with the back of her wrist and jumped down to the ground to collect her backpack. Rod and Binky looked at her—both squinting to block the tropical sun.

Phil raised a hand to her brow to block the sunlight and looked up. "Come on, boys. Let's get the pit stop out of the way. It's time to kill them dead."

Rod frowned at Binky. "You think she means it?"

Binky lifted mirrored sunglasses from where he'd hung them on his T-shirt collar and slid them on. Phil looked at her distorted image while the Binkster made a decision.

"Nah. She might want us to hold them down while she gets in her licks, but she's not a killer."

Rod tossed away the dregs in his cup. "Don't be too sure. Her field may be nineteenth-century-literary romance, but she's not romantic. I'm staying out of her way on this one. And I suggest you leave the guy with the tattoos for her."

As they buckled themselves in for the ride to the site, Phil reached under her vest. She touched her shirt pocket, checking that she had the last two squares of chocolate snugly wrapped in a paper napkin. She savored a brief fantasy of licking melted richness from the foil. She squelched the fantasy when it evolved to licking smeared chocolate off Rod.

Binky said, "I kinda wanted the one with the tattoos. He has a Screaming Eagle on his forearm. I'd bet my left nut that he's never jumped from a plane in his life. He had the pukes all the way to Mexico."

The Huey coughed to life. The rotors began to turn, and Phil quickly said before it wound up to its deafening roar, "Head northwest. What's a Screaming Eagle?"

Binky leaned toward her to shout his reply. "Hundred and First Airbourne."

"Tough luck. He's mine," Phil hollered back. "You can have what's left."

Binky's grin was feral and frightening. She envied that smile and tried to copy it. "Take me to their leader, Captain Binkerman."

"Aye-aye, ma'am. Roddie, are you buckled in?"

"Shut up. And stop smiling at my woman!" Rod hollered from the back.

Phil laughed. The Huey, revving up to take off, smothered Phil's denunciation of being objectified as anybody's woman. The helicopter lifted, pivoted midair, and dipped forward slightly as they flew out of the clearing.

The forest canopy sprawled underneath the bulbous helicopter nose of thick, tempered glass. A verdant field of waving green heads sailed by and underneath the chopper as Binky skimmed above the forest. Phil pointed at the waterfall coming up fast.

Binky nodded and headed slightly north to avoid the updraft. In minutes, the open expanse of the plaza came into view.

Chapter 35

Binky circled the plaza perimeter until Phil tapped his shoulder. She pointed to the highest pyramid. They swooped over its peak and saw a square, black hole in the plaza floor.

The helicopter's nose lifted into an abrupt climb. Phil twisted sideways in the seat. She searched out the window but couldn't find the reason why he changed course so abruptly.

Binky circled, took them to the far edge of the ruins, and turned the chopper to face the pyramid. Hovering caused an increase in the vibrations, distorting the view.

Phil inhaled a gasp. In the distance through the swirling dust, she made out her uncle. He straddled a plank, tied and taped to the wood with his legs dangling over the sides. The broad plank spanned the sacrificial pit in the plaza floor.

A memory flashed of standing beside the square hole when she was twelve, throwing pebbles into the darkness below, and the unexpected grip of her uncle's hand dragging her away from the eroding edge. His fear for her had left bruises on her arm. The scare hadn't stopped her from entering the maze and breaking her uncle's strict rule of never exploring alone.

Rod unbuckled his belt and left his seat to come forward. He squeezed her shoulder as he leaned over to look out. He grabbed an overhead strap when Binky set down the helicopter. Phil stared at her uncle through the safety glass, knowing this was a trap. She waited for the Huey to wind down.

When the noise subsided, Binky asked, "Is that a well or an old excavation site they have him suspended over?"

Phil unbuckled her seatbelt. "It's called the Well of the Eater of Souls. It's why some of the guides are nervous about coming here. Enemies and refuse were thrown into it."

Phil stood beside the helicopter and stared at her uncle. She tried to think through her fear for him and waited for the rotors to stop moving. Worry for her uncle overwhelmed the need to concentrate and the noise aggravated her ability to focus. There was no doubt in her mind that this was a trap.

She took off her vest, checked the pocket fasteners, and tossed it into the helicopter. "Do either of you have guns?"

Rod jumped down from the cargo bay. "Neither of us carry. The object is to get the weapon from the other guy."

Phil's heart sank and then surged with frustrated anger. "Dang it, you guys! This is serious. I don't need a display of male posturing right now or some kind of stupid pissing contest. That's my uncle out there, and you're telling me that the bad guys have all the guns and we don't!"

Rod sent Binky a what's-a-man-going-to-do-with-her look and shook his head. "I told you she had a temper."

Binky unwisely tried logic. "Excuse me, ma'am, but I would like to suggest a moment to cool off. It sounds like you might have a smidgen of transference tucked into that accusation."

Phil never responded well to any kind of male condescension. Screw them and her disposition. This situation called for a serious attitude. She rewarded them with a glare of disgust and headed for her uncle.

Rod yanked her back. She broke the hold, and he grabbed her other arm, this time wrapping her in a rough embrace and lifting her off her feet. He held her imprisoned against his chest.

"Phil, you can't go out there angry."

Tears began to spill down her cheeks. That made her angrier. "Let me go. I don't want to hurt you."

"I know, baby. Just calm down. Let's think this through."

Phil glared at him. After a minute, she nodded, and he set her down. She almost kicked him for being right but was stopped by the fact that she'd probably need all the help she could find to get Uncle Cal out of this predicament.

She inhaled a calming breath. "Very well, we know this is a trap. Binky, your education at Coronado involved making you into a glorified trap setter and springer. Am I right in supposing that the first objective is to get the bad guys to show themselves or their position?"

"No." When she glared at Rod for spouting an answer she didn't like, he said, "Tell her, Binky."

Binky had been surveying the ruins. He stayed focused on that task, taking too much time, in Phil's opinion. When he finished his survey, he said, "Highest priority is the safety of the people involved. Hostages come first and then the team."

Surly and impatient, Phil said, "I would've thought success was the primary objective."

That made Binky smile. "Success is never in question. That's a given. This looks doable. Dr. Hafeldt, get your uncle's attention. Let him know we've got everything under control."

Phil waved at her uncle and signaled that they were going to help him. "How do we get him off that plank? He's taped up like a mummy."

Binky squinted. "And he's got something strapped to his chest. Maybe a bomb set to go off if it's removed. Roddie, take a look. Your eyes are better than mine at a distance."

A moment later, Rod said, "Simple C-four set-up."

Binky pursed his lips. "Motion or removal?"

Rod shook his head. "Can't tell from here. We'll have to get closer, but I'm going to bet it goes off if removed. If they wired it for motion, it wouldn't take much to set it off. All he'd have to do is cough or sneeze and they'd lose their bait, so let's go with removal. It's the size of the charge that's got me worried. They've got enough there to blow up half of the plaza."

Binky agreed with a nod. He reached into the cargo bay and lifted a harness from the wall. He tossed it to Rod, who slipped it on.

"OK, doc, we got the bomb challenge covered. Let's say this is your show. What's next?"

Phil scanned the plaza to hide her relief. "Keep it simple. We draw them out, make them suffer, and take Uncle Cal home."

Rod said, "Sounds good. There are two hiding in the brush growing on the pyramid. They're both carrying standard issue. One is so nervous I can see the leaves shaking from here. What do you think of the plan, Bink?"

"Three simple components, get in, get them, get out. That always works." Binky asked, "And the third man?"

"That would be Richardson," Phil said. "I would expect that he's at the site. He thinks I've left something there for him." Phil handed her uncle's hat to Binky. "Take care of that for me. And keep an eye on my vest."

"Yes, ma'am," Binky murmured. His half-smile told her that he liked her spunk.

Phil nodded that she was ready to go and started across the plaza, Rod following, snapping the chest harness in place. Relentless heat compressed the air. A thin layer of withered ground cover crunched under their boots. Seared weeds struggled to grow between the pavement cracks. The scraggly growths swished and crackled as they walked.

Phil pretended to keep her attention entirely on her uncle, but she was peripherally scanning the area. Reed and Schulz were probably the two men hiding at the base of the pyramid, but that didn't mean that there weren't more elsewhere.

As they neared, she made out Uncle Cal's face. He was gaunt and dark from waiting under the merciless sun without a hat. His face, leathered from years in the sun, was beyond sunburn, but the constant pressure of the relentless rays could sap anyone's strength. She wished that she had remembered to bring water.

Rod spoke under his breath as they neared the edge of the hole. "Doc, when this goes down, it's going to happen fast. If I'm not close enough to do it, latch this big clip to the cable when the time comes."

"What cable?"

"You'll know it when you see it."

She dropped her chin slightly to let him know that she understood and pretending a lightheartedness she certainly didn't feel, called to her uncle. "In a bit of a pickle, are we? Where's your buddy, Richardson?"

He returned a crooked, weary smile. "Over at Fifty-four. He said you left him the key."

"He's in for a surprise. Will that bomb go off if we try to move you?"

"He said it's rigged to blow if we try to remove it. He's also got a device to detonate it by remote."

Rod bowed his head to whisper. "Where are the watchdogs?"

Uncle Cal replied, "Hiding on the pyramid behind me."

"How many?"

"Just two. The others ran off when they heard where we were going."

Rod said, "That's what we figured. I'm going to shimmy out to you. I'll see if I can disarm it."

Uncle Cal said, "Don't bother. It's rigged to go off that way, too. And so is the tape stuck to the board. I don't know if the ropes have anything to do with it."

Rod hunkered down and straddled the broad plank. "I can't believe that they're that smart. I'll just take a closer look before we get you out of here."

Phil curled her fingers into fists to stop herself from hauling Rod back. She knew nothing about explosives. She figured that Rod must know something, being trained by a Navy Underwater Demolition Team alumnus.

Rod began to inch across the stout plank to the center. The wood squeaked with each movement, protesting the additional stress. Dirt fell from the soles of his dangling boots. His focus never wavered from his goal.

Phil looked down into the black pit. Something glinted, a brief flicker of light and movement. Apprehension crawled across her skin.

"Rod, something is moving down there."

He never looked down. His attention stayed fixed on his objective. When he got to the center, Rod unfastened and took off the bulky harness taken from the helicopter. He checked over the apparatus strapped to her uncle's chest before carefully helping her uncle to slide his arms into the harness.

Phil looked up, distracted by furtive movement. The brush sprouting from the pyramid rustled. Schulz and Reed came out, both carrying pistols.

To draw attention from her uncle and Rod, Phil walked around to the opposite side of the pit. The Huey started up on the far side of the plaza.

Rod was backing off the plank as she reached the other side of the hole. He joined her by the time Schulz and Reed stopped near the edge of the pit.

Schulz's attempt to sneer was arrested by the abraded wound on the left side of his face. The skin of his cheekbone and jaw had been sheared off, exposing drying meat, a dangerous injury and a foolish one to leave uncovered in the tropics. She knew the exact spot in the maze where it happened. Payment for taking the wrong way out of the maze. She doubted that they knew how lucky they were to have survived that particular trap.

Phil held her position, shielding her uncle and hoping Rod would back off. "I see you found the sliding stones."

Schulz jerked up the muzzle of his gun and pointed it at her head. "I've used up all my patience on you, girlie. Where's the crystal?"

"With Richardson, who's double-crossed you, by the way."

She watched the wheels turn in Schulz's mind. "What's with the helicopter?"

Rod answered, "Our ride. Where's yours?"

"Since you've provided it, your chopper. Consider it confiscated. But before I go, I still get to choose which of you to shoot first."

Phil masked the chilling fear that seized and twisted her heart. A rush of protective need made her blurt, "That would be a dilemma for a brain your size, so let me explain. If you shoot me, Rod will get you. Shoot him, and I get you."

In the seconds it took for Schulz to play with a decision, Phil raced through the possibilities and rendered it down to two, simple choices—save Rod or her uncle.

The thumping reverberations of the approaching chopper was a constant distraction. In the end, fear or love didn't help her make the decision. The irascible temper she'd always had a hard time controlling did it for her. She gritted her teeth. She wasn't going to lose either of them to this snake.

Schulz misunderstood her glare and grinned but the expression on his battered face registered hatred. "Reed, plug the writer when I do the old man."

Schulz had to repeat what he said at a shout to be heard over the approaching helicopter.

The wind rush from the chopper tugged at her balance. The heavy cable hanging from the cargo bay came sweeping at them. The metal clip on its business end was easy to see, seize, and attach to the harness.

Schulz and Reed looked up at the hovering behemoth and swinging cable. Reed raised his pistol at the helicopter's belly, his fear and indecision making him dimmer than usual. He was about to shoot at the Huey without considering that the monster might crash down on their heads. There was also the danger of a contact spark igniting the fuel tank.

It was time for a distraction, an unbalancing act. Phil grabbed for her shirt buttons and started to disrobe. Schulz's stunned expression moved from confusion to wary surprise.

Reed began to fidget in despairing indecision. Rod yelled something that was swallowed up by the tremendous noise of the helicopter. Her open shirt flapped in the breeze.

Schulz's attention shifted back and forth between the helicopter, Rod, and then settled on her fingers reaching for the front clasp of her bra. Rod lunged and Schulz jerked the pistol in his direction.

Phil sprang forward and kicked the gun from Schulz's grasp. The pistol discharged upward. The metallic clank of the round slamming into the Huey was muffled by rotor and engine noise.

Reed stood rudderless, not knowing what to do. He gaped at his fearless leader pinned to the ground by Rod. Phil was moving to disarm or distract him, when in desperation, Reed used his pistol butt to clip Rod on the head.

Freed, Schulz sprang at Phil. She stepped back slightly and used his momentum to fling him at the hole. Schulz landed on the edge and grappled for a handhold, as Rod staggered upright. The thin line of blood that trickled from his scalp, instead of the bleeding gush of most head injuries, reassured her that his wound was slight.

"Save Uncle Cal!" Phil screamed above the chopper noise and turned on Reed, who glanced at her face and froze. Every protective hackle on her body was up and eager to retaliate. Reed's bumbling ineptitude was almost endearing, but he made Rod bleed. Nobody hurt the ones she loved and got away with it.

Rod snagged Schulz's pistol from the ground and tossed it into the hole. He leaped for the cable and used it to swing closer to Uncle Cal. He landed on the plank and snapped the clip to the harness. Standing with his feet braced on either side of her uncle, Rod grasped the cable in both hands. His weight balanced the plank and kept it from tipping.

Seeing that Rod and her uncle were good to go, Phil advanced on Reed. The Weasel tossed down his gun and backed away, his hands up in surrender.

Phil looked up. Binky stared down at her through the rounded glass nose. She waved him off and the helicopter lifted and moved slowly across the plaza, carrying away Rod, the plank, her Uncle Cal, and the bomb.

The look Rod shared with her was unbroken until she peripherally noticed Schulz crawling away from the edge of the pit.

She fastened her shirt and glanced over her shoulder to see what Reed was doing and scan for his discarded gun. That was when she heard a familiar scratching noise. She looked at the hole, where Schulz was getting to his feet.

Tarantulas swarmed up and out of the pit. The wave of frenzied creatures scurried by Reed, who shrieked and ran, dancing in horror to avoid the unavoidable. Confused tarantulas ran up his legs and leaped off his shoulders to rejoin the fleeing migration flowing from the hole. He batted at the riders clinging to his shirt and pants. Blinded by his terror, Reed joined the frantic swarm hurrying to reach the shelter of the trees.

Phil stood rooted in place as the deluge surged around her boots. She jammed her fingers into her shirt pocket and searched for the chocolate made squishy from her body heat.

The last of the tarantulas scampered by. The horde had fanned out over the plaza and disappeared, going over the wall, through the wall gates, and into the forest.

Schulz rushed at her, this time expecting her to step out of the way. Instead of racing full tilt, he was holding some in reserve. The slight hesitation in his attack warned her of his intent to tackle her. She was ready and stepped across his path at the last second.

With her hands smeared with melted milk chocolate, Phil grasped the back of his shirt and the nearest arm. She used his momentum to swing his body around and fling him back at the hole. Her throw fell short and he landed, sprawled on his stomach, at the edge.

Schulz glared at her from the ground, eager for another chance at slaughter. He pulled a knife from a leg holster. He stood the same time that a partially dismembered spider leg appeared over the edge of the pit.

The second leg and then the others joined the wounded member, anchoring its massive hairy body by spanning the hole. The back legs settled on the rim of the opposite side, tilting the main body slightly back and lower, poised to leap.

Phil staggered back at the grizzly sight of the utterly still spider . Schulz didn't look behind him. His skeptical expression showed that he thought her sudden shift of attention and the fear on her face was a ruse.

The spider's mandibles moved in a grinding motion, the sound of its jaws muted by the distant reverberations of the Huey. The helicopter noise ended.

The clacking crunch of the spider's jaws echoed in the sudden void of helicopter racket. A whirring growl joined noise from the grinding teeth. Phil recognized the threatening sounds from previous encounters, but this time daylight exposed an additional warning.

The darkness of the maze had spared them from seeing the white substance beginning to ooze and drip from the spider's back end—preparation for the cocoon. The rear legs twitched, limbering up to bind the prey. The main body pressed down and lower, preparing to spring.

Phil couldn't pull her attention from the spider. Horror numbed her brain and paralyzed her instinctive need for fight-or-flight. She wanted to leap for Reed's dropped weapon even as a distant corner of her brain registered that the pistol would be useless. Her hand wasn't steady enough to aim at its eyes or shatter the white protrusions between the jaws.

The silence following the cessation of helicopter noise seemed unbearably loud. The spider's clicking mandibles captured Schulz's attention. He made the mistake of moving and jerked around. The spider pounced.

Chapter 36

On the other side of the plaza, Rod jumped off the plank the instant the wood connected with the dusty paving stones. He released the clip to the cable and gestured for Binky to move away. When the whirling debris from the helicopter settled, Rod unbuckled the harness.

"Dr. Hafeldt, are you all right?"

"Could use some water."

"Let's get this bomb defused first. Did you watch them put it together?"

"No. Schulz just came in and strapped it on me. I overheard them talking about how to set it off. Mike has the detonator."

"Did you get a look at it?"

"No. Where's Phil?"

"She's taking care of Schulz and Reed."

"I wish you would've made her come with us."

Rod snorted. "Me and what army? Lift your right arm."

"She doesn't like spiders. A sea of them just crossed over the other side of the plaza." He watched a few strays scuttle by them, heading for the cover of a nearby building. "Wonder where they came from."

"I'm guessing from that pit on the other side of the big pyramid." Rod began to curse under his breath.

"What is it? Is there something I can do?"

"Bomb wires are usually different colored. Schulz has used wires that are all the same color. This is going to be tricky."

"I'm sure you'll figure it out."

Rod glanced at Uncle Cal. "You don't look worried about the fact that we could be in pieces any second now."

"I have complete confidence in you, Rod. Your mother assured me that you were marvelously resourceful."

"Let's hope her confidence isn't misplaced. Up with the left arm."

"Oh, I doubt very much that you could be anything less than brilliant with parents like yours. She said you were perfect for Phil. Ah, here comes your pilot."

Distracted, Rod hesitated for a second before resuming his study of the bomb. "What did you just say? That comment about me and Phil being perfect."

"Your mother and I had a nice chat about you and Phil being perfect for each other years ago. I wasn't at all surprised to hear from you. I supposed your mother thought it was time to get you two together. Although, when Phil said that you were supposed to be my bodyguard, I was a bit taken aback, but then, I shouldn't be that surprised. A thriller writer could come up with all sorts of interesting stories at the drop of a hat. But I am curious. Why a bodyguard?"

"To impress Phil. Anything to convince her to let me hang around. Dr. Hafeldt, tell me that you're joking. Tell me that my mother and you didn't get your heads together and arrange for Phil and me to meet. No, don't bother. I already know. Doing something like that is so my mother. I'm dead anyway. If this bomb doesn't kill us, your niece will."

"She's mostly talk, you know."

"I'm afraid that I'll have to disagree with you about that."

"You know, Rod, I've been worried about Philadelphia's solitary life for a long time. She wrote so often of how disappointed she is with the men she dates. A few have used her to get to me. The rest are either afraid of her intelligence or intimidated by her confidence."

"Those are the things I like best about her." The memory of Phil's joyous sensuality flashed behind his eyes. "Well, there are a few other reasons."

"After meeting your parents, I was sure the two of you would hit it off."

"Since it looks like I'm going to die either way, let's drop that subject and concentrate on this loaded-up puppy you're carrying. Did you hear them mention anything about a delay?"

"Fifteen seconds, I think."

Binky strolled up and squatted beside them. "Hello, Dr. Hafeldt. What's a nice cultural anthropologist like you doing rigged to a candy-assed bomb like this? I'm Binky, Rod's glorified errand boy. I'd shake your hand, but it might set you off."

Uncle Cal smiled cheerily, as if he didn't have a brick of C-four strapped to his chest. "A pleasure to meet you. Thank you for the rescue. Candy-assed? Rod intimated that the charge was not insignificant. Perhaps I misunderstood. Rod, did I misunderstand you?"

"You're a big help, Bink. Actually, Dr. Hafeldt, this is enough to take down a building. The scary part is what Schulz doesn't know."

Binky glanced over the bomb arrangement. "You're wrapped up like a mummy, sir."

Flipping open his knife, Rod started to work on the tape and ropes. "There may be a delay, but I can't see Schulz being smart enough to rig that."

"The safest bet with that thing is to do what you're doing. Cut off the duct tape and then remove shirt and bomb together. Fast. Follow with running like hell for cover. With the wires all the same color, there's no way to know which one is to the detonator."

"Sheesh, tell me something new, Binky. We've got fifteen seconds after it comes off and the hope that Richardson isn't in range. There's a chance he can detonate it whenever he wants."

Uncle Cal said, "I suppose it depends on the device's range. He's over at the maze. Is that close enough?"

Rod started cutting the shirt. "Plenty close. But I'm banking on whatever is inside the maze will block the signal. Get ready to run."

Uncle Cal tested his legs. Knee cartilage snapped and popped. "Perhaps the two of you should take refuge in that building over there. The entrance is on the eastern side. This thing could go off any second."

Rod stilled and sharply asked, "Did you just hear a click?"

Chapter 37

Phil was knocked off her feet when the bomb exploded. The blast shook the ground, lifting the fine layer of dust on the plaza floor.

The spider ducked into the pit. Phil's last glimpse of the creature included the ends of Schulz's legs sticking out of its mouth.

A second explosion erupted moments after the first. Black-rimmed clouds of red-orange flames billowed upward from behind the pyramid—the helicopter's fuel igniting.

Phil leaped up and ran toward the blast site, her mouth open in a silent scream of denial. Terror and disbelief followed her flight, escalating her anguish. She'd been so sure that Rod could defuse the bomb.

The helicopter explosion ignited the withered weeds and dust. Exposure to time and sun pulverized the plaza's seared brush into a combustible powder. A wall of flames raced across the pavement, heading directly at her.

Phil veered for the shelter of the vegetation growing on the great pyramid's exterior. She leaped between the slender trees, crouched under the brush, and covered her head.

The fire whooshed by both sides of the pyramid. The lush greenery sprouting from the gaps in the stones resisted the scorching heat. The part of the pyramid not facing the fire was left untouched, still luxuriant and green, with only the edges scorched.

Phil crawled through the brush growing on the perimeter. Between a break in the vegetation she saw residual smoke issuing up from the plaza floor. The ferocity of the fire had burnt off the powdered tinder, leaving a field of charred pavement in its wake.

She dashed out of the protection of the unscathed side of the pyramid, covering her mouth and nose with a sleeve as she ran. Ashes and smoldering cinders gusted up. Heat saturated the thick soles of her boots and prickled against the flat of her feet.

She stopped when she rounded the corner of the pyramid and saw the torched remains of the Huey. Everything in sight, from the city walls to the central pyramid was scorched. The rapid-to-burn and quick-to-die inferno had singed the plant life from the smaller mounds and buildings. The shriveled, blackened spikes looked like twisted candles on grotesque birthday cakes. Mocking and terrifying.

She made a frantic, visual search for bodies. Her heart held onto to hope. She ran toward the steaming helicopter. Ashes swirled. Tears burned on her cheeks. The streaks tingled where wet paths scored her skin. There was no sign of anything that resembled the terrible images in her head—pictures and news reports of what burned bodies looked like.

She coughed and started to call their names. There was always a chance. Perhaps they made it to the trees on the other side of the city wall.

A noise, the clatter of rock hitting rock, came from a blackened ruin on her left. She ran to the sound. The noise came again and she stopped, trying to get a fix on the direction. Then came the muffled sound of her name.

Phil turned around, shrieked a shout of joy, and rushed at the nearest ruin, an elongated building near one of the smaller pyramids.

Stones had collapsed over the building's entrance, an avalanche of fresh-looking masonry. She began to tug and throw the stones she could lift, casting them out of the way without thought.

Voices grew louder on the other side of the cave in. She ignored her abraded palms and torn fingernails and kept clearing away the rubble. Coughing and renewed shouting on the other side of the stones brought a fresh surge of strength.

She staggered back when the larger blocks overhead creaked and tumbled. A second avalanche produced a hole under the roof. Masonry and rubble clattered down from the opening. Hands appeared, shoving rocks out of the way.

Phil sank down onto a fallen stele where she watched them widen the opening. Binky's face appeared first. Then Rod and Uncle Cal. When they were able to crawl through the hole, Phil could only sit and watch. Her throat was parched. It hurt to swallow. She was too dry for happy tears and unable to hold back the grateful weeping sounds.

Rod knelt beside her. "You OK, doc?"

She couldn't smile. She croaked, "You're covered in dust."

His boyish grin broke her heart. "Babe, you should see your face. It's coated in soot and you sound like a frog."

Her uncle stretched out his hand. She gripped it and tugged him to sit beside her on the stele. "Uncle Cal. Thought I'd lost you."

"Not when you're around. And your reinforcements."

She looked up at Binky, the only one standing. "Thanks."

"My pleasure, ma'am. This was fun. Call me anytime."

She reached for the cell phone and then realized she wasn't wearing the vest. "Speaking of calling. My vest was on the Huey." She looked at her uncle. "The phone and crystals were in it. Where's your shirt?"

Rod squeezed her hand. "Taking off the shirt was the fastest way to get rid of the bomb. Your uncle insisted that we hide while he removed it. Then he ran for cover."

She felt a fresh batch of tears well up. "Oh, Uncle Cal!"

He patted her hand. "It was the best way."

She nodded. "But now what do we do to get out of here? We're out of water and our transport is incinerated."

Rod glanced up at Binky, who turned, scaled the rubble, and crawled inside the hole. He reappeared, carrying her vest and Uncle Cal's hat.

Phil started to laugh. She withdrew the phone from the vest pocket, punched in the numbers, and handed it to Binky.

"Mind arranging for a ride?" she asked, hoping her grin was still spunky.

He walked away with the phone to his ear. Phil kept her hand in Rod's and rested her head on her uncle's shoulder.

She watched Binky stroll through the entrance to the plaza and enter the shade of the jungle. "Will one of you tell me what actually happened?"

Rod said, "Richardson detonated the bomb, but we were already running for cover."

Phil glanced away. Anger tightened her lips. "I guess I should have expected it. I have a terrible need to give that guy a smack. It's too much for me to believe that anyone could kill merely for a chance at fame. Or money. Our justice system will almost certainly let him get away with this, so I'd better get my licks in while I can."

Uncle Cal slid his arm around her shoulder. "Have I done anything to help mold you into the cynic you are today?"

She sighed. "No, that's something I accomplished all by myself."

"Here comes Binky," Rod said. "He's carrying something."

When Binky got close enough, she asked, "Been gardening?"

Binky handed her a spongy root. "Chew on this. Transport will be here in thirty minutes."

As roots go, and she hadn't sampled many, this one tasted tangy. The bittersweet flavor stung, but the wet in her sticky mouth and parched throat was heavenly. "Can I eat this thing?"

Binky said, "If you're that hungry, go for it. Hey, Roddie, isn't there another man out there?"

Rod started to peel the handful of roots Binky had brought back. Skinned, the root looked like a bleached carrot. "There's two. Reed is probably half way to Cuba by now, but he's harmless. Richardson's the detonator. He's the only one still out there that we know of. Any sign of a guy who looks like Mr. Honeydew?"

"Nope. He has to be outside of the ruins. I thought I saw something moving east of the clearing before we landed."

Rod passed a denuded root to Uncle Cal. "Chew on this. It'll hold you until our ride gets here."

Phil swallowed a bit of the stringy pulp and decided not to do that again. "If Richardson's anywhere, he'll be off that way. There's a stele not far from the eastern perimeter. You might find him there."

Binky took off at a jog. Phil watched him go, chewing the juice from the root. She wondered if she would have the good fortune to be able to trot off like that when she was on the downhill side of forty. But that was then and this was now, and there were some dangling threads that needed snipping off.

She flipped what was left of the masticated root over her shoulder, preferring to wait for water. "Uncle Cal, I'm curious as to what you meant when you said that you were glad that Rod turned out perfect."

"Well, Rod and I had a nice chat about you while he was taking off the bomb."

Out of the corner of her eye, she saw Rod freeze. This wasn't going to be good. Her uncle, who was a great deal like her father in many ways and was oblivious to a tempest gathering power.

Phil reined in her flying emotions. It could be that Rod wasn't the sort of lying toad that would use her to get to her uncle. Pigs could fly, too.

She refused to think about how often she'd been used in the past to get to her uncle. Because of her knack for hitching up with self-involved men, she would have to let this story play itself out. It would be too humiliating if all Rod wanted from her was an in with her uncle and perhaps then felt obligated to throw in a little sex out of pity.

Oh, please, no. Not pity sex. What could be worse?

Uncle Cal held a root close to the end of his nose so he could see it to peel. Myopic to the end, he rattled on happily, breaking off little bits of Phil's heart as he unwittingly exposed the pathetic state of her nonexistent social life.

"You know how worried your father and I have been about you. He called—oh, it must have been a few years ago by now—and asked if you had told me anything about your personal life, if you were dating anyone. That sort of thing.

"I told him that you'd stopped dating after that episode with Terrance Granger. And there was the unfortunate affair with Jeffrey Ferrall prior to that. Your father hadn't heard about Jeffrey, and I had to explain how he'd spent months winning you over just for a chance to look at my Amazon field notes. What some people will do to get an idea for a story. This whole thing about 'publish or perish' has gone too far."

Phil knew her uncle well enough to recognize that he'd lost his train of thought and was about to start a rant about the dismal condition of the institutions of higher education. With her uncle, there didn't have to be a connection between the two. Her father was the same way.

"Uncle Cal, if you please, get back on task."

"Oh, yes, the users and your love life. Or lack of it. As I was saying, your father and I were concerned, and he asked me to do something. That was right about the time when he was settling in to tackle a new project. He knew his head would be buried for some time.

"So, when I was in D.C. to wrap up that donation to the Smithsonian, I went to a party and met Rod's mother. Extraordinary woman! We got to talking. She about her son and I boasted endlessly about you. Of course, she was worried about her son for the opposite reason. Rod was playing the field a bit too indiscriminately for her tastes, and she was ready for more grandchildren to spoil. It sort of came to us out of the blue. The more we talked the more we agreed that you and Rod were made for each other."

"Excuse me, Uncle Cal. Clarification on two points. You pretended not to know who Rod was at the cabin. And what makes you think we're such a great match?"

"Phil, you categorize men as if you were sorting through a pile of rotten tomatoes, pitching out anything that's slightly bruised and squashing the rotten ones. Your problem is that you tend to fall for the rotten ones before you squash them."

Phil glared at Rod. "I'm not going to argue with you about that. So you and Rod's mother arranged for us to meet?"

"Actually, she did the arranging."

Rod sounded relieved when he announced, "Here comes Binky with Professor Honeydew."

Chapter 38

The sight of Michael Richardson erased all thoughts of her uncle's matchmaking. Phil relished the feeling of dangerous intent narrowing her glare into a squint. An evil smile curved her lips as she wondered if the spider would have room for dessert.

She began to consider the opportunities the upcoming situation offered. For a girl who'd been forced to revisit the most terrifying experience of her childhood, and endure three encounters with the Spider From Hell, the retributive possibilities seemed endless.

Binky carried a duffel bag and Richardson's weapon in his left hand. He herded his prisoner toward them with blunt shoves into the center of Richardson's back. Binky's cocky smirk showed how much he delighted in the taunting of his arrogant captive with each jarring push he administered.

Richardson had not entirely escaped the flash fire. Scorch holes pocked his clothes where sparks had landed. It was hard to take Richardson's outrage over the rough treatment seriously while the hair on his head was still smoldering.

Binky gave his prisoner a final shove. Richardson stumbled to a halt in front of them. He grasped the hem of his jacket for an authoritative tug into place and lifted his chin. Tendrils of smoke continued to waft from his frizzled bean.

Binky opened the duffel bag and withdrew a bottle of water. He tossed it to Phil, who snapped it open and chugged. She handed off the remainder without looking to see who took the bottle. Her attention remained fixed on Richardson.

With his nose in the air and his round face covered in soot, Richardson flipped a hand at Binky. "I insist you call off this troglodyte."

Phil stared, debating if she should let Binky squash the pompous twit into a pile of not-so-pretentious mush.

But Binky wasn't insulted. He dulled the sly gleam that usually lit his eyes and contorted his face into dim-witted confusion.

Hands on his hips, Binky struck an adversarial pose and topped it off with an absurd pout. "You hurt my heli-cawter, mister! That not nice. Binky had feelings for Huey."

Richardson looked horrified.

Binky stepped into Richardson's space, a blatant threat. He towered over his cringing captive and flexed a few muscles for fun and effect.

"Binky no like you. Me think maybe you look better without arms."

Richardson left horror behind and went straight for babbling, terrorized idiot. Phil decided that playtime was over. She was ready for the real stuff.

"Enough of the Mongo routine, Binky. Before the Feds get here to take this creep away, I want my piece. Everybody turn around. I'm going to do this the old-fashioned way."

Mike Richardson relaxed when the men obeyed. His benign smile, one of renewed smugness and superiority, was his undoing.

Phil already had her target in mind, having spent considerable time going over this moment of payback. She cocked her arm, gathered strength from every fiber of her being, and plowed her fist into his left eye. She had the sublime satisfaction of watching him land on his rump on the unforgiving plaza stones. A cloud of ash billowed.

The guys, who were *guys* after all, cheated and had turned around to watch. Ruddy color surrounded Richardson's eye that was rapidly swelling shut. She turned away, feeling for the first time that the ordeal was finally over.

Phil wrapped her arms around her uncle's waist, squeezing him close. He was safe. Not even a bone broken.

His hand smoothed the wild strands of her hair. "Poor girl. You've had a time of it."

"I'm fine. Just ready for a bath. How long before we're picked up?"

Binky lifted his head. The only sound in the plaza was Richardson coughing and Binky's murmur.

"Incoming."

Two dark specs in the sky turned into helicopters, sleeker, newer models than the old, reliable Huey. Phil hid her face from the whirling ashes until the Black Hawks landed and the debris settled.

Bill stepped down from the lead chopper. Mirrored sunglasses went well with his basic military camouflage unit and glossy boots look. A team of humorless drones jumped down from the second chopper and fell into formation behind Bill.

Two men in suits watched from the cargo bay of the lead Black Hawk. Whatever agency they represented restricted them from leaving the helicopter. Phil suspected FBI, since kidnapping was involved.

Bill halted in front of them, removed his sunglasses, and surveyed those present. He assumed the "at ease" position—feet placed well apart and hands clasped behind his back. His glance took in but did not express his thoughts about the group's bedraggled condition. He replaced the sunglasses.

"Good afternoon, people. I'm looking for Dr. Michael Richardson."

All eyes turned to Richardson, who scrambled to his feet. "Here, sir! I am Dr. Richardson. Thank heavens you've come! Please, assist me. These people have assaulted me. That brute over there has my possessions. He kidnapped me, dragged me here against my will!"

Bill remained statue still. There was no way to tell behind the mirrored lenses where he was looking. His blank expression never changed.

Richardson flung out an arm, pointing at Phil. His voice went up another notch with his next accusation. "And that female over there—she hit me. I can't see out of my eye! Look for yourself at the damage she did to my person. Arrest her. Have her restrained."

Phil stood up. "Excuse me, but did I just hear you call me a *female*, as if I were an insect or alien species?"

Richardson scuttled closer to Bill and his solemn troop of mercenaries. "You see how violent she is? Restrain her. She's going to hit me again."

Phil flexed her fingers. "Gentlemen, what you don't see, you don't have to report."

Bill raised one finger and twirled it in the air. The military types smartly presented their backs.

Rod's broad smile was startling white against his sooty face. "Get'im, doc. Make me proud."

Richardson started to back away. "Now, Philly—"

Phil grabbed a handful of Richardson's jacket to pull him into the blow and rammed her fist into his mouth. Her knuckles were skinned but she had the satisfaction of feeling his front teeth get knocked loose. This time he landed hard on his tailbone and flopped backward to crack the back of his head on the pavement.

Phil stood over him, wishing he'd get up so she could hit him again. "That's for the put-down and messing with my family! *And don't ever call me Philly!* Do I look like a slab of cheese?"

Richardson moaned and sat up. He spat teeth into his hand. Tears streamed down his face as he stared at the white chunks in his palm.

Bill whistled through his teeth and the inert mercenaries came alive. He signaled to the pilots and the helicopters spurted to life. The soldiers hauled Richardson away and flung him into the chopper with the somber-suited agents.

Bill came closer and shouted at Phil, "I need to take Dr. Hafeldt with me. We'll meet you in Cancun."

Phil pressed a hand on top of her head to keep her hat from blowing away. "I'm going to give Uncle Cal the crystals."

"We'll talk about that later."

She looked at Uncle Cal. When he agreed to the plan with a nod, she handed him the crystals. She kissed his cheek, waved them off, and watched Bill assist her uncle into the first Black Hawk.

A "female" piloted the last helicopter. She waited patiently while Phil glanced around the scorched plaza.

Rod hollered over the noise, "At some point, we've got to talk. How about on the beach at Cancun? Mommy is part owner of a beachfront hotel. Bet I could get us a room."

"A room, Chaucer, as in sharing one?" she shouted back. "I don't think so. My idea of a vacation is somewhere I can be all alone to sit and watch the world go by."

"You want it, you got it, doc. One single room with view coming up."

They hurried to the helicopter. She reached for Binky's hand and he hauled her up between the open doors. He moved forward to take the empty co-pilot seat and waited for Rod's thumbs-up to tell the pilot they were buckled in.

Phil peered out the portside window at the plaza below. The chopper banked, showing a panoramic view of the damage. The rains would wash away the evidence of the fire. The tropics would quickly rust the incinerated chopper's metal skeleton. Nature would replace the burnt forest. The maze would wait in the sly silence of its underground lair until someone else came along to try and unlock its ancient secrets. She never wanted to see a block of granite again.

She refused to talk during the flight. When Rod said something, she pointed at her neck. It wasn't a lie. Her throat was too sore from breathing in smoke and soot to scream out an answer.

An indication of how much Bill and his hush-hush agency thought of her uncle was revealed by their treatment when they arrived at the airstrip. A smoke-glassed limo was waiting to whisk them away.

All the aches and pains of the recent days seemed to hit all at once. She hated the fact that she had to limp to get from the helicopter to the car. It didn't help that the sole of her left boot was completely burnt off. The other one flapped as she walked. She must look pathetic, but then Rod and her uncle didn't look much better.

There was one survivor that had to look worse than she did. She pictured Richardson's blackened eye and missing front teeth and squashed down a wave of guilt. Striking out at Richardson was the only time she could remember using her martial arts training vengefully, but Richardson deserved punishment and would probably get away with nothing more than a judicial slap on the wrist. At least he would have the dental work to remember her by. She hoped it would deter him from continuing his irrational vendetta.

Binky was still annoyingly spotless and seemed to be hitting it off with the helicopter pilot. He handed her a slip of paper before climbing into the limo's front seat with the driver. The pilot pulled off her helmet, revealing her Hispanic heritage and the fact that the age spread between her and Binky wasn't that much.

Rod opened the back door to the limo before Phil could reach for the handle. It wasn't until she sank down onto the silky leather seat that she noticed how she smelled. Uncle Cal sat next to her and Rod joined them. Apparently familiar with limousine travel, Rod opened a panel tucked into the wall that separated the driver from the passengers and dialed a number.

One of Bill's special-ops team had given her uncle a camouflage shirt to wear after checking the bandage on Uncle Cal's arm. The dried edges of the clear tape patch were curling up but the crease wound underneath looked clean. Every time she saw the bandage she relived the horror of seeing him shot.

The black crystal peeked out of one of the front pockets of the camouflage shirt. The single hum told her that he'd given Bill the blue one, which was fine by her.

Less noise. She didn't want to have anything to do with crystals for a while.

She smoothed a hand over her flying hair and swiveled on the seat to face her uncle. "I need to put some closure on that talk we had back at the ruins. I'm not happy about you meddling in my love life, Uncle Cal."

"I told you that it wasn't my idea. I merely helped it along. Gave it a boost, you could say."

Lowering her voice, she accused, "You fixed me up with a writer of high-concept novels."

Uncle Cal put on a face she hadn't seen in years. She withdrew a bit from his stern disapproval and looked out the window.

"Philadelphia Hafeldt, I'm surprised at you. That's a very snooty remark. Who died and made you the book police?"

Phil subdued her anger. Shame humbled her tone. "It's so embarrassing! He's got to be my age. We're too old for blind dates."

"You're both thirty and ready to settle down. Don't scowl, Phil. It makes me miss the little girl I used to have for the summers."

"You didn't have to stop seeing me." She hadn't meant to say that but now that it was out, she couldn't seem to stop. "You didn't even come to my graduations!"

"Phil, sweetheart, I didn't want to stop having you with me every summer. We almost lost you that time in the maze. Your parents were very angry with me and rightly so."

"Dad said you were too busy. But a letter or card would have been nice. Were you injured or incapacitated? I didn't hear anything about your hand being broken."

"I suppose it's as simple as letting guilt get in the way. Phil, taking you inside that maze was irresponsible. I've never forgiven myself for that."

Phil slipped her arms around his neck. The soldier that gave up his shirt liked to wear a lot of designer cologne. She gave her uncle's cheek a quick peck before withdrawing.

"Consider yourself forgiven. But not if you don't keep in contact. I want to hear from you more often than requests for camping equipment and packing cases."

Uncle Call patted her hand. "Bill made that easier. He gave me a cell phone that doesn't need recharging."

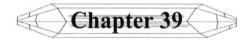

Chapter 39

The first thing she did when she reached the hotel was draw a bath. She shampooed and scrubbed off layers of grime, then luxuriated in a long, bubbly soak.

Room service provided delectable foods. She groaned through a tray of broiled seafood and only managed a few spoonfuls of toffee chocolate-chunk ice cream before passing out.

She didn't move until the sun began to lighten the sky, lulled by the surf's distant shush. Excited laughter in the hallway pierced the drugged sleep. She inhaled a deep breath of sea air.

The last days caused a serious depletion of her caffeine level. She made coffee in a stupor due to an inability to fully return from ten hours of dreamless sleep. The only thing that penetrated the haze was an acute reverence for the saintly person who placed a courtesy coffeepot on the bathroom counter.

The complimentary coffee pouches eked out a mediocre brew, but she didn't care. Java in any form was a blessing and near-religious experience after the recent turmoil and deprivation. The bliss of this caffeinated moment ranked right up there with making out with a certain lying writer of thrillers. But she couldn't think about him right now.

The mental haze began to lift after the first cup. Fortified, she noticed a flashing light on the bedside table. The hotel phone blinked red on and off. Messages waiting.

She listened to the instructions and activated the speaker so she could keep sucking down life-giving pseudo-expresso.

The first message was from her uncle. "Good morning, Phil. I knocked on your door, but you didn't answer. I hope I didn't interrupt anything."

Phil made a what-on-earth-are-you-talking-about-face at the phone. Did he really think she spent last night getting it on with Bobbio? It had taken the last of her energy just to crawl out of the bathtub and stagger to the bed.

"By now Rod must have told you everything. If he's still there with you, I want him to know how much I appreciate everything he's done.

"I'll contact you at work in a few weeks. Rest up and I'll talk to you soon. Love you, honey. Say hi to your father for me."

The tape clicked. A dial tone sounded. She waited for the next message to run.

"Hello, Dr. Hafeldt. This is Bill. Your uncle and I are on our way to the airport. I've left another cell phone in the hotel safe under your name, which will be the only way for you to contact your uncle. The other one has seen some hard use. Use the same number. Keep in contact, and thanks for helping us locate your uncle. We'll take good care of him."

Tape click and dial tone. Next message.

"Hey, doc. Call me when you wake up." He hung up.

"In your dreams, you prevaricating pile of monkey ca-ca," she muttered and savored the control of deleting his message.

Betrayed again. Her uncle admitted to being in cahoots with Bobbio's mother. And what was that all about? Now that she'd had time to think of it, she had to wonder how Rod must feel to have his mother arranging suitable dates. How medieval.

Her uncle was family; she couldn't hate him or be free of him and had no other choice but to forgive and love him forever. But Roderick Wakefield Gameson, alias R.W.Chaucer, Bud, Bobbio, Rob, Buddy, Roddie, and—her personal favorite—Not Bob, was another story. It suited her to be mad at him.

She poured another cup of coffee and looked in the refrigerator. A carafe of fruit juice waited for her on the top rack. The freezer held a bowl with crushed ice flanked by tall frosty glasses. Healthy snacks everywhere. No goodies with massive caloric content in sight. The plush hotel accommodations provided everything else from cosmetics to designer shades and a nifty beach bag full of books. She wrinkled her nose when she discovered one of Rod's tucked in with the rest.

An ocean-scented breeze glided through the open door to the balcony, floating the sheer curtains in slow motion. Two padded deck chairs waited for her presence.

She stuck the carafe of juice and a glass in the bowl of ice and padded across the polished wood floor to the balcony.

The knobby texture of the ecru Egyptian cotton slipcover on the chaise felt downy against her back. She stretched out and wriggled her bare toes. A manicure and pedicure were definitely in order. Later. After a snooze in the morning sun.

The wind shifted, bringing the scent of masculine cologne from the occupant of the room next door. *Spicy. Nice.*

The hedge barrier between the balconies offered visual privacy but did little to block sound coming from the other side. She hoped her neighbors would keep it quiet.

She adjusted the distance of the carafe and bowl of ice she'd set on the wicker table next to the chaise. She sipped juice, content to do nothing but sprawl in comfy leisure and absorb the spectacular view.

This was precisely the way to start a vacation after an exciting adventure. Next week was soon enough to think about reality. Then she'd go back to work, eking out a life putting out fires and saving the day. Nobody thought of librarians in quite that way but the fact was that her job was mainly solving other people's search problems.

She slipped on a pair of sunglasses to block the glare off the ocean. Someone was bodysurfing in the aqua waters. She squinted and recognized Binky. She watched him play, a middle-aged man, assured of himself, and in his element. An affectionate smile curved her lips. A woman appeared, surging up out of a breaker. Binky tackled her and they disappeared under the bubbling waves.

Someone tapped on the connecting door. She ignored it, hoping that the noise would eventually stop if she pretended she wasn't there. She wasn't in a mood to be chummy with strangers. Even the kind who wore sexy cologne.

Discreet clicking noises started when the knocking stopped. After another scrape and click, Rod opened the door. He pushed aside the billowing sheers and stepped out onto the balcony.

"Mind if I join you?"

She heaved a sigh. "Why ask for permission at this point? There's fruit juice in the carafe."

"No Margaritas?"

She pushed her sunglasses down her nose and gazed up at him over the rims. "Is your arm broken that you can't call room service?"

He grinned his killer grin and strolled into the bedroom. His muffled instructions filtered through the open door. She stared at the ocean and ordered her heart to stop thumping.

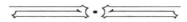

Rod stood between the sliding door to the balcony, oblivious of the magnificent view. All he could see was Phil. She looked delicious stretched out on a padded chaise, wearing the fluffy white bathrobe the hotel provided. She'd folded back the cloth to soak up the sun, exposing her endless legs that were bruised and scratched.

He remembered his first sight of her, lurking in a corner of her uncle's apartment, getting ready to send him to his Maker with a fertility mask.

His attraction and fascination for her had been immediate. Something about the suspicion in her too-blue eyes wrung his heart. He had decided then and there to do everything he could to get her and keep her. Tough, brainy women were hard to find.

Many women hid their intelligence or confidence. Phil hid nothing. He loved that and was amazed how desperate he was to keep her. The tricky part was how to convince her that he liked what drove some men away and that he had nothing to do with his mother's matchmaking scheme.

The other tricky part about catching Phil was that she was as stubborn and sly as his mother—undoubtedly one reason he liked her and her smart mouth.

And her legs.

And the way she blew the top of his head off at the waterfall.

If he had to play dirty to keep her, he would. He wasn't his mother's son for nothing. And he was beholden to his father for explaining how to survive and maintain clever women like his mother and now Dr. Philadelphia Casca Hafeldt.

He strolled over to the chaise, pushed her hip over, and stretched out beside her. "Guess who I saw in the lobby?"

She took a minute to answer. "I'll bite."

"Estelle."

That got her attention. "How did she track you down?"

"Another one of her grandsons is a computer geek. She promised not to attend his graduation if he found us."

"How could he do that?"

"Not all that hard these days. Probably tracked Mom's plane."

He suppressed a shout of victory when Phil turned onto her side and draped an arm across his chest.

After a few minutes of making him crazy with twirling her fingers in his chest hair, she asked, "Does she know our room numbers?"

"Yes, but I made her promise not to interrupt us."

"I can just imagine what she thinks that means."

So could Rod but he was saving that for later. "I told her I was thinking of starting up a new business,

Finders Keepers. She wants to invest. Would you? This partnership comes with free back rubs."

"Is this a ploy to keep me hanging around?"

"Absolutely."

Phil snuggled closer. "It's working. Start rubbing."

He kneaded the toned muscles of her back until she was limp. He whispered in her ear, "Doc, I've never had nooky under mosquito netting."

"What makes you think you're going to experience it now?"

He trailed his fingertips up and down her arm. When he said nothing, Phil raised her head.

Suspicion narrowed her eyes. She propped herself up on an elbow. With her nose pressed to his and cross-eyed she accused, "You're thinking up something underhanded, Chaucer."

He shrugged the shoulder she wasn't snuggled against. "Just thinking. You know that friend of mine that's really into the Atlantis stuff?"

Her reply was slow and cautious. "Yes?"

"He said he'd pay big bucks to anyone who could find the Lost Mines of Peru. Heard anything about ancient gold mines in South America?"

She returned her head to his shoulder. "There's been some information written about it."

"Think one of those skulls might be hidden there?"

"It's a possibility."

"Wanna be a partner in my new company and dig up some lost gold? Maybe pick up an emerald skull along the way?"

When she didn't say anything, he added, "Or…you could do something really dangerous and exciting…and marry me."

She rubbed her cheek against his shoulder. Rod couldn't stand the wait. "Well? What do you say?"

"I'm thinking."

He smiled when she began to mutter under her breath, vocalizing the pros and cons. At least it wasn't an outright rejection.

"Come on, Phil. Let's get hitched. It'll be fun."

"That's no recommendation for a lasting relationship."

He tucked a finger under her chin and lifted so he could study her face. "Don't be a scaredy cat, doc. Come on. Say yes."

She made a funny moue with her lips and refused to look him in the eye. After resettling her cheek on his shoulder, she finally said what was on her mind. "You know that thing by the waterfall?"

"You mean when the rockets went off, and I lost all credibility as a considerate lover?"

"Oh, I didn't think you were inconsiderate."

"Sheesh, Phil, I know you came. You go off like the Fourth of July. I was talking about my extreme lack of finesse. I didn't have to be so rough."

Her head was down, so she didn't see him working to suppress a grin when she quickly said, "I didn't think you were rough. It certainly didn't hurt."

Now that he had steered her into convincing herself, while assuring him, he stayed quiet and let her get the sticky parts out in the open.

She started with the chest hair twirling again. It was nearly impossible to keep focused.

Her voice was small, unrecognizable, when she asked, "Then it wasn't just you feeling sorry for the poor, little librarian, who wasn't getting any?"

"Doc, get serious. Have you ever, at any time, seen me acting sorry for you? Why would I give you a reason to permanently injure one or more of my important body parts?"

He felt her lips move into a smile against his skin. She leaned back to look up at him. "And my quirks don't turn you off?"

"For the most part, they turn me on. What other quirks are you talking about?"

"I have a thing about errors on printed receipts."

He toed off his loafers and hugged her closer. "That's good. I never bother to look at them."

"And I can't help it when I take down the muggers first. It's the training, you know."

"I like watching you whack guys. Saves me the trouble. Can't stand it when women squeal over nothing. Any other chick would have shrieked her head off or fallen down dead in a faint from what we handled in that maze. You were awesome."

She chuckled and nuzzled her nose into the crook of his neck. He sent a thankful prayer winging to heaven, blessing the wise counsel of his daddy.

"So, what'd you say, doc?"

She sighed. "About what?"

"Getting hitched."

"Oh, that." She paused. "Yes. I think so. Maybe. But only if we can honeymoon in Peru. But shouldn't we talk about—"

"Later, doc. It's time to light up my beautiful firecracker."

More Books by M.L.Rigdon

Award winning fantasy
Seasons of Time Trilogy

PROPHECY DENIED
BEYOND THE DARK MOUNTAINS
HER QUEST FOR THE LANCE

Contemporary Romantic

NEVER LET ME DIE

Dr. Philadelphia Hafeldt

THE ATLANTIS CRYSTAL
SEDUCTIVE MINES

Young Adult
Songs of Atlantis Fantasy Trilogy

THE VITAL
MASTERS OF THE DARK
CANTICLE OF DESTRUCTION
DRAGON AIR (Coming Soon)

Writing Historical Fiction as: Julia Donner

THE TIGRESSE AND THE RAVEN
THE HEIRESS AND THE SPY
THE RAKE AND THE BISHOP'S DAUGHTER
THE DUCHESS AND THE DUELIST
THE DARK EARL AND HIS RUNAWAY
THE DANDY AND THE FLIRT
LORD CARNALL AND MISS INNOCENT
THE BARBARIAN AND HIS LADY
A ROGUE FOR MISS PRIM
AN AMERICAN FOR AGNES
A LAIRD'S PROMISE
TO JILT A CORINTHIAN
MORE THAN A MILKMAID (2019)

SEDUCITVE MINES

Amazon River, Peru, South America

The handcuff chafed her right wrist. Dank, river stench saturated the humid night and lumpy mattress under her back. The inside of the boat smelled like fish and mildew. It rocked slightly, creating a surge of nausea from the remnants of whatever drug she'd been given.

Phil stayed still and thought her way through the fog of the narcotic. Clarity returned while she identified the sounds of the jungle—the dense silence disturbed by a startled howler monkey and a jaguar's distinctive, yowling scream. The birdcall of a nightjar verified which jungle and a general sense of time. In the morning, the color of the water, black or light brown, would let her know if she were east or west on the Amazon. Unless born here, the largest river in the world rarely allowed a newcomer the pinpointing of an exact location. It knew how to hide its dangers.

She drifted off and came awake when predawn light filtered through the mesh screen over the small porthole. Plunking sounds, the plops of things falling into water had brought her back to life. Again, more plops and plunks—ripe produce, falling from trees into the water to fruit-eating fish. That meant the boat was close to shore.

Phil swallowed what little moisture there was in her mouth. When was the last time she'd had anything to drink? She turned her head to look around. Movement sent a spear of pain slicing through her skull. Flinching from it created another streak of piercing agony. Bile threatened to gush up her throat. She concentrated all of her attention on not moving. Unfortunately, the river had other ideas. A wave from a disturbance in the water caused the boat to lift and sink. Something thumped against the wood portside. Perhaps one of the Amazon's mysterious pink dolphins? She hoped so.

She relaxed and allowed her body to ride another rolling shift. Her pain response wasn't as severe, but enough to gauge that it would be some time before she'd feel fit enough to escape. She had some idea about the identity of the person, or persons, who had done this to her. No need to worry about that now. Her suspicions would be confirmed sooner or later.

Carefully moving stiff fingers, she curled them around the safety bar that ran the length of the cot. The hardwood pole felt sticky, its seat at the head and foot of the bed slightly loose. That would prove helpful.

Another series of waves rolled by, sloshing against the portside. A passing vessel? The disturbance had to be caused by a craft larger than a dinghy. She hoped there was a dinghy, or a kayak, on board. At this time of year, the Amazon wasn't flooded. Traveling through the jungle on foot without the proper gear was unsafe in the extreme.

She had to stay out of the water. Using a floating log wasn't safe. Tree bark could be infested with toxins and clinging insects that took root under the skin. On foot, there was the constant threat of frenzied attacks from venomous ants, but the primordial soup gliding beneath hid monsters large and small—catfish with toxic

316

spines, sly caiman, always hungry piranha, and microscopic-sized fish that liked to swim into orifices. Swimming snakes weren't a bother. If they were on the river, they were heading somewhere fast to avoid the predators below.

If she could have, she would've smiled. It was like coming home.

She spent her recovery time mapping out ways to break free and identifying all the sounds, scents and impressions of the two summers she'd spent in the Amazon with her uncle. Thinking of him, she couldn't stop a grin from forming, but it fled her lips when she heard voices outside.

Then the boat listed to one side from the weight of being boarded.

CHAPTER 1

Two Days Earlier
University of Chicago
Regenstein Library

"So, Phil, are you going to call off the wedding or marry Rod of the gorgeous bod and spend your honeymoon hunting lost Peruvian gold?"

Philadelphia Hafeldt glowered at her best friend. "Gee, Maddie, thanks for dropping by. I can see you'll be loads of help."

Maddie closed the office door and sashayed to the nearest chair. "With what? Wedding jitters?"

"I left jitters behind and segued directly to hysteria this morning.

Your response of looking utterly unimpressed with my panic isn't making it easier."

Maddie's reply was a throaty, sultry chuckle. "Blasé comes with my new look. You never did say what you think of my makeover."

Phil rolled her eyes. Three years ago, Maddie took a job in the Big Apple and returned to Chicago wearing NYC's ubiquitous black. Three *weeks* ago, she invested in an expensive wardrobe and makeover. The trouble was that Madelyn Dare had so completely made herself over that Phil had trouble finding her friend under the new guise.

Staring at her laptop, and the page she hadn't altered in twenty minutes, Phil muttered, "I didn't expect you to come back looking like Lady Gaga does Jessica from *Roger Rabbit*."

Phil yearned for a glimpse of her friend's familiar red-gold hair in a frumpy braid, her smiling freckled face, and wrinkled, Village-People getups. It wasn't easy to accustom herself to Maddie's shift from one end of the fashion spectrum to the other.

Phil wiped back wisps of honey gold hair from her forehead. "I miss the old you."

Maddie's expression softened for a moment, then morphed back to sultry wench. She twitched a shoulder in a careless shrug. "I don't. I'm having too much fun. Subject change. What's up with the Peruvian gold thing? I thought you were into the mysteries of the Maya."

Phil scowled at the computer. "It's the mines I'm after. They've pretty much figured out everything about the lost gold. It's in some pit or cave around La Libertad, Utcumbama."

Maddie parked her rump, clad in a tight pink leather skirt, on the edge of the desk. "Refresh my memory. What you study is completely different from my field. I rarely listened in history classes. All I remember about Peru is Pizarro making some guy fill a room with gold."

"Yes, Emperor Atahualpa. The Ransom Room. The justice in that bit of nastiness came later. Pizarro was sorely ticked after he'd killed the king and taken the ransom. He found out later that the king's subjects were bringing in tons more overland. When they heard about the king's execution, they dumped all of it and went back home."

"Then if lost gold isn't what you're after, what is?"

Phil debated how much to tell her. She hadn't even told Rod what she was really after. "I want to find the actual mines. With that much gold being excavated, there had to be a large settlement or city near it. They've found a four thousand-year old tomb that predates Inca. I'm thinking of starting there and moving inland."

"Listen, hon, the last time you went into an ancient tomb, you almost got stuck there. And you hate confined spaces. Caves are bad enough, but *tombs*? And what's wrong with your eye?"

Phil slapped a hand over the tic having its way with her left eyebrow. "Nothing."

Maddie gave Phil a sideways I've-got-your-number look. "I've never seen you in such a state. Are you absolutely sure you want to marry a guy you've only known a few days?"

"Not a few days. It's over a month. Just about six weeks."

"Don't get defensive with me, Hafeldt. You met him only a month ago and accepted his proposal after three days. He must be something else to get my careful Phil to say yes at cyber speed. But the bigger question is—where's he been hiding the last five weeks?"

"He had a deadline to meet and went to his family's place on Mackinac to finish up the last chapters. He's picking me up this morning to meet his…mm—ma—ma—mother."

"For heaven's sake, Phil! She's Homo sapiens, not an alien. Hey, are you going to hyperventilate?"

"Maddie, I so do *not* want to meet his mother."

"That much is patently obvious. She can't be *that* bad." Maddie paused to study Phil's hunch-shouldered posture. "OK, so she's that bad."

"You have no idea. I did a search. There are pages and pages about her online. Think Miss Universe of Wall Street meets my mother."

Maddie huffed a dramatically exasperated sigh. "Time to get over your lousy relationship with your mom. Rod's mother isn't *yours*. She's probably nothing like her. You can get through a first time meeting with her. Just keep in mind your reward is God's gift to womankind."

"And you know this, how?"

"I took the time to check out the photo on the back of his last book. And by the way, when does the *yummy guy* get here?"

The thought of that event punched Phil's stress level up another notch. She pressed her fingertips against her left eyebrow. The way it twitched, she feared it might jump right off her head.

Rod getting a load of Maddie presented whole new worry and she hated herself for harboring it. She had to be adult about this and accept the terrible truth—she was a teensy bit jealous about how sexy and stylish Maddie's makeover had turned out. She no longer had a geeky-looking best friend. It had been easier to confide in the old Maddie.

"Earth to Phil."

Aggravated with her smallness of character, Phil snapped, "What?"

"When does Mr. Hottie show up? I'm dying here to meet the yummy guy and he better be as good as you've described him, especially since he's been the main course in all of my late night fantasies."

Phil felt her insides tighten. "He should be here any time now."

Maddie, who liked things neat and orderly, loved to sprinkle her conversations with initials and crooned dreamily, "Wish I had a YG."

Phil dropped her hand from her eyebrow and choked out a cough of disbelief. "What are you talking about? Ever since you had that makeover yummy guys trail after you everywhere you go!"

Maddie silently laughed and shook back her auburn hair in true shampoo commercial style. "And it was worth every penny. You should try it."

Phil scowled and replied with a negative shake of her head. No matter how hard she tried, Phil couldn't picture herself in a glitzy outfit fending off slavering males. She'd always dressed conservatively—practical clothes, sensible shoes. Yes, she looked dull but she took comfort in how Rod acted more interested in getting her out of her clothes rather than changing her fashion sense. What little she had.

Maddie had adopted her present shameless siren routine after years of being ignored or getting dumped when men found out that she was a brilliant mathematician. Quantum physics and advanced math elicited the sort of shivers of delight Maddie had never found in lovers. Her problem—as Phil's had been before Rod—was that she could never find a man centered enough in his own masculinity to feel confident around a smarter female. Lately, she'd been forced into thinking about herself BR—Before Rod.

Phil did a mental eye roll. She'd also picked up her friend's love of turning everything into an acronym. She straightened up in her chair.

"I don't think a makeover is what I need. Besides, Rod says he likes me looking natural." Phil glanced away from her friend's knowing gaze, wondering if what she'd just said was actually true.

Maddie laughed. "Natural? Hah! That's what they all say. Studies prove that men are sight-driven. The better the package looks, the faster their blood supply travels south. I'm living proof."

"I don't think I could make the drastic changes you have."

"Then don't go that far. Perhaps an evaluation and nothing else? You've already got a dancer's figure from all the workouts you do."

Not convinced, Phil scrunched up her face. "I can't imagine me doing the siren look."

"Then go for the svelte, lethal, career woman thing. That's very hot right now. And speaking of hot, how much longer do I have to wait to meet your YG?"

Most of the time, Phil thought Maddie's acronyms were funny, but she was beginning to feel squishy inside from imagining how Rod was going to get his socks knocked off from meeting her. Phil didn't want to think about the strain an embarrassing situation like that could cause two of her three, most favorite people in the world.

Phil shoved her fears aside with a tiny shake of her head. "Like I said, he should be here any second."

"Promises, promises. I'm not leaving until I see him. Does he know about your thing with crystals?"

Phil propped her elbows on the desk, bowed her head over the computer keyboard, and rubbed the knot forming behind her skull.

"He knows, Maddie."

"And?"

Phil looked up. "Actually, he says he likes all the weird things about me. When we go out to eat, he hands me the check to make sure there are no mistakes."

Maddie raised her eyebrows. "He doesn't mind your OC thing with overcharging?"

"He thinks it's cute. Quirky. And he gets a charge out of the fact he can let me take care of muggers. He's always asking if we can go down dark alleys, hoping some idiot will jump out from behind a dumpster. Says it turns him on when I make tough guys cry. He buys me immense slabs of chocolate, orders me double cheeseburgers with extra pickles, and watches me eat the mess, while he munches on veggies."

Maddie processed this amazing news with a skeptical expression. "*Fascinating*! He knows crystals sing inside your head, gets off on your love affair with junk food, and isn't intimidated when you feel it's necessary to kick some jerk's ass all the way to Canada. You've made oblique references to the fact that he's more than satisfactory in the bedroom department and that he's easy on the optics. Am I on course so far?"

"Pretty much. And I think he's hiding that he's a closet trekkie-type."

Maddie shook her head. "Then *why* so glum? On top of all that, he's supporting himself on his writing, which means he can't be entirely bereft of gray matter."

Phil huffed a silent laugh. "I think he may have more degrees and credentials than the two of us put together."

Maddie narrowed her eyes. "Phil, as a rule, I advise avoiding long-term commitments with good looking men and prefer the tried and true use-'em-and-lose-'em theorem, but your Rod sounds like the axiomatic keeper." She lodged a hand on her hip. "So tell me the problem here."

"Oh, Maddie, there are so many! His mother. Giving up my job. Getting down to Peru. Finding a boat and a guide. His endless string of old girlfriends—"

"And let us *not* omit your fear of involvement, stemming from previous relationships with seriously sucky guys."

Phil's shoulders slumped. "There is that."

Maddie came around the desk and stuck an admonishing finger in Phil's face. "Time for a reality check, chick. *You* quit this job. He didn't ask you to do that. We've already settled the non-issue of his mother. Peru will be there next year, if it doesn't work out this year. What else?"

"I need something to protect my brain from the synthetic crystals. I've got a hunch a big one is going to show up somewhere during this trip."

"Another skull?"

Phil wasn't surprised Maddie had figured out her true quest. "It may turn out to be true rock, like the others, but if it's synthetic, something that size will amplify the singing sounds in my head. The noise almost knocked me out last time I encountered one that large, and where we're going, we both have to be in top form. I wouldn't have made it out of the Yucatan labyrinth without Rod."

Waylaid by a challenge, Maddie grinned. "What a delicious problem. It'll take some thought."

Eager to change the subject from makeovers and mothers, Phil suggested, "What about lead shielding?"

"That may work for Superman, hon, but even as physically fit as you are, I can't see you accessorizing with a forty-pound ball of lead wrapped around your head. Give me a few days to work up something else."

"We're supposed to leave next week right after the ceremony. Not much time."

"Enough for me. It's your habit of avoidance that's making me nuts. It's time for us to move on. Is there a bathroom behind that door?"

"That's a storage closet, but there's a full length mirror on the door."

Maddie immediately opened it to savor her appearance. "You'd think they could come up with a better solution for a temporary office than this."

While Maddie primped, Phil stared at the neglected work on the screen. Multi-tasking wasn't going to be an option today. Too many problems whirled in her mind. Too many decisions to make.

She couldn't shake the manic compulsion to have all of her emotional and professional ducks lined up in the right rows before fulfilling any long-term promises. Especially one like marriage to writer R.W.Chaucer—a.k.a. Roderick Wakefield Gameson, uber-rich playboy.

His image on the dust jacket of his last book bloomed—dark eyes and hair, a knock-your-socks-off smile. No matter how she tried, she couldn't erase the brain spam of her former mistakes with men, which were nothing less than monumental. She puffed out a sigh. Her life was turning into a soap opera.

On the other hand, backing out on the wedding would get her out of having to meet her future mother-in-law, a very scary lady. It would be easier to face a dozen muggers. With knives.

But there was the other, safer commitment that she really wanted to keep—a dream on the verge of coming true—a trip to Peru and the upper Amazon, a journey into the unknown—Rod's honeymoon gift to her. She could feel her spirit stirring, salivating for an exciting adventure.

Even more delicious and boggling, Rod felt the same about the trip. One of the things she found endearing about him was his boyish excitement about an expedition into an unexplored sector of Peruvian jungle. On a danger scale of one to ten, hacking their way through uncharted jungle ranked around seven or eight. Maybe nine.

A twinge of concern sidetracked her joy: the prospect of a courthouse quickie marriage induced a terror factor of twelve and a commitment to failure. Actually, a failure to commit. She suspected that Rod suggested the courthouse solution to get her hitched before she backed out. And he was right. Her feet were feeling mighty chilly, especially when he hinted that his mother would love a private, family wedding at their summerhouse on Lake Michigan, if the courthouse idea didn't work out.

She massaged the back of her neck. The problem was not with Rod. It was herself with Rod. He had an insidiously delectable way of eroding her will and titillating her passions for adventures, sensual and tropical. She couldn't get over the fact that he found her addiction to chocolate and the rest of her peculiar ways appealing.

Her last fiancé, the snarky Peter Ferral, settled for eroding her confidence, using veiled ridicule and subtle comparison. Not Rod. He was right up front with everything. He manipulated her the old-fashioned way—with sizzling animal magnetism.

Add to the mix the fact that R.W. Chaucer was Everywoman's fantasy in the sack. If he hadn't showed up at Uncle Cal's apartment for an appointment, would Rod have ever noticed her across the proverbial crowded room? That's how Ferral cozied up to her, trying to get to her famous uncle through his niece.

So, what was a girl supposed to do? Let a man like Rod walk out of her life and share his indisputable talents with some other orgasm-starved female?

Not in this lifetime.

Phil exhaled a despairing sigh. When had she become so shallow? So weak. So famished. *Gee, a five-pound box of chocolates sounds good.*

She searched her desk drawers for a snack as she thought about the other problem she hadn't mentioned—the weird phone calls she'd been getting at home on her land line. They usually ended with a hang-up after an extended silence. She'd begun to look forward to the calls with their vulgar noises and labored breathing, sort of like soft porn without the projectile implants and supernaturally waxed, tanning-bed bodies. Unfortunately, the crude calls stopped when she could no longer hold in the laughter.

She never for a moment believed that her number had been picked at random by a frustrated asthmatic. Sly female intuition whispered that the crank calls had something to do with Rod and the various women who leaped out at him wherever they went. Former girlfriends seemed to lurk around every corner, which was so-not-good for her problem with a lack of trust when it came to men and relationships.

Phil supposed the simplest solution for the crank calls was to invest in a phone with caller ID, but that solution wouldn't soothe her suspicions about who the callers might be. And if she mentioned a name, would Rod have fond memories, comparatively speaking? Did she really want to go there?

Maddie interrupted Phil's pathetic train of thought when she closed the supply closet door and strolled to the office window. She stuck a manicured fingernail through the slats of the privacy blinds, pressed down, and perused the traffic on the library's main floor.

"Oh, my!" Maddie whispered. "Phil, we've got an SGLG at four o'clock. Drool factor of ten."

Not really interested, Phil looked up from the computer screen to please her friend. "A what?"

Maddie pulled the slats lower, providing Phil with a gap to view the SGLG—seriously good-looking guy.

Phil craned to look through the opening in the flimsy blinds. Her spirit sank to her shoes. "Oh, no! It's Peter. Not now!"

The ugly worm of an unwanted suspicion wriggled in her brain. Would Peter sink to making crank calls? Sure he would. The man was the walking definition of jerk. The next question that popped into her head was what did he want?

Made in the USA
Middletown, DE
02 October 2020